# CARTER

## HOPE CITY

## MARYANN JORDAN

Kris Michaels Maryann Jordan
M+J
PUBLICATIONS

ISBN ebook: 978-1-947214-58-3

ISBN print: 978-1-947214-59-0

❀ Created with Vellum

*Young. So fuckin' young.*

"Hard to tell, Detective. Maybe not as young as you think."

Realizing he'd spoken aloud, Carter Fiske looked up at the medical examiner as he squatted by the body on the floor. Natalie Bastion had only been working in Hope City for a few months, but considering she came from the Medical Examiner's Office in Chicago, he figured she knew a thing or two about dead bodies.

He turned his attention back to the young man. Ill-fitting jeans. Well-worn, black, long-sleeved, thermal shirt. Heavy, scuffed boots. But his coat was new. Over-sized, but new.

He stood, perusing the scene. The kitchen was gutted—and not by the fire next door. The row town-house was stripped to its bones, appearing uninhabited for God knows how many years. Water pooled in the dips in the floor and still dripped off the walls where it blasted through the broken windows.

A splat landed on his head and he jumped, cursing as he wiped the moisture from his face. A flash of a smile crossed Natalie's face, and he couldn't remember seeing her smile before. Inwardly rolling his eyes at being the cause of her fleeting amusement, he continued to scan the area.

"Not going to be much scene evidence in here," he surmised aloud as two more firefighters poked through the aftermath. The 9-1-1 came from a driver on the street, and once the Fire Department determined suspicious burn patterns, the arson detectives had been activated. Then, when checking another unit and the body had been found, Carter received a call.

"I'll push this up in my queue, give you what I can just as soon as I can," Natalie said. Completely covered head to toe in hazmat gear, she appeared almost ghostly in the dark room.

"Anything you can tell me about those?" He tipped his head toward the bag of pills that she had found in the deceased's coat pocket. The reason he had been called in.

"They appear to be prescription, but anything beyond that would be premature." Natalie stood and nodded to her two assistants, indicating she was ready for the body to be transferred to the morgue. Handing the bag of pills to him, he sealed them into an evidence container. She followed her assistants as the body was removed, snapping off her gloves and plastic booties once she was outside.

Following her down the steps, he observed the firefighters emptying and rolling up their hoses. Portable lights were being hauled to the end unit, and he grinned, recognizing the arson detective standing nearby.

"Good to see you, Sean."

Sean McBride turned to the side and threw his hand out in greeting. "Carter, good to see you, too. I wondered who they'd call in for this."

He dipped his head toward the burned hulk of the end unit. "You've been busy lately."

"That's a fucking understatement," Sean agreed.

"Is Jonas around? You still partnered with him?"

Sean nodded. "Yeah. He's getting the lights set up. We've got extra and can send some to you, too."

"Thanks. I was just going to call for some."

Sean held his gaze for a moment and asked, "What do you think?"

His hand moved to the back of his neck, squeezing some of the tension away. "Medical examiner didn't see any signs of fatal injury, and I'm not seeing any signs of violence. I've got several cases dealing with drug overdoses of homeless persons, so this may just add one more to my load."

"Hell, you probably see more of my brother right now than I do."

"You'd be right." Sean's brother, Kyle, was also a detective with the HCPD, working with the Drug Task Force. "We're both working the homeless drug cases. Up to our ears in this shit. We're checking with some of the homeless shelters, but it's a slow go."

"Hey, I've got someone who could help. You might want to talk to my sis—"

3

"Got the lights!" Jonas called out. "Does Carter want any?"

They were interrupted by the arrival of the portable lights. Sean directed the ones he and Jonas needed to gather evidence in the blackened hole of the first unit. After a quick clap on the shoulder, Carter walked back into the unit where the body had been discovered, setting up several lamps as well.

With more illumination, he turned around in a slow circle, his gaze searching the room. The walls dripped with water. The ceiling was dark with smoky soot. The floor gave no signs of evidence as to the identity of the deceased or his life here in this abandoned townhouse. The kitchen cabinets and sink had been removed, and Carter considered that the entire block of houses had probably been gutted of anything considered valuable.

*Over a hundred and fifty years of life inside and they end up as dead as their last resident.* Old architecture was fascinating, a tidbit he tended to keep to himself. *Buildings can be so resilient, outlasting their many owners.* But now, at the end of this house's life, there was nothing but empty decay, ready for demolition—once it was no longer a crime site.

He crossed the room while pulling on a new pair of gloves and opened the door to a small closet. Inside, he discovered a cardboard box. Snapping several pictures, he knelt closer. The top of the box formed a shelf, containing a crumpled paper sack. Carefully opening the sack, he found several plastic baggies, all empty except for one which contained bread crust. The paper sack had a large *"PB"* written in black marker on the outside. He placed each item into an evidence bag, labeling them.

"Whatcha got?"

Looking over his shoulder, he smiled at his partner, Rachel Seas, stepping into the kitchen, jerking her head to avoid a water drop falling from the ceiling. It was on the tip of his tongue to warn her to be careful on the slippery floor, but he hesitated. At over eight months pregnant, she would soon be out on maternity leave and his caution ratcheted upward with each passing week. The balance of not treating her like glass warred with his natural protectiveness.

Before he had a chance to answer her question, she added, "I never thought an empty room could be a mess, but hell, this is nasty."

He chuckled as she walked closer, peering around him to see what he was bagging. "There was nothing in the room other than the deceased. The ME just left with the body but showed me a bag of pills that were tucked in his coat pocket. This is the only thing I've found in here so far."

"Any ID?"

He shook his head. "I was just getting ready to go through the other rooms to see if I could find any other evidence that might tell us who he was or what he was doing here."

"Could've just been looking for a place to sleep."

Nodding, he silently agreed. Leaving Rachel to continue looking around the small first floor, he walked upstairs, finding it much like the downstairs. Shining his light around, he saw the space was completely empty. The bathroom cabinets and fixtures were ripped from the walls. The upstairs windows were broken and water on the floor kept him from seeing if the dust had been disturbed before the fire next door. He continued around each room but found no evidence that anyone had been there recently

After a thorough search, he walked back downstairs where he found Rachel as empty-handed as he. "Nothing?"

"Anything on the floor would have been washed away with the fire hoses. Upstairs?"

"Same. I found no evidence that he or anyone had been upstairs." Carter stretched his back, feeling as well as hearing his neck crack. "I'll take what I found in the pantry to the lab. I'll get the rest from Natalie, and hopefully, we'll be able to get an ID along with cause of death."

She lifted an eyebrow and grinned. "Are we going to hit the homeless shelters again?"

"Yeah, even if we haven't had much luck with the last two."

Patting her stomach, she said, "Since I'll be on maternity leave soon, I hate to leave it all to you. Hopefully, we'll get a break soon."

"Are you sure that little one doesn't want to wait longer to arrive?" He pretended to grumble and watched her fight a grin.

The two stepped out of the back door and walked past the charred walls of the first unit. Its interior was well lit from the portable lamps, and he spied Sean and Jonas kneeling, scraping bits of evidence into jars.

While they might have much more evidence to collect, he did not envy them. The serial arsonist plaguing Hope City was not going to be easily caught.

Walking to the perimeter, he offered a chin lift to the police officer standing watch. Ducking under the yellow tape, he bypassed the few reporters who had gathered for information about the arsonist.

Placing his evidence in the back of his SUV, the young face of the deceased stayed vividly in his mind. If he truly was homeless, Carter wondered who would mourn his passing. Certainly not the media, clambering for headlines. With the recent high-profile murder of one of Hope City's richest men, Carter knew his unidentified body would receive little interest or fanfare. Slamming the door of his SUV, he also slammed the door on those thoughts. As far as he was concerned, the young man who'd died alone, possibly after doing nothing more than finding a warm place to sleep, deserved Carter's full attention. *And that's what he'll get—my full fuckin' attention.*

It was after midnight by the time Carter stepped out of the elevator onto the second floor of the police laboratory. Walking down the long, tiled hall, he bypassed a number of doors on either side that led to various labs. Coming to the door he needed, he moved through and looked into the large room. The laboratories were staffed 24 hours a day, but the midnight shift was skeletal. Glad to see a familiar face, he smiled as he approached one of the desks.

"Hey, Jerry, got something for you."

"How you been, Carter? Haven't seen you in a few weeks. Not here nor at the pub."

He handed the evidence bags to Jerry, observing as the lab technician labeled them before handing him the release forms to be signed. Jerry had been working in the lab as long as Carter had been in Hope City, the two of them hitting it off right away, including shared beers at the Celtic Cock. "I've been around but haven't been to the lab in over a week. Before that, I think you were on vacation the last time I came by."

Jerry grinned. "Took our youngest to check out some colleges. My wife is having a hard time with him getting ready to leave the nest, but I'm looking forward to a little peace and quiet."

"You're so full of shit," he laughed. "You'll be crying in your cornflakes worse than your wife when he leaves."

Once the paperwork was finished, Carter got back to business. "Let me know what you can get from any of this. The ME has the body right now, so I'll get their prints sent to you, hopefully tomorrow. Once I pick up the personal effects, I'll get those to you also."

"Will do. I'll be on the lookout for them."

Jerry stood and the two men shook hands before Carter walked back to the elevator. As he headed to the parking lot, he saw Sean, his arms full of a fire evidence collection kit, walking in. Sighing as he climbed into his SUV, he thought of the hours they kept. Glancing at the time on the dashboard, he calculated that if he was lucky, he might be able to get a few hours of uninterrupted sleep.

## 2

Carter parked in the first-floor parking garage of his condo building. Perfectly situated near the Inner Harbor, his seventh-floor condo sported wide windows with views of both the Inner Harbor to the east and the professional football and baseball stadiums to the west. He had been lucky to snag it when he did, renting it from a young couple who had spent a considerable amount of money on upgrades before being forced to rent quickly when the husband was transferred.

The carpet had been ripped out, replaced with hardwood floor. The walls were painted a soft gray, complementing the granite countertops and black, tiled backsplash in the kitchen—at least that was what the real estate agent said. A far fucking cry from the gutted townhouse he'd just been inside.

Minimalist in his own furnishings, the two-bedroom condo gave him plenty of space to move around while being comfortable enough to call home. Something he appreciated at all times but especially when he'd been out in the dark of night, staring at the face of death in a young person.

After shutting the door behind him, he tossed his keys, wallet, and badge onto the kitchen counter to his right. He stood for a moment, squeezing the back of his neck, hesitating over the decision to have a whiskey, a beer, or just a glass of water. At a slight movement out of the corner of his eye, he jerked his gaze into the open dining and living room.

Before he had a chance to speak, the beautiful, elegantly-dressed woman sitting on his sofa beat him to it. "Well, it certainly took you long enough to get back here."

Her words dripped with disdain, and her anger was evident by her narrowed eyes and tightly-pinched lips. When he saw her last, they had been in the process of stripping each other in his bedroom. When the call came in, he distinctly remembered her silently fuming as he redressed and him telling her to leave since he had no idea when he would be back.

"I've been sitting here for," she began, then swung her arm out to look at her watch with exaggerated movements, "four hours." She lifted her hands to the side, still glaring. "When is this ever going to change?"

Fatigue had already morphed into surprise and, with her words, was quickly morphing into anger. "What the fuck, Allison? I told you to go home when the call came in. If you've been here for hours, that's on you. Don't sit around, then start bitchin' at me when I walk through the door and you're not even supposed to be here."

"You don't get it, do you, Carter?" Standing, she

placed her well-manicured hands on her narrow hips. "I don't know how to make it any plainer."

His head jerked back. "Make what plain?"

"Argh," she growled in response, her mouth twisting into a sneer. "You must not be a very good detective if you can't figure this out."

"Allison, I'm really not in the mood to try to guess what the hell you're pissed about. If you've got something to say, then just say it."

"Typical." Shaking her head back and forth slowly, she continued to glare. "Okay, fine. I'll spell it out for you. We've been seeing each other for six months. I can't believe you haven't noticed that I've been calling more, texting more, even insisting on cooking dinner for you. I thought we were taking the relationship forward."

"Allison, there is no relationship to move forward." As soon as those words left his mouth, he wanted to retract them. Not because they weren't true but because the look on her face gave evidence to the screech that followed.

Lifting her fist, she shook it in the air. "No relationship?"

Turning to face her fully, he now placed his fists on his hips, his jaw tight with anger. "Let's recap, shall we? We met at a party. We flirted. We slept together that first night after both of us clearly stated that we were looking for fun only. In the last six months, we've had dinner occasionally, usually followed by fucking—"

"Don't be crass!"

"Crass is all I got right now, Allison. Hell, you've

even called us fuck buddies. So why are you coming at me with this relationship bullshit when I'm exhausted?"

"I thought casual was just how we started. I expected after a while we'd become more. But with you, it's always about your job. How am I supposed to feel? You leave here because you get a call out, and I'm expected to just go?"

*Count to ten, boy, before you explode.* His father's wise words came back to him, and he closed his eyes, mentally counting. He cast his mind back to the previous months, searching his memory banks to see if there was anything he'd missed but came up blank. In the last six months, they had gone out occasionally for drinks or dinner, never spending the night after having sex, no matter which bed they were in. And they rarely talked, at least not about anything important. Certainly not building a relationship.

Taking a deep breath, he let it out slowly before he began. "Allison, I'm sorry if you thought our relationship was moving in any direction other than what it was—casual and convenient. You knew I worked for the Police Department when you met me, and you know that I can get a call at any time. You're standing here all pissed at me because I'm out doing my job. You're also pissed at me because I didn't read your mind about expecting a change in our relationship when we never even hinted that that was what either of us wanted."

Her jaw tightened as her lips pinched. "I know you can get called out at any time, Carter. But that's another problem. You don't have to be."

His head jerked slightly to the side, hearing her words but not understanding her meaning.

"My father's law office employs several private detectives. And, I have no doubt, they get paid more than you do." Her lips curved slowly at the sides, a smile that reminded him of the Grinch, full of plots and plans but no true happiness. "I thought I would wait until our relationship moved forward to let you know that you could work for him. But maybe now is the time to bring it up." She stepped forward and placed her hand flat on his chest, her gaze dropping from his eyes to his mouth. "Think about it. Working for a prestigious law firm or wasting your skills on the great unwashed of Hope City. After all, it's not like you're a high-profile homicide detective. Jesus, Carter—a drug cop? Having to work with the homeless? That's barely a step above being a street cop." Biting the corner of her lip, she smiled again.

As she stepped closer, he jerked his hands up to clasp her shoulders and keep her from pressing against him. Allison had certainly shown a great interest in his detective career when she thought he worked on high profile cases. But she'd lost interest very quickly when she'd discovered he was not a homicide detective, certainly not one working on a media-laden case.

Thoughts slammed through his mind so quickly they crashed together, but one image came to the fore-front… the unknown young man who now lay in the morgue.

With his hands holding her in place, Carter stepped backward, needing the distance. He watched her brow crinkle in surprise. "You need to leave, Allison. I won't be calling and won't accept calls from you anymore. What we had will never become anything more and now only leaves a bad taste in my mouth."

Understanding moved over her face, and her incredulity would have been funny if he'd found any of their conversation amusing at all. Tilting her head toward the front of his condo, she lifted an eyebrow. "I walk out that door, I'll never walk back through. Do you understand what I'm saying to you?"

He nodded and held her gaze. "Yes, and that would be good."

She jerked backward as though slapped. With narrowed eyes, she turned and reached for her coat and purse. Watching her stalk toward the door, he expected a parting shot and was not surprised to receive one.

"The best thing that could've happened to you and your career is leaving." With that, she left, slamming the door behind her.

He stood, his feet rooted to the floor, his chin to his chest, staring at his feet before lifting his hand to the back of his neck, once more squeezing in an effort to relieve the tension. Tension that came not from the scene in his apartment but from the scene of death still needing to be processed.

Allison didn't get it; she never would. He was not a detective for glory. There sure as hell would not be riches or accolades. But that young man had had a life in front of him, now cut short, and Carter wanted to find out why—and where the hell the bag of prescription drugs had come from.

It now felt like a whiskey night, and he headed into the kitchen. After grabbing a glass, he poured a generous amount of the amber liquid and walked past the sofa Allison had reclined on, moving instead to the large picture window that faced the Inner Harbor. Taking a deep swallow, he welcomed the burn from the peaty drink. The city below twinkled with lights, their reflection on the undulating water hiding the ugliness he knew was present in the light of day.

Unlike some people he knew, he wanted a relationship. Someone to come home to. Someone to share his life. But damn. *Never met that person. Who knows if I will?*

Tossing back the last of his drink, he shoved those thoughts from his head and settled his mind firmly on what needed to be done the next day. Reports to write. Evidence to look at. A trip to the morgue. And another trip to the homeless shelter. Scrubbing his hand over his face, he sighed.

He shook his head on that cheery note and placed his now-empty glass into the sink before going into the bedroom. Looking at his clock, he knew a couple of hours of sleep was all he would manage before he needed to be up and going again. He stared at the empty bed and felt nothing but relief that it was just him crawling between the sheets. *Better to be alone than with someone who can't handle who I am.*

---

Carter's alarm jarred him awake, and he stared bleary-eyed at the time as he turned it off. Sitting up in bed, he propped his elbows on his knees and rubbed his palms over his eyes. *Five hours of sleep. Thank God.* When he became a detective, one of the byproducts was insomnia. Plagued with the inability to let go of the cases rolling through his mind, he would get up and read until falling asleep or it was time to get up. It was rare for him to get more than two or three hours of sleep at a time.

Invigorated from a hot shower, he relished his relaxed morning, not having to rush out the door. The autopsy would not be performed for several more hours, giving him plenty of time to get to the station, meet with Rachel, and then head to the morgue.

Not thrilled with cooking for one, he enjoyed the perk of a coffee shop on the first floor that not only served great coffee but cooked fresh breakfast sandwiches daily. Once dressed and ready to go, he headed downstairs.

"Good morning, Detective Fiske." The greeting was called out as soon as he entered the coffee shop.

Flashing his grin at the college student working behind the counter, he soon had his coffee and sausage-and-egg biscuit. "You're the best, Jenny." He was not immune to the hungry look she gave him but made sure to keep it friendly-but-distant. *Been a lot of years since a college girl was part of my take-out order.* The previous night's scene with Allison bolted through his mind, and he shook his head as he carried his breakfast to a seat at the counter by the window. Sighing, he sipped his hot brew and pushed thoughts of too-young and too-demanding women from his mind.

Dusting a few crumbs from his lap, he headed out into the morning commuter rush and was soon pulling into the parking lot of police headquarters. Up the stairs and down the hall, he greeted others as he made his way to the bullpen, the large room that housed numerous desks.

"Good morning, sunshine," he said to Rachel, setting a takeout herbal tea in front of her.

"Oh, God, thank you. I really need this!" She sipped the now-cooled brew, nodding in appreciation. "Got a call from the ME. Autopsy on our John Doe is being done this morning."

Another detective walked in and looked over at the coffee he was drinking. "Damn, man, don't I get one of those?"

Carter looked over his shoulder and watched as Kyle McBride stalked toward him. "You're rarely in the office. If I had known you were going to grace us with your presence this morning, I would've called for a fuckin' caterer."

Kyle made it to him and playfully punched him in the arm enough to jostle his coffee.

"Watch it! You make me spill a drop, I'll find a way to get you permanently assigned as a resource officer."

Kyle threw his head back and laughed before turning to Rachel in greeting her. "What are you doing hanging out with this loser? Anyway, by the looks of you, you're about ready to pop."

Shaking her head, Rachel groaned, "Too much damn testosterone for this early in the morning, boys." She turned her attention back to Carter. "Trip to the morgue at 10 o'clock?"

Carter nodded and glanced at the clock. "Hopefully we can get an ID then."

Kyle leaned his hip against the desk. Sean's younger brother was part of the drug task force, and while they looked like brothers, that was where the similarity ended. Sean was precise and methodical whereas Kyle lived by gut determinations. At work, Sean was rarely seen without a button-down shirt and tie, even if it was loose around his neck. Kyle gave off the vibe that the idea of a tie would choke him.

"Early morning trip to the morgue. Fuckin' way to start the day. Prescription pills? How many does this make?"

"This is the third one that's landed in my lap. The first one from two weeks ago was identified. It was ruled accidental overdose. He had a packet of prescription drugs in his pocket, like my guy from last night. Oxycodone, maybe Fentanyl. Same with the second one last week. Looked a lot like what my John Doe had in his pocket, but I'll know more after the autopsy. Last two had been homeless, and it looks like this one was also."

"You're still dealing with the homeless shelters?"

Chuckling, he nodded. "Yeah, but that hasn't been easy going."

"You know, my sister works at—" Kyle's phone vibrated, and he looked at the screen. "McBride. Yeah. Yeah. Shit, on my way." He took to his feet and immediately weaved through the desks toward the exit, calling over his shoulder, "School resource officer called in a drug bust at Carver High School."

After watching Kyle disappear down the hall, he turned back to the files in his desk. *Might as well get a little work done before heading to the morgue.*

## 3

"Mom!"

Tara jerked at the sound of her daughter's yell, poking her eye with the mascara wand as she leaned close to the bathroom mirror. *Shit.* Blinking, she turned and offered a one-eyed glare toward her six-year-old daughter standing a few feet away in the bathroom doorway. Grabbing a tissue, she blotted her teary, now mascara-smeared eye and sighed heavily.

"Colleen, how many times have I told you to please not scream in the house unless it's an emergency? I'm not deaf. I promise you do not have to scream to get my attention."

"But I can't find my pink sneakers!"

"Then wear another pair. I saw your blue ones in your closet."

Colleen scrunched her nose and shook her head viciously from side to side. "No! Today's color day. We're supposed to wear our favorite color!"

Now that her vision was clearing, she stared at her

daughter. Pride might be a sin, but she was thrilled her daughter was a miniature version of herself, seeming to gain little of her father's DNA. Long, thick, dark hair. Blue eyes. And a smile that could light a room. *Well, maybe that didn't come from me, considering I can't remember the last time I lit a room with a smile.* As her gaze moved over her daughter, she observed the pink shirt, pink ruffled skirt, pink tights, and pink ponytail holder in her hand.

Smiling at the amount of Pepto Bismol pink one little girl could wear, she asked, "I suppose that pink is your favorite color?"

Rolling her eyes while bouncing on her shoeless feet, Colleen said, "Mom! You know it is! That's why I have to find my pink sneakers!"

Trying to remember where she saw them last, she shook her head slowly. "Honey, this is why I tell you to keep things in their right place." One look at her daughter's quivering chin and she bit back the suggestion that Colleen was just going to have to wear the blue ones. Dabbing underneath her eyes, removing the last traces of smeared mascara, she said, "Let's see if we can find them in your room."

With a twirl that sent the ruffled skirt swirling, Colleen darted out of Tara's bedroom. Following, she glanced at the clock by her bed and knew that their morning was going to be rushed. It would have been helpful if Colleen had told her about color day the night before. Once inside her daughter's messy room, she could not help but sigh as memories flooded.

Tara might have been the third child in her family,

but she was the oldest sister, with three siblings younger than her, including two sisters. She remembered often having to help Erin and Caitlyn get ready for school, their room looking very similar to Colleen's.

The bedspread was half on the floor, and she knelt nearby, pulling up the corner. Bending, she could see the toe of a pink sneaker peeking from underneath. *Not so hard to find, after all.* Snagging both shoes, she stood with them dangling in her fingertips. Before she had a chance to speak, Colleen squealed and rushed over, grabbing her around the waist and squeezing. Laughing, Tara bent to kiss her daughter's head, leaving her lips pressed against her hair for a few seconds longer.

"Okay, munchkin, finish getting ready. I've got to do the same and then I'll fix you breakfast."

Hurrying back into her bathroom, she managed to swipe on her mascara, and with a quick brush of blush on her cheeks, she hurried into the kitchen. Colleen was a picky eater, but Tara managed to get her daughter to agree to cinnamon apple oatmeal on school days, leaving the sugary cereal for weekends.

The two bowls of oatmeal were quickly fixed and just as quickly eaten. Keeping an eye on the clock, they had little spare time. "Make sure to go to the bathroom, brush your teeth, and get your backpack. We leave in five minutes."

As Colleen rushed out of the kitchen, Tara rinsed the bowls before heading into her own bathroom. Finishing her business, she glanced into the mirror as she washed her hands. A sigh slipped from her lips as she peered at the reflection staring back at her.

Her long, dark hair was pulled into a sensible, low ponytail at the back of her neck. Her pale-blue blouse was unadorned, and her neatly-pressed navy pants were more of a practical uniform than fashionable. Small, silver hoop earrings and a silver Celtic cross necklace were her only nods to jewelry.

Drying her bare hands on the towel, she could still remember the day she removed her wedding ring. At thirty-two, she was hardly old, and yet she sometimes felt ancient. *"You're no fun, anymore, Tara."* Those parting words by her ex-husband still occasionally rang in her ears.

"Mom!"

Startling at the shout for the second time that morning, Tara walked briskly out of the bathroom, tucking her maudlin thoughts away. *We're better off without him.* Sliding her feet into her low-heeled pumps, she grabbed her phone from the nightstand and headed down the hall toward the front door. "You ready?" she asked while taking their coats from the closet.

"I forgot to have you sign my folder!" Colleen was kneeling on the floor, rummaging through her backpack.

"What have I told you about waiting until the last minute to do any of your schoolwork, including getting me to sign things?"

Colleen turned her expressive blue eyes upward, and Tara sighed once again. Kneeling next to her daughter, she quickly laid her hands on the bright red first-grade parent folder. Opening it, she could see that Colleen had brought home a reading sheet, a math sheet, and a parent permission form for an upcoming field trip. A quick glance showed that she had everything correct on the reading and math sheets, and she initialed in the top corners. Reading quickly, she smiled at the idea of a field trip to a science museum and signed the permission form. "Looks like you've got a fun trip coming up."

With the papers signed and secured back in the backpack, Colleen was once again bouncing as she put on her coat. "Our teacher said that we're going to get to see a cool exhibit on space! I told her that I already know all about space! Grandpa taught me everything!"

"I'm right here, sweetheart. You don't have to yell even if you're excited. Remember, indoor voice."

"Oh, yeah," Colleen whispered, still bouncing.

Opening the front door, they walked outside, and she locked the door securely. Turning toward their car, she observed a thick frost covering the windshield. Dropping her chin to her chest, she sighed heavily for what seemed like the millionth time that morning. "I wish we had a garage."

Once Colleen was inside the car, Tara started the engine and blasted the heat. Grabbing the scraper, she scraped enough frost that she could safely see out the windows. Nurturing was easy. Independence was natural. *But damn, a partner that cared would have been nice.*

Now, five minutes late, she prayed that there would be little traffic getting Colleen to school. *Hmph, right.* The streets near the school were lined with cars and school buses, and there was nothing that could be done except get in queue and creep forward. As soon as they were at the drop-off spot, she leaned around as Colleen unbuckled. Her daughter popped through the opening between the front seats and gave her a tight hug. Kissing the top of Colleen's head, she leaned back, and they held each other's gaze. "Love you biggest," they said in unison.

Colleen grinned and whirled around, threw open her door, and hopped out. With a wave, Tara watched as she ran to her friends, and they entered the school building. Not wanting to hold up the line, she quickly moved forward.

Flipping on the radio as she drove to work, she listened as the DJs ran off a list of famous people whose birthday was that day. She was acutely aware of what day it was, silently commemorating it each year. She remembered the winter wedding eight years ago. She had finished her master's degree in social work, was newly employed, and ready to marry her college boyfriend. Young, in love, excited for the next logical step in their relationship. The only good thing that came out of that relationship was Colleen, and she was a priceless treasure.

*Honk!*

Jumping, she saw that the red light had turned green. *Jesus, I'm as distracted as Colleen! I need to get my mind off the past.* Glad she only had a few more blocks to go, she quickly drove to the large, brick building housing the Ever Hope Homeless Shelter.

One of the reasons she hated to be late was due to insufficient parking in the area. Driving around, she finally found a space just big enough for her to park.

Mentally fist-pumping for her excellent parallel parking procedure, she grabbed her slim briefcase. Clicking the locks, she glanced down and saw that she was still a foot away from the curb. She grimaced. At least her car was straight and not sticking out into the road.

Entering through the front door, she waved toward the two employees sitting at the reception desk. "Good morning," she called out. Enrico and Suzette Juarez had worked at the shelter for the past two years, and she considered them invaluable. Suzette won her over when they interviewed for the positions. *"Our kids are grown, and sitting around watching TV all day will make me lose my mind or want to hit my husband. So, I told him we were going to work where we could make a difference!"*

Enrico was a retired Marine, having served in Afghanistan. He was often the first contact some of their homeless veterans had at the center, and she had no doubt they stayed to get help because of him. Suzette's smile put many of the homeless mothers with children in tow at ease.

Not having time to chat, she hurried past the entrance to the free clinic and down the hall to her office. Because she dropped off Colleen every morning at school, she never made it to the shelter in time to oversee breakfast being served but was resolute in starting her day in the dining hall nonetheless. Tossing her briefcase behind her desk, she turned, almost slamming into Michael, one of the other social workers.

"Sorry!" she gushed.

"No worries. You're flustered this morning. Have a rough time getting out of the house?"

He turned and walked down the hall with her as she nodded. "No matter how much I try to get Colleen organized at night, there's always something the next morning that needs to be done, needs to be signed, or needs to be found."

He chuckled. "Just wait till she gets older. My wife is always complaining that our kids wait until the last minute to tell her that they need Styrofoam balls and pipe cleaners to build a solar system."

She smiled and nodded but inwardly winced at the thought of Colleen getting older and only having a single mother to try to keep everything straight. But, on the heels of that thought, she knew she would not trade a moment with her daughter and that her ex-husband had given up everything when he walked away. Glancing to the side, she also knew that laid-back Michael had a wife at home that was a ball of energy, probably doing most of the work.

"Good morning, Mrs. Wilson," came the greeting from several people as she entered the dining hall. Most of the residents had finished breakfast already, many having left to go to work or class. She hated missing the children before the school bus came to pick them up but was glad to greet them at the end of the day when they were dropped off.

Stepping into the kitchen, she eyed the cook and volunteers. "Everything go okay this morning?"

Mrs. Rossini had been cooking breakfast at the homeless shelter for the past four years. With a round body and a wide smile, she was considered the shelter's resident grandmother. But Tara knew that in the kitchen, Mrs. Rossini was a taskmaster. Shelter residents were required to assist at meals on a rotating basis and their cook took her duties seriously. Smiling at Tara, she nodded her head emphatically. "Yes, yes, all is well. It's cold outside today, so I made sure the little ones had a hot breakfast."

Patting the older woman on the shoulder, Tara thanked her before heading back to her office. Once there, her first order of business was to look over the list of any new residents who came in the night before. The shelter ran at capacity, the winter months making the demand worse, and they were unable to take everyone who sought shelter.

Bethany walked in and she smiled at the bright-eyed, eager young social worker fresh out of graduate school. She hoped Bethany would be able to keep her enthusiasm, knowing she would need it over the coming years in this profession.

"Just before I left yesterday, another group of WinterPole coats came in. I was able to distribute some of the smaller ones to the kids getting on the bus this morning, and the adult sizes I put in the supply closet."

Tara nodded, her smile firmly on her face as she considered the best way to distribute the bounty. "Let's see who we have to turn away that doesn't have winter clothing."

Watching Bethany leave her office, she settled her mind to the multitude of tasks in front of her.

# 4

Carter parked outside Hope City's Medical Examiner's building. It was housed near the campus of the university, and from the outside resembled a modern office building. Walking inside with Rachel, they moved to the reception desk. "Hey, Tim," he greeted the familiar young man as he signed in and collected his visitor badge.

"Detective Fiske. Detective Seas." Tim wiggled his eyebrows at Rachel, adding, "Gorgeous as always."

She laughed, shaking her head and patting her stomach. "Just what I needed to hear."

Carter rolled his eyes at the young man's ineffectual flirting. "Natalie Bastion is expecting us."

"She's in autopsy three."

Moving through the doors in the back, he and Rachel stalked down the hall. She laughed again as he wiggled his eyebrows, mocking Tim.

"I swear, the people they hire here seem to be getting younger and younger. Last time I was in here there was a girl at reception that looked like she was barely eighteen."

"Are you sure you're just not getting older, Rachel?" he asked.

"Shut up, Fiske. The last thing I want to think about is how old I'm getting."

Coming to the door indicating Autopsy 3, she pushed through and he followed. They were in a small observatory room, the seats leading down to a large glass window overlooking the actual autopsy. He walked past the four rows of inclined seats and observed Natalie in what appeared to be the final stages of the autopsy.

He pressed the buzzer located on the panel and a chime sounded, drawing the doctor's attention up to the window. She lifted her hand in acknowledgment and pulled the surgical mask down to her chin, still keeping her face shield in place. "Five minutes," she called out. "I'll meet you in the consultation room and can give you my results and his personal effects."

He felt Rachel shift beside him, turning to go back up the steps, but his gaze remained on the young man lying on the autopsy table. His chest had been opened, now stitched in the familiar Y. Under the harsh lighting in the autopsy arena, the corpse appeared even younger than he had the night before. A large tattoo covered his left bicep, but Carter was too far away to discern a pattern. He knew Natalie would have pictures and all the information they needed.

With a last look at the young man's face, he sighed before turning and following Rachel out the door. In the two years that he and Rachel had worked together, he appreciated that she intuitively knew when he did not want to be peppered with questions. And every time they viewed an autopsy was one of those times. They walked down the hall in silence to the consultation room for Autopsy 3.

"Quick break," she said.

As Rachel hurried down the hall to the ladies' room, he entered the consultation room. A few minutes later, both she and Natalie entered at the same time, Rachel with an air of relief and Natalie with her hands full of several bags and a file.

Not wasting any time, Natalie sat behind the desk and nodded toward the bags. "Here are his effects. There was no identification on his body. No wallet. No cell phone. I'll send his fingerprints to the lab and see if we can get an identification."

Opening the file, she flipped through several pieces of paper. "Obviously, my full report isn't written yet, but this is what I do have. Male. Approximately 18 to 25 years old. 5 feet, 11 inches. 173 pounds. Cause of death was smoke inhalation. There were drugs in his system but not enough to cause death. Definitely enough to make him drowsy and could have been a contributing factor as to why it appeared he made no move to get out of the smoke coming from the fire next door."

"Do you know what kind?" he asked.

"Selective serotonin reuptake inhibitors. Prescription antidepressant."

"Fuck."

Natalie continued reading. "He had eaten recently,

probably just last night. Overall health was good. There were no obvious wounds. He did have a tattoo on his left arm. I'll send the pictures to you to see if that will aid in identification. He had scarring on his left leg and tiny fragments of shrapnel embedded in the bone."

"Military?"

"Quite possibly."

Carter listened as she finished the recitation, nothing else giving them any more pertinent information or clues to the young man's identity until she mentioned what was in the bag.

"You'll notice when you look at his clothes they appear worn, somewhat dirty. Not filthy but not recently washed. The coat, on the other hand, is almost brand-new."

"Probably stolen," Rachel said on a sigh.

"Maybe, except I noticed the brand. It's a Winter-Pole, and there was an article in the paper a few weeks back about how the WinterPole company has a manufacturing plant here in Hope City. Wanting to give back to the community, they were donating a large number of winter coats to the homeless shelters to be distributed. I have no idea if that will help but thought I'd mention it."

"What about the tattoo?" he asked.

Natalie leaned back and shoved her glasses up on top of her head, rubbing her eyes. Fatigue showed briefly before the mask of efficiency dropped back into place. "I'll have it in my report that will get emailed to you but let me go ahead and send you a quick message."

Gaining his cell phone number, she sent the photograph of the tattoo to his phone.

Pulling it up, he stared at the black, monochromatic image of a fallen soldier memorial tattoo. Boots at the bottom. Rifle propped up, rising from the boots. Combat helmet resting on top. Heart pounding, the image hit him in the gut. For a few seconds, the analytical façade fell away at the memory of some of his fellow soldiers who did not come back. Blowing out his breath, he waited for the tightness in his chest to loosen.

He cleared his throat, swallowing past the lump, and pulled the mantle of detective around him once again. "This doesn't mean he was a veteran, but it gives us a good place to start." Standing, he shook Natalie's hand and thanked her. With the evidence bags in his arms, he and Rachel walked out of the building.

"Let's stop at the lab," he said, climbing into the driver's seat. It did not take long to arrive, and they quickly headed inside. Meeting Jerry, they waited as he pulled up his report.

"Mostly prescription drugs. Benzodiazepines, including diazepam, alprazolam, and clonazepam."

Carter's breath whistled between his teeth. "Opioids."

"Yep. And fentanyl. No identification on the pills."

Grimacing, he thanked Jerry as Rachel accepted the report. Arriving at headquarters, they walked straight to the evidence storeroom. After signing in, they moved to a table at one end of the room. Opening the bags, they pulled out John Doe's clothing and spread it out. It had already been processed by the Medical Examiner, but he wanted to look at it, hoping there was something he could discern.

Natalie, of course, had been right. The jeans were worn, but not filthy. There were no socks, but his boots were standard-issue military.

"He could have gotten those anywhere, so the boots don't mean he was in the military either."

Rachel nodded. "His pants and shirt appear to fit a man of his size. This coat, though, is an extra-large. Unless he just wanted to purchase a large coat, this might give credence to the possibility that he received it and was given no choice in size." She shrugged before adding, "Of course, he could've just stolen it from someone else."

Snapping pictures of the clothing, he put them back into the bags and gave them to the evidence officer. Once the bags were logged in and signed for, they walked back up to their desks.

A few hours later, Natalie sent an eCopy of her report. Printing out the information, he added John Doe's pertinent details to the large board next to his desk.

This John Doe was the third death on his caseload ... unusual for a non-homicide detective. Each with a bag of prescription drugs on their possession. Standing, he moved around to the front of his desk and leaned his hips against the side. Arms crossed over his chest, his gaze roved over the board.

Carl Burnley was the first, his body discovered on a park bench three weeks earlier. Autopsy revealed high levels of opioids in his system and he had a plastic sandwich bag in his pocket containing a variety of pills, a combination of opioids, antidepressants, and fentanyl.

Five days later, Jonathan Rothberg was found in an alley, his makeshift home created from cardboard boxes. His autopsy also revealed high levels of opioids in his system and a similar plastic sandwich bag containing prescription pills in his pocket.

Both men had identification on them, making confirmation easy. He and Rachel had divided the list of homeless shelters in Hope City and visited, searching for information about Carl and Jonathan, but they came up blank. Now, armed with a photograph of their John Doe, they would need to visit again.

"Carter..."

He turned and looked over his shoulder as Rachel approached. Her face was scrunched, and she walked with a slight limp, one hand on her back and the other hand resting on her protruding stomach. He pushed off the desk and stalked toward her, concern spearing through him. "Are you okay? Shit, is it time?"

She shook her head, blowing out a breath. "No, it's not labor. But I'm having some back pain."

"We need to get you to the doctor." His hands shot up to offer support, clasping onto her arms.

"Rick's on his way up—"

"I'm here."

Carter swung his head around and saw Rachel's husband, a cyber-investigator for the HCPD, stalking toward them. Relief flooded him as he moved to one side of her as several others crowded around. "Call me," he directed to Rick, receiving a nod in return.

Their captain stepped out of his office, concern etched onto his face. After speaking with Rachel and Rick, he looked up and held Carter's gaze. Stalking directly to him, Mike tilted his head toward the whiteboard and asked, "You got this for now?"

He nodded. He didn't mind working by himself but knew it would take longer to cover the investigation. "Yeah. I'll let you know if I need help, but for now, I'm going to re-canvas some of the homeless shelters to see if we can get an ID on John Doe."

His captain remained silent, his gaze still on the board. "I've got a bad feeling about this. Like it goes much deeper than a couple of homeless men hooked on opioids."

An hour later, Carter parked outside of Ever Hope Homeless Shelter. Rachel had visited this shelter last week, but with her out of commission, it fell to him. He gazed at the large brick building that appeared to take up a full city block. Toward the right corner was another door, the sign overhead indicating it was a clinic.

Climbing the steps at the front of the shelter, he walked into the reception area. The floors were spotless tile, and the pale walls were decorated with various artwork as well as informational posters. A man with a wide smile looked up as he approached. Pulling out his badge, he said, "I'm Detective Fiske, HCPD. I'm looking for any information you can give me about a person we're trying to identify."

"I'm Enrico, and I'll be glad to help, sir." Enrico cocked his head to the side. "The police have been here several times lately. Did the other detective have her baby?"

Smiling, he shook his head. "You must have talked to my partner. No, she hasn't yet, but it looks like I'll be the one investigating now."

Enrico's gaze grew wary. "That doesn't sound too good, Detective Fiske. The police having to come here to keep investigating makes me nervous."

*Kyle started to mention a sister this morning.* "I don't suppose someone named Ms. McBride works at this shelter?"

"Ms. McBride? No sir. We don't have anyone here by that name."

*Just my fuckin' luck.* Not replying, he reached into his pocket and pulled out a photograph he'd printed of the young man and had cropped so that only his face was visible.

Enrico sucked in a quick breath. "Shit, man." He dragged his gaze from the photograph up to Carter's face. "This man is dead, isn't he?"

"Do you recognize him?"

Nodding slowly, Enrico said, "Yeah, I've seen him around. But not real recently. I can't think of his name, but the head social worker would know. Her name is Mrs. Wilson. She's who you'd need to speak to." He picked up the phone and dialed. "Bethany? Is Tara around? Yeah, okay."

Looking up, he pointed to a hall leading toward the back of the building. "Admin offices are back there. You can head on back and talk to Bethany Barker. She's one of the social workers here. If she can't help you, she'll find Mrs. Wilson."

"Thanks, Enrico." He moved around the reception desk and started down the hall. A moment later, a pretty blonde came into view, her smile wide as her eyes shifted quickly from his head to his boots. Not a stranger to nor immune to a woman's approving gaze, he merely nodded toward her.

"Hi, Detective. I'm Bethany Barker, one of the social workers. Well, a social work intern. What can I help you with?"

*Intern. I thought she looked young. Or I'm getting old.* "I'm trying to identify someone and am checking with various homeless shelters in the area to see if someone can put a name to the face." He held out the picture and watched as she eagerly reached out to take it.

Gasping, she paled immediately. "Oh, my God! This... he's... this person is dead?"

She looked as though she were going to faint, and he grabbed the picture from her hands as she slumped back against the wall.

"Bethany, what on earth is going on here?"

Looking over his shoulder at the sound of the sharp voice and tapping of heels on the tile floor, he observed a woman approaching, her maturity and beauty much more to his taste than the rail-thin cheerleader still sucking in air as she pressed against the wall.

Thick hair so dark it was almost black pulled back in a low ponytail. Luminous blue eyes and pink lips that made him forget what he needed to ask her. As she walked toward him in her simple blouse and pants that did nothing to hide her curves, she had legs that seemed to go forever and yet she would still tuck under his chin.

Her gaze shifted from his face over to Bethany and she repeated her question. "What's going on here?"

"I'm sorry, Tara," Bethany cried. "He showed me a picture of a dead man, and I just wasn't expecting it."

If he thought the new woman was going to give in to histrionics, he was greatly mistaken.

"A picture of a dead man is hardly going to be able to hurt you," Tara said, taking Bethany by the arm and leading her into a conference room. "Michael," she called out. Another man popped out of an office, his gaze moving between the trio but settling on Tara.

"Bethany is not feeling well. Could you give her some water and sit with her for a few minutes until she's recovered? I need to deal with..." She hesitated, looking up at Carter.

"Detective Fiske, Ma'am."

She offered a curt nod his way before turning back to Michael. "I need to deal with the detective." She left the conference room, turning sideways as Michael rushed forward toward Bethany. Barely sending a glance Carter's way, she walked down the hall and entered a small office. Sitting down at a desk piled with folders and papers, she waved toward the chair in the room.

"You are..." he began, feeling the need to take back the reins of the encounter with the efficient woman.

"Forgive me," she said, her voice smooth. "I'm Tara Wilson. My official title here at Ever Hope Homeless

Shelter is Head Social Worker. My unofficial title is *Fixer of All Things That No One Else Can Figure Out How to Fix.*"

His lips quirked and he murmured, "I can only imagine you're right."

"I assume you need me to look at the photographs that sent Bethany into a fit?"

He reached across the desk and handed the picture to her, watching carefully for her reaction. Not certain what he expected from the cool and collected social worker, the flash of recognition in her eyes followed by slumped shoulders was a surprise.

A sigh escaped her lips, and she nodded slowly. "Yes, I recognize him. Rocky." She sucked in a deep breath through her nose before letting it out. Her fingertips ran lightly over the picture, almost reverently. "Rocky Stallone."

"Would you be able to accompany me to the morgue for an official positive ID?" He watched as her gaze shot up to his, emotion working behind her eyes. She looked as though she wanted to argue against his request but finally nodded.

Through tight lips, she replied, "If that's necessary, then yes."

They stood and he waited while she slipped on her coat and bent to gather her purse slowly, her mannerisms not as snappy as before. Walking toward the front, she stopped at the reception desk and spoke to Enrico. "I'll be back as soon as I can."

Whatever questions were on the tip of his tongue to ask, Carter kept them to himself. She did not seem amenable to conversation, and until he had an official positive ID, he decided to keep his questions to himself. He escorted her to his SUV, and they drove in silence to the morgue. Inwardly sighing, he could not help but wish he'd met the intriguing woman under different circumstances.

# 5

Sitting ramrod straight, Tara clutched her purse in her lap. She had never been to a morgue and on the drive over had no idea what to expect. She was surprised when Detective Fiske only drove about six blocks before parking outside of a building near the university. Not waiting for him, she alighted from his SUV and followed him inside.

A young man sitting at the reception desk grinned, saying, "Every time I see you, Detective Fiske, you've got another beautiful woman with you."

She blinked at the comment, her back stiffening. Next to her, she could have sworn she heard the detective growl.

"Keep it professional or you might find you don't have a job."

The young man swallowed deeply, mumbling his apology. She watched as the detective signed in for both of them and handed her a temporary badge. Continuing to follow his lead, she walked down the hall.

She opened her mouth to ask if she was going to be viewing the body up close as she had seen on TV or in the movies. She sucked in her lips and pressed down, refusing to give an indication of weakness in light of Bethany's actions just from looking at the picture.

He opened the door and stepped in, holding the door for her to follow through. She released a breath she had been holding to see that they were in a conference room.

"Ms. Wilson, let me explain how this is going to go. Pictures of the deceased will be shown on the screen," he said, waving to a widescreen TV on the wall. "There will be a multitude of pictures from the front and sides. If you are uncertain that he is who you think he might be, please say so. On the other hand, if you are able to positively identify him, we will have a form for you to sign. Do you have any questions?"

"Will it all be based on what I say?"

"We have his fingerprints and it will be cross-referenced with your identification."

She nodded, then added, "Rocky was in the military. The Army."

At her added information, his eyebrows raised. "Then that will be an added place that we will be able to obtain cross-referenced identification."

He leaned forward and pressed a button on an intercom panel sitting on the table. "We're ready."

She stared down at her clasped hands resting on the table for a few seconds, then, steeling her spine, lifted her gaze. There, on the screen, was the face of a young man she had gotten to know. Her heart squeezed as she continued to watch as several more pictures moved across the screen. The left side of his face. The right side. His shoulder and upper arm covered in a tattoo. And then another picture that was taken straight on. She recognized the small scar that cut through his left eyebrow, remembering his story of having his eyebrow pierced, then getting rid of it when he joined the Army.

"Ms. Wilson?"

She startled, her gaze shifting from the screen to Detective Fiske, seeing sympathy in his eyes. Her head nodded up and down in jerks, and when she attempted to speak it came out as a croak. Clearing her throat, she said, "Yes. That's Rocky... um... Richard Stallone. He said that his Army buddies nicknamed him Rocky because of his last name."

Her lips were suddenly dry, and she blinked, battling back the moisture that threatened to gather in her eyes. She swallowed deeply before asking, "How did he die?"

"From smoke inhalation. There was a fire in the building next to him and he appeared to have never woken from his sleep."

Her stomach clenched as her heart began to pound. *Christ, he just wanted a warm place to sleep. Why didn't he take the bed we offered? Why didn't I insist?* Sucking in another breath through her nose, she wondered how many other Rockys were out there that she couldn't reach, couldn't help. *"You can't save everyone." How many times have I heard that? It's the mantra of social workers everywhere.*

Biting the inside of her cheek to quell the desire to weep, she glanced to the side toward the detective eyeing her carefully. She could see the questions building in his eyes but cut him off before he had a chance to begin. Lifting her chin slightly. "You have papers for me to sign?"

He held her gaze, and she fought the desire to look away. Finally, as though giving up the silent battle of wills, he nodded. He pulled a sheaf of papers from inside his coat pocket and began explaining each one. Uncertain her fingers would hold a pen, she was glad that he wrote down the name Richard Stallone, adding a line underneath indicating Richard had been in the Army.

After reading through the papers and asking if she had any more questions, he handed her the pen, and she signed and printed her name. They stood in unison, walking back through the hall and out the door.

They had almost made it to his SUV when she halted, her feet stumbling. Her mind churned with memories of Rocky in the group counseling class she led. *I thought he was making it.* Those thoughts swirled with the images she had just seen. The never-ending list of those she needed to assist was growing, so she forced her gaze to lift to his. "If there's nothing else, Detective Fiske, I believe I'll walk."

"Ms. Wilson, please allow me to drive you back to the shelter. I know this has been a shock, and I appreciate your cooperation. I'll have more questions for you, but they can wait."

"I appreciate that." It seemed surprising for her voice to be as strong as it was, as though they were discussing something more mundane than the death of a young man. But right now, she simply wanted to be alone. "I do prefer to walk, though. Thank you." Without giving him a chance to argue, she turned and quickly headed down the street, pulling her coat around her, warding off the chilly wind.

At the end of the street, she gave in to the desire to look over her shoulder, shocked to see the detective still standing by his SUV, his gaze pinned on her. She turned the corner, no longer wanting anyone's eyes on her. She finally felt the sting of tears and bent her head as she dug furiously in her purse, her fingers grasping a tissue. Dabbing underneath her eyes, she wiped her nose before continuing to walk down the street.

Burned into her memory was the picture of Rocky in death, so in contrast to the smile she'd eventually managed to coax from him. She first met him when he'd come in six months earlier, just for a meal. When she tried to get him to place his name on the bed list, he'd insisted that there were others who needed it more than him. She did manage to get him to come occasionally to the group therapy session that she had and worked to set him up in their employment program. Recognizing signs of bipolar disorder, she had made sure to get him to visit the free clinic next to the shelter. Dr. Tiller, the clinic's physician, had hoped to get Rocky on a regimen of medication to help stabilize his moods, but Rocky always refused.

*"He never woke from his sleep."* Detective Fiske's words rattled in her head as she continued walking down the street. Rounding another corner, she looked up and saw Ever Hope in front of her. People were going in and out

the front door as always. The scene was so familiar, and yet now, she simply stood and ached for the young man who had met an untimely demise. *Oh, Rocky. I'm so sorry I didn't do more for you.*

She had no desire to go back into her office. Not now. Feeling the overwhelming desire for a break, she glanced at her watch and decided to take an early lunch break. Passing by the front of Ever Hope, she continued walking until she came to her car. She did not have to ponder where she was going; she simply drove and was not surprised when she pulled into the driveway of her parents' large home.

Walking around to the back door, her mind was flooded with memories of growing up in this neighborhood. The Kings lived next door, a couple that were best friends to her parents. With their five children and the six McBrides all about the same age, there was always someone to play with, fight with, confide in, or babysit. The oldest girl of all of them, she often kept an eye on everyone.

She knocked on the back door before opening it, entering the large kitchen, not surprised to see her mom busy making lunch.

"Tara! What a nice surprise!" Her mom's eyes immediately narrowed as she glanced at the time on the microwave and asked, "Is everything okay?"

Not attempting a pretense of a smile, she shrugged. "I just spent the morning in the morgue."

Her mother immediately moved to her, pulling her in for a hug. She looked so much like her mother but had more height from her dad. Sharon's dark hair was now an elegant silver, cut in a bob. Her figure was still beautiful and her eyes as blue as ever. Her father, Colm, was tall and lean. A former FBI investigator, he now worked as a consultant after a medical retirement the previous year.

As she rested her cheek next to her mom's, Sharon declared, "You're going to have lunch with me."

The two worked side-by-side in the kitchen, making sandwiches and pouring chips into a bowl before settling at the table. She explained why she had been at the morgue, sighing at the end of her tale. "No matter how much I do, it doesn't seem like it's enough."

Her mom sat quietly for a moment, the two women comfortable with the silence. Finally, with a smile moving over her lips, her mom said, "After having two boys, I was so excited to find out I was having a girl. At first, you were the little princess. Sean and Kyle were so sweet with you, and your father nearly popped with pride every time he showed his little girl off. But after three more children, your place in the family went from being the baby princess to being the oldest girl. It's funny how we don't think about birth order and how it affects our lives, but I firmly believe it's a factor. You were never bossy, but from a very young age, you slid into the role of taking care of everybody, including your two older brothers."

Uncertain where her mother was going with her reminiscing, she continued to sip her iced tea, enjoying the recollections.

"I worried that I placed too much responsibility on your shoulders, but you seemed to relish helping your siblings. I think your brothers became better men because you took the time to let them know how young women should be treated. I know Erin and Caitlyn were so lucky to have their big sister's guidance as they grew up. Goodness, even the King kids benefited from your counsel. You kept the peace among eleven children more times than I can imagine."

"So, what are you telling me, Mom?"

Chuckling, her mom nodded. "Your father and I were not surprised when you became a social worker, Tara. Helping others is not just what you do, it's who you are. You can touch their lives, but you can't save everyone. To hold that up as the bar you're trying to attain will only make you unhappy." Her mother patted her arm before standing and taking their plates to the sink.

Driving back to work, her mind rolled to Detective Fiske, doubting he would label her as helpful. *I'm usually so much nicer to people...* She did not have to think long and hard about her reaction to the tall, blonde detective. When she first saw him at the shelter, her heart jumped to life, a reaction she'd had many years earlier when she first met Colleen's dad. Blonde. Handsome. A charming smile. But Detective Fiske had such confidence. Since the end of her marriage, she kept a tight rein on her heart, and that had worked very well—until Detective Fiske walked through the door.

---

The next day, Tara sat in her office, staring at the files

that needed reviewing and clients that needed to be seen. When she had returned from the morgue and her impromptu lunch, Bethany had immediately rushed in, full of questions as her hands fluttered nervously about her head. It seemed as though Bethany cared more about the excitement of having been presented with the picture of a deceased person than she actually cared about Rocky. Giving short answers, Tara had left work early, wanting to have time alone before Colleen got home.

Now, utterly lethargic, she felt as though molasses ran through her veins. Growling under her breath, she stood. *This isn't helping anyone.* She stalked down the hall to the nearest classroom, sitting in on Michael's class on employment skills. Throwing herself into the discussions, she assisted with mock interviews, finding the tight band around her chest easing slightly.

When the session was over, she walked out of the classroom, her arms full of files and books. Looking up, she observed Detective Fiske walking toward her. He was handsome, no doubt about it. She should not have been surprised that Bethany could not stop talking about him after she gathered her wits. Tall, thick blonde hair, and blue eyes. If he ever needed to give up police work, he could be a model for Ralph Lauren—their mature line. She shook her head, frustrated at the trail her mind had taken. She had not had this strong a reaction to a man since Calvin. *And look how that turned out.*

Instead of smiling in recognition, she stopped and sighed heavily. "Detective Fiske, to what do I owe the pleasure of another visit?"

"I needed to ask you more questions."

She knew he had a job to do but felt the weight settle on her shoulders once again. Her lips pinched together, and she looked toward the other social worker. "Michael, would you handle the next class while I take the detective back to my office?" Barely giving Carter a second glance, she said, "Follow me."

Once inside, she divested the load in her arms onto a table pushed to the corner, then sat at her desk. As he sat in the other chair, she remained quiet, waiting for him to speak.

"I want to thank you for your identification yesterday," he began, his gaze intense. "I know that was difficult for you. The information that he had been an Army veteran was incredibly helpful. We were able to ascertain that he was indeed Richard Stallone." Before she had a chance to respond, he continued. "He was wearing worn clothing, except for a new WinterPole coat—"

"He didn't steal it. We received a shipment to give out, and he was given one." Her voice was harsher than she meant, but the idea that Richard would be accused of stealing irritated her.

"I didn't say he stole it."

Pursing her lips, she inclined her head in agreement. "That's true, you didn't." Sighing again, she said, "I'm glad that you're concerned about him, but I don't understand. If smoke inhalation killed him, what else is there to investigate?"

"Richard is the third death of a homeless person in

the last few weeks. My partner came by to ask about the other two."

Tara's brows lowered. "They didn't speak to me, but then if I'm unavailable, someone else would have checked."

He flipped through his small notebook, and she observed just enough to see that his handwriting was chicken-scratch. He appeared to understand his notations as he flipped through several pages, landing on the one he was searching for.

"Yes, she spoke to Michael Gorney. She had him check on Carl Brumley and Jonathan Rothberg." He lifted his head and met her gaze.

She nodded. "Michael fills in for me when I'm out or in a meeting. That was the man who was taking the class for me just now."

"Would you mind taking a look?"

Tara shook her head slowly, reaching her hand out.

He pulled a photograph from his pocket and slid it across her desk toward her. "This is Carl Burnley. We have no known address for him, but we know he was a veteran. The picture you're looking at was from his driver's license and is several years old."

She let out a long sigh of relief, her breath shaky, her tension peaking as she feared she would be staring at another photograph of a corpse. She picked up the photograph and studied it. Shaking her head, she lifted her gaze and said, "I don't recognize him."

## 6

Carter was not sure what he'd expected when he walked into Ever Hope Homeless Shelter yesterday but had hoped that Sean and Kyle's sister worked there and would be able to help him. The idea of a detective's sibling being more efficient with the police had settled in his mind. But since there was no McBride at the center, he had to admit the intrepid Tara Wilson handled herself with professional efficiency. Her composure at the morgue impressed him. And now, if it wasn't for the slight shaking of her hands, he would never know that she was stressed.

Earlier, as he walked behind her down the long, tiled hall, his gaze was drawn to her ass even though there was nothing overtly sexual about her clothes. Plain, pale-yellow blouse paired with black slacks. Her feet tapped along the tiles, encased in low heeled pumps. Even her office was professionally efficient, both neat and cluttered at the same time. Files and papers were stacked on her desk, but as she sat in her chair and directed her gaze toward him, he had the feeling she could lay her hand on any report needed.

After she viewed the photograph of Carl, he pulled out a second picture and slid it toward her. "This is another young man found dead. Jonathan Rothberg. As far as we can tell, he also had no address, leading us to believe he may be homeless. Unlike Carl, he wasn't a veteran. I'm hoping to see if there's anything you can tell me about him."

She took the old photograph from his hand and gave it the same careful scrutiny she had with Carl's picture. Shaking her head, she said, "No. I don't recognize his face." Without another word, she opened her laptop and quickly began to type. She continued to shake her head as she looked up from her computer to hold his gaze. "Carl's not in our system."

"System?"

"There are multiple homeless shelters in Hope City. Those that are sanctioned and funded by the city, such as ours, and those run by private groups and churches. We do have a shared database for listing anyone who comes to stay with us, although it is not inclusive."

"So, if he was homeless, he would be in your database?" he asked.

"The city shelters are very good about keeping track of the information. Some of the others are less... um... accurate."

"Why would a shelter not be accurate?"

"Some are emergency shelters or cold-weather shelters run by churches. While we appreciate all efforts to aid the homeless, some do not keep records the way we're required to. They may also hand out sleeping bags and food while not offering a bed."

"Are you able to service most of the homeless through the city's shelters?"

She tilted her head to the side, her expressive blue eyes peering straight into his. It was hard not to notice her beauty, but at the moment, her pink-tinted lips were stretched into a thin line.

"Detective Fiske, on any given day there are almost three-thousand persons considered to be homeless in Hope City. Seventy-two percent of those are men, and at least ten percent are veterans. Over twenty-five percent are considered to be chronically homeless, which means it's not temporary. In our city, there are only about twelve hundred emergency beds. You can do the math. That means many, many homeless persons are either turned away because there's not enough room or they never make it through our doors."

"And Jonathan?"

Tara's attention refocused on her computer. When she looked up and held his gaze, he was struck with the clearness of her blue eyes and beautiful face in contrast to the hard set of her jaw. She tilted her head and he realized he was staring. "Did you find anything?" His voice was rough, covering his perusal.

"Yes. Last year, he spent two nights at the emergency shelter over on 43rd Street. From what I can see, those were the only two nights that he spent at a shelter."

"What about clinics for treating or offering prescription drugs for the homeless?" He watched her blink at the change in direction of his inquiry.

"Our center is next to a free clinic if that's what you're asking. It's not the only clinic in the area that provides services to the poor and uninsured."

"So, Carl Burnley or Jonathan Rothberg could have been seen at the clinic without ever having come to stay at this homeless shelter?"

She leaned back in her seat as she nodded. "What are you not telling me, Detective Fiske?"

He held her steady gaze, his admiration increasing. *Smart, intuitive. And beautiful.* He considered how much to reveal, then decided she might be more accommodating if she knew what he was up against. "All three men had opioids in their systems and pills in their possession."

It took just a few seconds for her eyes to widen and she gasped. "Rocky? Rocky also?"

"Yes, Ms. Wilson. This is why we're investigating. All three were carrying prescription pills in baggies—way more than they would be taking."

She looked down at her hands clasped together on her desk as she pursed her lips together again. "I see. I'm not sure what you're looking for, but over forty percent of those who seek shelters have a substance use disorder." Lifting her head, she speared him with her glacial stare and added, "The streets are full of ways for them to get their next fix. I'm not sure looking at the clinics that offer needed services is the right place for you to focus your energies."

"What can you tell me about Rocky? Was he being seen for a substance use disorder? Or given opioids for pain? Other drugs?"

A long silence ensued, and he wondered if she was going to answer his question. While she stared at her hands on her desk again, it gave him full access to study her discreetly. She didn't wear a wedding ring, and he wondered if she, like him, was married to the job. *A demanding job that probably at times seemed as thankless as mine.* He noted the dark circles underneath her eyes, possibly indicating little sleep the previous night. A stab of guilt moved through him that he needed her at the morgue. *I've no doubt that was sure as fuck not what she expected to have to do when she came to work yesterday.* She lifted a hand and rubbed her forehead as though in pain. "Ms. Wilson, are you okay?" He blinked in surprise when her gaze hit him.

"I'm sorry, Detective Fiske. My mind wandered. All I could think about was Rocky finding a place out of the elements to stay warm but having the bad luck of being near a fire." She opened her mouth as though to say more, then gave her head a little shake. Clearing her throat, she said, "You asked about drugs. I can't tell you what he had taken. The times he came in to talk to me he was clear-eyed and coherent. I know he suffered from PTSD, and I referred him to the clinic. I spoke to Dr. Tiller about Rocky, and the last conversation we had about him I was told he was prescribing an antidepressant."

"For those who can't afford medication, how does the clinic handle that?"

"I know the basics of how the clinic functions, Detective, but you would need to speak to them about the particulars. The free clinic is a completely separate entity from the homeless shelter. Their facility is adjacent to us, but we are not connected to them financially or procedurally. We make recommendations that some of our homeless visit the clinic, but we have no control over whether they do or what happens once they are there. Their medical records are private unless they sign for us to have access, which we only need if they are receiving counseling from us."

The phone on her desk rang, and she answered it, pressing the speaker. "Yes, Enrico?"

"Ms. Wilson? You're needed for an emergency intake. It's a family with small children."

"I'll be right there." She disconnected the phone, placed her palms on the top of her desk, and pushed herself to a stand. Another sigh slipped through her lips. "If that's all, Detective Fiske, I have to get back to work."

He stood and said, "Thank you for your time, Ms. Wilson. I'll speak to the clinic, but I'm sure I'll have more questions for you later."

Without waiting, she strode past him, and he could hear her heels clicking as she walked down the hall. Following, he shook his head at his royal dismissal, wondering if there really was an intake or if she had a system in place for a coworker to call her when she wanted to be interrupted.

Once out into the reception area, he inwardly winced at his assumption as his gaze landed on a young couple with two small children standing with Enrico. The man wore no coat, and the woman only had a thin sweater. The two children were bundled in oversize coats in an obvious attempt by the parents to keep them warm.

As he stepped around, he looked over his shoulder and watched Ms. Wilson approach. Her stern expression had softened, and her wide smile lit the room. His feet came to a halt as he watched the transformation. After greeting the man and woman, making eye contact as she reached out and shook their hands, she then squatted so that she could greet the children. Their eyes were big as they partially hid behind their mother's legs. It only took a moment for her soft voice and kind words to have the children smiling back at her.

The front door opened, letting in a blast of cold air, and he was jostled as several people walked in. Turning quickly before he was caught staring, he walked down the front steps and turned to the left toward the clinic.

"Detective Fiske? Ms. Robinson has a few minutes for you now."

He had spent almost an hour cooling his heels in the waiting room of the free clinic but had not wasted his time. It gave him the opportunity to read their brochures, study some of the patients coming into the clinic, and do a little research on his phone.

Smiling, he followed the receptionist to an office that was connected to a room filled with medical records. The woman sitting at the desk looked up and smiled, then stood and offered her hand.

"Detective, I'm Marsha Robinson."

Her handshake was firm and her smile warm. Waving her hand toward one of the empty seats in her office, she invited him to sit. "I confess I don't have very much time to give you right now, and I know you've been waiting, so please don't consider me rude if I ask that we go directly to your questions."

Appreciating her efficiency, he said, "I'm investigating the recent deaths of three men who happened to be homeless. Only one of them was seen at the shelter next door, but all three had opioids in their system. I'm here for two reasons. One, I'd like to find out specifically if any of those three men were seen here or got their drugs from this clinic. And while I understand the basic workings of a free clinic, I'd like you to explain how the pharmaceuticals and prescriptions work for your clients."

Just as she opened her mouth, he anticipated her objection to the first reason he wanted to talk to her and added, "Their deaths have been ruled suspicious, therefore, they're under investigation."

"I understand, Detective. I can give you the information and explanation you ask for, but I must tell you that opioids or any narcotics are not kept nor dispensed here at the clinic's pharmacy."

He simply nodded at her statement but waited to hear about the three men. He slid a piece of paper across her desk with their names and watched carefully as her gaze moved over the list. She said nothing but turned to her computer and began to tap.

"Carl Burnley filled out our intake paperwork three months ago, but there's no record that he came back in for any treatments." She continued to search on her computer before adding, "Jonathan Rothberg filled out our paperwork about the same time, but he was unable to provide any documentation. He would have been given a list of what he needed to bring in, but there's no record that he returned to us."

Jotting the information in his notebook, he asked, "And Richard Stallone?"

A slight smile curved her lips. "Ah, Rocky. He came in for an initial intake four months ago. He brought in the required paperwork, and I have him being seen by Dr. Tiller twice in the past three months. Before you leave here today, we can set up a time for you to meet with the doctor."

"Appreciate that." He waited until she turned away from her computer, her attention focused on him again. "And the pharmacy here? How does that work?"

"Often, the cost of prescription medications is prohibitive to our clients. We have a licensed, in-house pharmacy with a wide variety of medications for diabetes, high blood pressure, depression, cholesterol, asthma, and many other common illnesses. We do not carry or dispense narcotic or controlled substances at all, Detective Fiske."

"You mentioned medications for depression." He looked back down at his notebook and flipped through a few pages. "Do any of those include a Selective Serotonin Reuptake Inhibitor?"

"I'm afraid that's a question for the pharmacist or Dr. Tiller. I'm not familiar with all the medications that are offered. If you like, I can take you back to the pharmacy. They might have time to talk with you now."

Nodding his agreement, he stood, allowing her to proceed before him. He glanced at his phone but had no message from Rachel or her husband. Firing off a quick text, he knew Rick probably had his hands full but hoped to hear something soon. Rachel was a good partner, and even though he knew her maternity leave was coming up soon, he had not prepared mentally to be working the case alone so soon. Lost in thought, his feet stuttered to a halt to keep from running into Ms. Robinson as she stopped at a half-door.

"This stays locked and our patients are not allowed here. If a prescription is needed, the nurse comes and gets it, then delivers it to the patient."

He glanced through the top half of the door into what appeared to be a regular pharmacy. Multiple shelves were filled with boxes and bottles, and a woman and a man were working at a large counter, counting pills.

Continuing to follow Ms. Robinson, they stopped at another door with a nameplate declaring *"Pharmacist, Robert Atkins."* She knocked on the door and, receiving a reply, opened it.

"Robert, this is Detective Fiske. He's investigating the deaths of several people, one of them our patient, and he had a few questions for you." She waved Carter forward, and he heard her padded footsteps fade as she walked back toward her office.

The man sitting behind the desk jumped to his feet with a wide smile on his face. Sticking his hand out he pumped Carter's hand up and down several times. "Detective, nice to meet you." Clapping his hands together he rubbed them vigorously. "Sit, sit, and we can talk drugs!"

Unable to keep the surprise off his face, Carter knew his eyebrows had reached his hairline as he sat down and cocked his head to the side. *This should be interesting...*

## 7

Carter's gaze quickly assessed the pharmacist. Robert was much younger than he'd anticipated, probably in his early thirties. His dark hair was a little shaggy, and his brown eyes darted about the room. Wearing a bright green button-down shirt, the color stood out starkly from his white lab coat. Casting his gaze about Robert's office, it appeared to be used for storage, one table along the side of the room stacked with boxes.

"I'm investigating the death of three men. All three had been homeless at the time of their death. The last one had a large dose of antidepressant in him, and all three men had opioids in their system. What ties them together particularly is that they also all had plastic baggies filled with a variety of opioid prescription pills in their possession."

Eyebrows raised, Robert sobered. "I'm truly sorry to hear that, Detective. I don't actually come in contact with any of our clients and can tell you that we don't prescribe or carry any opioids in our pharmacy. We do carry antidepressants. We have a number of drugs for pain and arthritis. Most of them are non-steroids, but we also have muscle relaxants and some steroids."

"What about patients who come to the clinic already on opioids?"

"That's a question that I would leave for Dr. Tiller, as far as specific drugs for specific patients. In general terms, I can tell you that the drugs we do offer would be used instead of opioids, but it's more difficult to wean someone off an opioid addiction."

Nodding, he stood and offered his hand. Once again, Robert shook it firmly. "Thank you for taking time to answer my questions."

"No worries, Detective. Like I said, it was a nice break in my day."

He turned to walk out of the office, glancing toward the table that was piled with boxes. "I assume all of these are pharmaceuticals. Are you the one who checks them in as they come?"

Nodding, Robert said, "I check them off the invoice list initially to make sure we have everything. Then they're turned over to the pharmacy staff where two of them work together to get them catalogued and on the shelves of the pharmacy."

Offering a chin lift, he walked out into the hall and back toward Marsha Robinson's office. Seeing her door open, he knocked on the doorframe and waited for her to look up. "Thank you for your assistance today. Who should I see about setting up a time to talk to Dr. Tiller?"

"I've already arranged it. If you can come early tomorrow morning, he'll see you before he starts seeing patients. You would need to be here around seven."

"I'll be here. Thank you." With another nod, he walked back through the crowded waiting room and out into the cold air. His phone vibrated and he pulled it from his pocket, checking the incoming text. Richard had replied, letting him know that Rachel was being sent home but would be on bed rest until the baby came. Blowing out his breath, he fired off a quick text, wishing her well. Stalking back to his SUV, he headed to headquarters. With the news about Rachel, he needed to check in with his superior.

Glancing at the front of the homeless shelter as he drove by, the vision of Tara Wilson's beautiful smile as she knelt and chatted with the two children stayed firmly planted in his mind.

---

"Why don't you come over for dinner? Caitlyn said she was going to drop by. We can make it a McBride girls' night."

"Are you sure?" Erin asked.

Huffing, Tara said, "Erin." She may have only said her sister's name but had no doubt her tone of voice would carry her feelings. Sure enough, Erin laughed.

"Is Aunty Erin coming, too?" Colleen yelled from across the kitchen.

"I'm sure you had no problem hearing my daughter and the excitement in her voice considering that most people in the world probably heard her. Come on over anytime. I've got plenty." Disconnecting, she looked at Colleen and smiled. "Looks like we'll have all girls here tonight."

Colleen began twirling and Tara opened the refrigerator door. Her parents had bought her a new pressure cooker for Christmas, and she had discovered its wonders. Pulling out the ingredients for beef stew, she began cutting the vegetables.

Colleen quickly abandoned the kitchen, giving Tara a few minutes to herself before her sisters arrived. Her workday had been busy with the cold weather forcing more people to seek shelter. But as she dumped the vegetables and beef into her cooker, it was not the homeless or her job that filled her mind. It was Detective Fiske.

*But why?* With three handsome brothers, three handsome King brothers next door, and their friends, it was not as though she didn't have any good-looking men in her life. Brothers. Friends. Coworkers. But no one seemed to stay on her mind the way he did.

"Aunty Caitlyn!"

Assuming Caitlyn had walked through the front door, Tara wiped her hands on the dish towel and made her way toward the front. Caitlyn was just a little shorter than Tara but had the same dark, thick McBride hair and blue eyes as the other siblings. Being the youngest, she always went her own way, and while Tara colored between the lines, Caitlyn reveled in coloring all over the page. Right now, she sported a flash of pink highlights in her hair. Tara could only imagine the boys at the high school where Caitlyn taught looked upon their teacher with a little bit of awe and a lot of lust.

"Hey, baby girl," Caitlyn called out, bending to give Colleen a hug. Tara reached her, and the sisters hugged as well.

"Guess who's coming?" Colleen prodded, bouncing on her toes. Without giving Caitlyn a chance to answer, Colleen said, "Aunty Erin!"

Caitlyn's eyebrows lifted and she smiled, looking at Tara. "Good. I've been so busy lately I feel like I haven't had a chance to see anybody."

The two women walked back into the kitchen, where Tara checked on the pressure cooker. Looking over her shoulder toward Caitlyn, she said, "You've been busy this school year. What's different?"

Tucking her hair behind her ear, Caitlyn huffed. "It's a new principal. I was so excited for him to start this year, having heard good things about him. But it seems to be mostly talk. He wants everybody to be super busy on paper. Volunteer for committees. Stay after school for tutoring. Making sure the students can pass their state tests. Nothing about that is inherently wrong, but he doesn't seem very interested in the students as individuals. If I go to him with a concern about a student, he brushes me off. I know the counselors are just as frustrated as the teachers are." Lifting her shoulders in a shrug, she began to set the table. "I'm already hearing rumors, though, he's hoping to get moved to the school board office next year. I hate having to get used to a new principal, but maybe that's for the best."

Before Tara had a chance to respond, Colleen's squeal of delight was heard once again. "Aunty Erin!"

Caitlyn laughed and shook her head. "Is she always so exuberant?"

Passing her sister on the way to the front door, she popped Caitlyn with the dishtowel. "You won't remember it, but you were just as bouncy and excitable as Colleen when you were that age."

Caitlyn wrinkled her nose and Tara laughed. When Tara reached the front door, she found Erin hugging Colleen.

"Mom! Aunty Erin brought cupcakes!"

"You didn't have to bring anything, Erin, although Colleen and Caitlin will love them. I love them too, but my hips will hate me in the morning."

"Oh, my God, Tara. Your hips are fine! Honestly, after getting out of the Army, I'd like to get a few curves back."

"Good grief," Caitlyn said, walking to the front and hugging Erin. "Listen to us talk about being too thin or too curvy. McBrides have good genes. We just have to embrace them!"

"When did you become such a sage?" Erin asked.

"Try working with teenagers with body image issues!"

Tara nodded, agreeing. "You're absolutely right. As far as I'm concerned, we're all perfect the way we are." Glancing down at the plate of cupcakes she was now carrying, she added, "But I *will* stop at just one!"

The women laughed as they walked into the kitchen,

sitting at the table while waiting for the stew to finish cooking. The conversation was easy, each chatting about their week.

"Well, I'm already looking forward to spring break," Caitlyn said. "There are some teachers who are going to take a cruise and asked me to come along. I'm thinking about it, but I may just want to do nothing for a whole week."

"Ooh, the possibility of a shipboard romance," Tara said. "Sounds lovely."

Erin smiled at the others, but the smile did not reach her eyes. Tara cast a gaze toward Erin but said nothing. Erin had been home from the Army for almost two months, but it was as though a shadow had moved over her. Erin had begun to talk to Tara, not just because she was an older sister but because of her counseling background. She had encouraged Erin to seek professional counseling, but so far, her sister just wanted to talk to her. And whatever her sister wanted, if Tara could give it to her, she would.

"Mom said that you had to deal with the morgue this week," Erin said.

"What happened?" Caitlyn asked before glancing toward the den to make sure Colleen was not listening. Caitlyn and Erin moved from the table into the kitchen to make sure their conversation was private.

She sighed heavily, sweeping her hand over her hair, pulling out the ponytail holder, hoping it would relieve her headache. "It was someone that I had worked with at the shelter. I was able to give them his name and the fact that he had been in the military. The detective took me to the morgue where I was able to identify the body, and then they were able to confirm with the military."

Both Caitlyn and Erin reached out and placed their hands on her arms, giving a supportive squeeze in unison.

"That must've been so hard for you," Caitlyn said.

"It was, but the detective was kind. I mean... you know... efficient. But, yes... kind."

She watched as Caitlyn and Erin looked at each other, their lips curving slightly. Turning, she opened the refrigerator to get the milk for Colleen, hoping her sisters would leave her fumbling words alone. She should have known that would never happen.

"You seemed awfully flustered when talking about the detective," Caitlyn said, moving to one side of Tara.

Erin closed in on the other side. "Anything special about him?"

"No, I'm not flustered. And no, there was nothing special about him."

"Hmmm, methinks thou doth protest too much." Caitlyn grinned as she tapped her forefinger on her chin.

"So, what does he look like?" Erin asked.

Whirling around to glare at both of her sisters, she said, "Truthfully? Tall, fit, blond, handsome, and charming. Remind you of anyone?"

"Damn," Erin huffed.

Caitlyn's smile had dropped from her face, replaced by concern in her eyes. "Tara, honey, not every handsome, charming man is like Calvin."

Dropping her chin to her chest, she sighed. "I know. Really, I know." Lifting her gaze back to her sisters, she added, "But right now, being a mom to Colleen is way more important than putting my trust into another man."

Before they had a chance to continue their conversation, Colleen burst into the room, a wide smile on her face. "I'm starving!"

"Well, good, let's eat!" Tara said.

Later that evening, after Caitlin and Erin had left and Colleen had been put to bed, Tara poured a glass of wine and sat on the sofa, her mind whirling. When Colleen was younger, Tara was always so tired at the end of the day that she often fell into bed soon after finishing household chores once Colleen was asleep. Now, with Colleen a little more independent, she found that her evenings gave her more time to think. And once more, she found her thoughts moving to the handsome detective.

Even though there was a physical similarity between him and her ex-husband, there was one obvious distinction—the detective did not mind work. With her father and two brothers working in law enforcement, she knew how committed they were to their jobs and how hard they worked, often in difficult conditions. Snorting, she thought of Calvin. Hard work and commitment turned out *not* to be his strong suit.

Draining her wine glass, she shook her head as she placed it in the sink and walked upstairs. She had no reason to see Detective Fiske again, so she was determined to put him out of her mind. *No more wasting time thinking of someone that would never be more than a passing acquaintance.*

---

## 8

Walking past Ever Hope the next morning on his way to the clinic, Carter wondered if Tara was inside. *Probably too early.* Disappointment speared through him and he jolted at the realization of how much he wanted to see her.

Continuing past, he approached the clinic door. It dawned on him that if the clinic was not open yet, he might not be able to get in. His concern was unfounded as a young woman wearing nursing scrubs pushed the door open as soon as he appeared and showed his badge.

She locked it after he followed her inside. "Hello, Detective. It's a cold one out there today, isn't it?" Her nose was red, and her hands were encased in gloves. Holding her fingers up and giving them a little wave, she said, "To save money, we cut the heat down in the evenings, and it takes a little while in the mornings to get warm.

"Are you one of the nurses here?"

"Oh, I'm sorry. I should've introduced myself. I'm Kate Burks, and yes, I'm one of the full-time nurses."

"Nice to meet you," he said. "You mentioned that you're full-time. Are there part-time nurses here as well?"

She nodded and smiled as she walked through the clinic and flipped on light switches. "Yes, there are several part-time nurses, but others of us are full-time. I don't usually open, but Polly is going to be late today. She's been around for a long time and knows the ropes. This is only my second year here." Continuing to lead him toward the back, she called over her shoulder, "Polly told me that you'd be coming this morning to meet with Dr. Tiller. He comes in through the back door and should already be in his office."

He followed her down several twisting halls, coming to an open door with Dr. Tiller's name on the plaque.

"Dr. Tiller? The detective is here." Kate smiled at Carter as she stepped to the side, allowing him to pass into the office.

He heard her soft footsteps retreat down the hall. Dr. Doug Tiller stood from behind his desk, leaning forward with his hand extended. Carter took stock of the doctor as they shook hands and settled into the offered chair. "I'm Detective Carter Fiske. Thank you so much for taking the time to see me this morning." He noted Dr. Tiller's office was much larger than Robert's. Medical certificates hung on the walls as well as photographs of the doctor with various politicians and some of Hope City's wealthier residents.

He had already investigated the clinic from their

website and knew that Dr. Tiller was a second-genera-
tion physician, his father having served the community
before joining the board of Hope City General Hospital.

Carter often found people did not resemble their
years-old social media photographs, but Dr. Tiller
looked very much like his picture on the website. Tall,
thin, and angular face with wire-rimmed glasses
perched on his nose. His dark hair was just starting to
gray at the temples. His blue eyes peered back at Carter,
and he observed dark circles underneath as though the
doctor was not sleeping well at night.

"Marsha took the liberty of indicating what you had
questioned her about yesterday," Dr. Tiller began. "I
assume you are asking about the men whose deaths you
are investigating?"

"Yes. Carl Burnley. Jonathan Rothberg. Richard
Stallone."

"Carl Burnley was not seen at this clinic after he
filled out the initial paperwork, so I never met with
him. Jonathan Rothberg also came in to fill out the
initial paperwork, but never returned with any documentation. Our clinic requires proof that they reside in
the Hope City area, even if this is a letter from one of
the shelters. We also require documentation of any
income, federal income tax returns, green card if necessary, food stamp notice of action, etc. Marsha informed
me that he did not bring in any documentation, therefore he was never processed into the system."

"And Richard Stallone?"

Dr. Tiller opened a medical file on his desk, glancing
at the contents before lifting his gaze to Carter's. "I

pulled his file. We do have this information on the computer, but I'm old school and tend to jot my notes on paper first. In the last several months, he has been seen three times. He suffered from mild PTSD and was prescribed an antidepressant. Upon follow-up, he stated that he felt better and was meeting with one of the social workers at the shelter next door. When he first came to us, he also had pain from an injury he had sustained while serving in the military. He was also prescribed Celebrex and Tylenol for pain."

"Do you recall if he asked for anything stronger? Narcotics, for example?"

Dr. Tiller leaned back in his chair and reached up to pull his glasses from his face. Taking a handkerchief from his coat pocket, he began to clean the lens. Sighing heavily as he placed his glasses back on his face, he said, "I can truthfully say that I have no recollection of that. I don't have a record of him asking nor do I have a note that tells me he might have an addiction. I will also say that with the number of patients I see in a day, week, month... I don't always remember each one."

"Each of these three men had opioids in their system at death, and Rocky also had antidepressants."

Dr. Tiller's eyes widened slightly, and he shook his head slowly. "An overdose?"

Shaking his head, Carter replied, "No, not an overdose. But enough to make him fall asleep and not wake up when a fire occurred in the building he was sleeping in. He died of smoke inhalation."

A wince crossed the doctor's face as he continued to shake his head. "Such a tragedy."

Changing direction in his questions, Carter said, "I spoke with Robert yesterday about the pharmacy. Knowing how much drugs cost, I wonder how the clinic is able to provide essentially free pharmaceuticals."

"The majority of our money for this clinic comes from private donors. Some comes from federal, state, and local grants. My father was on the board for Hope City General Hospital for many years before founding this clinic about eight years ago. The homeless shelter next door was already in service, and when this side of the building was available, the city purchased it for the use of the clinic. My father still does a lot of fundraising, and that's how we're able to provide medical services, including drugs to low-income patients. We're fortunate that Kilton Pharmaceutical Company is located in Hope City. They're able to provide some of the drugs in our pharmacy as part of their outreach and community program."

"Dr. Tiller?"

Both men looked for the door, seeing Kate peering in. "I hate to interrupt, but Beth Washington of Kilton Pharmaceutical is here. Since I'm not usually at work this early, I'm not sure what her procedure is."

"Thank you, Kate. She normally meets with Polly, but since she's here I'll deal with her. Please tell her I'll be with her in a moment." Dr. Tiller stood and said, "I'm afraid that's all the time I have this morning, Detective Fiske."

Inclining his head slightly, Carter said, "I appreciate your time. I'm sure I'll be in touch with more questions as the investigation continues." It did not miss his attention that the doctor grimaced slightly.

He followed the doctor back out to the reception area where Kate was chatting with another young woman. In contrast to Kate's ponytail, nursing scrubs, and Crocs, the pharmaceutical representative was attired in a tight-fitting skirt that came to just above her knees, a sweater that accentuated her figure while still maintaining professionalism, heavy makeup, and styled hair. At her feet was a rolling case that he assumed was filled with pharmaceutical samples.

Beth's eyes landed on Dr. Tiller first, and she smiled. When her gaze moved past the doctor and halted on Carter, her white-toothed smile was almost blinding. "Oh, my, Dr. Tiller, I certainly didn't mean to take you away from your meeting." Her voice lifted at the end as though she was inviting an introduction.

With a nod toward Kate, Carter walked out of the clinic. The back of his neck burned, and he was sure if he turned around, he would find the gaze of Beth's eyes boring into him. Shaking off the strange sensation, he mentally added her to the list of people he might want to interview, especially if she provided free samples of various drugs to the clinic.

People were already beginning to gather outside the homeless shelter as he made his way down the sidewalk.

"If you're here for the bag lunches, those are not distributed until 11 o'clock and the tables are set up on the back of the shelter near the delivery entrance. Please do not stay here until then because it creates too much of a crowd on the sidewalk. You may come back at the appropriate time."

Without being able to see the speaker, he already knew it was Tara. Her voice carried an air of authority, and he wondered how she managed the many aspects of her job. A few of the people were going inside the shelter, but most were beginning to disband.

"Back off, fucker!"

"Keep your fuckin' hands off of me!"

A scuffle broke out between two of the men on the sidewalk, but before Carter could reach them, Tara shoved her body in between the two men, pressing against both of them with her palms on their chests.

"Stop this minute!" she shouted. "You're here to receive help, not start a fight. For goodness' sakes, there are children around!"

Carter pushed through the crowd, his heart pounding as he saw the size of the men compared to the woman standing in the middle. Tara was not petite, but both men were a head taller, with quite a few pounds over her. As he made it to the trio, he pulled his jacket back, exposing his badge, two seconds away from calling a unit to haul them away.

"Shit, man," one of the men said, staring into Carter's tight-jawed, angry face.

"We was jus' playing," the other one mumbled.

Carter opened his mouth, but Tara got there first. "Thank you, Detective. I've got this."

His hands landed on his hips and his eyes bugged. It took all of his self-discipline, but he kept his mouth shut while still maintaining his presence in the middle of the group.

Tara's gaze left him and moved to both men, lowering her hands from their chests. "You know the rules of the shelter. Those rules apply whether you are staying in the shelter or getting a bag meal. This is your one warning. Come back at eleven, around the back, and you'll receive a lunch."

Both men dipped their chins and said, "Yes, Ma'am," in unison before they continued down the sidewalk side-by-side.

Tara shifted her purse back up on her shoulder, clasping her hands in front of her, avoiding looking directly at Carter. His feet apart, he crossed his arms over his chest and continued staring silently. She appeared to take a moment to compose her face and lifted her gaze.

"Good morning, Detective Fiske. I didn't expect to see you here so early."

Eyes wide again, he shook his head in disbelief. "That's it? You put yourself at risk, sticking your neck out by stepping in the middle of two men getting ready to throw punches, and all you can say is *good morning?*"

"I'm perfectly capable of determining what situations I can handle and when I need help. I knew those two men. They're actually friends who sometimes like to act as though they're teenagers, even though they're about twenty years beyond adolescence. I assure you that if I had not known them or felt as though there was a threat to others around them, I would have no problem letting you step in. In fact, I probably would've dialed 9-1-1 myself."

He tilted his head slightly, his chin tucked so that he could peer down at her. Once again, her dark hair was pulled back from her face. She was wearing slacks and low-heeled pumps but was wrapped up in a red wool coat that came to her knees. Most heavy coats made a woman appear shapeless, but this one was tied at the waist, accentuating the curves he'd noticed the other day. Silently counting to ten to get his mind back on the matter at hand and not on her curves, he jolted when he realized she had spoken again. Blinking, he said, "Come again?"

Her lips curved into a delicate smile, and she repeated, "I wondered what you were doing here this morning. Did you need to see me again?"

"Yes. Actually, I did." His words were a lie, but now that he was standing on the sidewalk with her, he wanted to find out what she was talking about when she mentioned a bag lunch. "I was just at the clinic, but I now have a few more questions for you."

She inclined her head toward the door and said, "We can speak inside."

He searched his mind quickly for a reason why he would need to talk to her but was distracted as she greeted the other shelter employees, several of the families, and some of the other shelter residents. Once in her office, she slipped off her coat and hung it on the back of the door.

They sat and she turned her attention to him. "Is this about Rocky?"

"Yes. You mentioned bag lunches outside. What did you mean by that?"

Her brow lowered, surprise settling on her face. "Bag lunches?" Gaining his nod, she said, "We're unable to provide everyone with a hot meal three times a day or even once a day unless they're staying with us. But there are groups of churches that have volunteers who make sandwiches. Hundreds of sandwiches. They put them in a paper sack along with anything else that their members have donated. Chips, an apple, maybe a cookie. Three days a week, the bags are brought to several distribution places around the city, and we're one of them. On those days, at 11 o'clock, we offer a bag lunch to the homeless that come by. Occasionally, we've run out, but for the most part, we're pretty good about estimating what the need is."

He scribbled in his notebook, and when he looked up at her again, her head was tilted to the side.

"If you're wondering if Rocky participated in the bag lunch program, then I can tell you that he did. He felt bad about taking a bed at the shelter when there were others that he said needed it more. But three times a week, he was always here to get lunch. Considering that he was also here for some of our counseling programs, I saw him quite a bit."

"Are the bag lunch days set?"

"Yes. Every Monday, Wednesday, and Friday. We have to be careful because the city doesn't want a large gathering of homeless persons on the sidewalk or standing in front of our center. I understand that, and even though many of them know that we don't open the door until 11 o'clock, they'll gather early." She offered a little shrug. "Sometimes, I think it's a social time for them."

"Do they eat the lunch here? At the shelter?"

"Oh, no!"

Her emphatic denial caught his attention, and he looked up from his notebook again, tilting his head to the side in silent question.

"I'm sorry, that probably sounded inhospitable. It's a service that we can provide due to the number of volunteers. But we're not equipped to handle hundreds of people coming through to eat lunch. The rules are they must line up in an orderly fashion, move through and pick up a paper lunch bag. They are not allowed to pick and choose what they want, although a large PB is written on the outside of the sack if it contains peanut butter—"

"PB?" Jerking his head up, he pinned his gaze on her.

"Yes… due to nut allergies. Some people love peanut butter, but because of allergies, we have those bags labeled."

"Please, continue."

"Once they get their bag and a bottled water, they continue down the sidewalk. We do keep some outdoor trash cans available in case someone decides to eat quickly and throw their trash away." She rubbed her forehead and sighed. "There are those in the city that hate the lunch bag practice because of the litter, but we're constantly reminding everyone to put their trash away. The city put extra trash cans across the street at the park, and I believe that has helped."

He tucked his notebook into his pocket and pinned her with his stare. "There was a paper sack found near Rocky with a plastic baggie containing only a bit of bread crust. There was PB written on the bag."

Her voice soft, she smiled sadly. "I remember he liked peanut butter. He said it reminded him of home." She blinked rapidly and looked down at her hands resting on her desk. "That's when I asked about home... family. And when he told me that he had no living relatives."

He watched as sadness moved over her face. He was certain Tara Wilson knew everything that happened with the shelter and the residents. *Probably feels a lot more than she realizes.* "Ms. Wilson, I have several more stops to make this morning, but I'd love to have a chance to talk with you more. Perhaps we could meet for lunch?"

As soon the words left his mouth, he blinked, uncertain where they came from. *No, this is good. A chance to question her when she's not distracted by everything here at the center.*

She sat up straighter, meeting his gaze. He was sure she was going to dismiss his offer, but she surprised him. "Actually, lunch away from here would be a novelty for me. I don't usually get to do that."

Smiling, he stood and extended his hand. "How about we meet at noon at..." He halted, quickly trying to think of a place they could eat that was both nice, quiet, and not on the typical detectives' radar.

"How about Sherman's? It's a small deli that's only a few blocks from here," she suggested.

He smiled and nodded. "Perfect." She placed her hand in his, and as he wrapped his fingers around hers he felt the warmth from her touch. Dropping her hand, he added, "Ms. Wilson, thank you for your time."

"I'll see you at noon, Detective Fiske."

Walking out of the shelter, he welcomed the cold wind that slapped against his face. Turning his collar up on his jacket, he breathed in deeply, clearing his mind from the fog that had settled ever since she agreed to have lunch with him.

He was almost to his SUV when he observed the pharmaceutical representative standing at her car, the trunk open. He hastened his steps and could see that her trunk was filled with boxes of drug samples. She was placing her satchel between the boxes, but there was not enough room for her to get the lid closed. She flipped open the top of the satchel, and he could see it was empty.

A middle-aged woman hustled down the sidewalk, her nursing scrubs bottoms evident underneath her long coat. She greeted Beth with a wide smile, receiving one in return. "Polly! I'm surprised you weren't here this morning."

Beth reached into one of the boxes, and from the angle Carter was observing, he saw her offer the nurse a hug and then hand more pill bottles to the nurse, who dropped them into her large slouchy bag worn across her body. "I gave everything else to Dr. Tiller, but knew you'd need these, too."

"Oh, thank you. With so many sick now, these will be perfect to hand out." As soon as the transaction passed, the two women waved goodbye as old friends and the nurse hurried into the clinic.

Beth continued shifting boxes of drug samples around, putting some of them in her satchel to make more room. Slamming the trunk lid closed, she walked to the driver's door. He walked up the sidewalk, waiting until she had driven away before making his way back to his SUV. He added her to his list of people to investigate. *Someone's getting these drugs into the hands of homeless people without going through proper prescription methods.*

## 9

Tara sat at her desk, unheeding of the files and forms scattered about. Ever since the detective had left her office, her mind continually rolled from her work over to him. *Jesus, it's not even a date! It's nothing more than a work lunch.*

Ignoring the words passing through her head, she reached inside her purse and pulled out a small mirror. She was not vain, but neither did she have false humility. When she was younger, she captured the attention of men fairly easily. *Like my sisters do.* She smiled. But it had been many years since she cared about catching a man's eye and was rarely out where it mattered. *I'm never looking for a date when at Pirate Ship Pizza!*

Tossing her mirror back into her purse, she wrapped her hands around her cell phone. Calling her parents' house, she was not surprised when Erin answered.

"Hey, I just wanted to see how Colleen was doing." Her daughter had woken up with a fever, and while

Tara was glad she rarely needed her parents to babysit, she was equally thrilled that her mom was available that day.

"She's fine. Mom got some ginger ale and crackers down her earlier, and right now, she and Dad are watching cartoons."

"Okay, thanks. Give Colleen a hug from me, and I'll swing by to pick her up after work."

There was a slight pause before Erin asked, "Is everything okay? Your voice sounds funny."

"No, no, everything's fine. I'm just... Well, I don't know what you hear. I'm fine." Tara rolled her eyes at her babbling.

"Okay, Sis, give it up. You know you can't get anything past me," Erin demanded.

"The detective came by again this morning and he asked me to lunch—"

Erin emitted a squeal, and Tara could not remember the last time her sister sounded so excited. "It's not a date. It's just lunch."

"I don't care what you call it," Erin said. "I'm just excited that you're going out for lunch instead of eating in your office or on the run. And the fact that it's with a man you described as handsome, well, that's all the better. You can even impress him with your McBride police pedigree."

"Oh, no. I don't want this getting back to Sean or Kyle. Detective Fiske is just asking me... Tara Wilson, not a McBride a few more questions about the homeless shelter and some of our residents. And for God's sake, don't say anything to Mom. I may be thirty, but you know how she is, she's been wanting me to date, and I don't want her to get the wrong idea about this. Like I said, it's just a business lunch."

Erin laughed, another sound that Tara had not heard much of since her sister got out of the Army.

Disconnecting, she looked up as someone knocked on her door frame. Seeing Polly from the clinic, she smiled. "Hey, Polly. How are you?"

Polly sniffed as she smiled in return, wiping her nose. "I don't want to get too close because I think I'm coming down with a cold. I came over to help with the lunch distribution, so I thought I'd pop in and say hello."

"I doubt there's any germs you can give me that I haven't already been exposed to with Colleen. In fact, she's with my mom today because she woke up with a fever."

Polly's brow furrowed and she asked, "Do you think it's an ear infection? Or sinus infection?"

Shrugging, she shook her head. "I have no idea. Her nose was running just a little, but it may be an ear infection. I'm so lucky she's rarely been sick, but she came in the other day and said her best friend at school was sick."

Polly reached into her pocket and pulled out a pill bottle, giving it a shake so the pills rattled. "Listen, I know that it's hard to get a doctor's appointment at the pediatrician's office. I've got some antibiotics here if you want to take them." She looked at the bottle and then reached back in her pocket, pulling out a different bottle. "Oh, here, this is the one. This is for children."

"Are you a walking pharmacy?" Tara asked, her eyes wide as she looked at Polly's bulging pockets.

"Good grief, honey, we get so many samples from the pharmaceutical reps that come in. Dr. Tiller gives them out all the time. I had grabbed a bottle for me this morning, and then realized I had the children's antibiotic. Because I'd already opened it up, I just stuck it back in my pocket when I grabbed the adult dosage." She blew her nose, then added, "Honestly, Tara. We get this all the time. Please, take it and use it for Colleen. It'll save you a trip to the doctor."

Shaking her head, Tara declined. "Thanks, Polly, but I don't really want to give Colleen any medication unless I know what's going on with her. It looks like her fever is already down, so I may not even have to take her to the doctor."

"Well, I hope she feels better. I'm going to head out to the back and see if they need any help."

Polly waved and walked back down the hall, leaving Tara staring after her. A niggle of doubt about Polly's motives moved through her, but with a shake of her head, she dismissed it. Polly was one of the most helpful, caring nurses and had certainly been a friend over the last several years. In fact, Polly used her lunch break on the days when they offered bag lunches to help with the distribution. It also gave her a chance to invite some of the homeless to the free clinic if she noticed that they appeared sick.

Looking at the clock, she had over an hour before she needed to meet at the deli. She rarely helped with the bag lunch distribution since it did not fall under her responsibility but occasionally liked to see how things were going. But with her desk still filled with files and forms, she heaved a sigh and turned her attention back to her work. *I'll check on them before I head out to the deli.*

Thirty minutes later, she buttoned her coat and grabbed her purse before walking down the hall. It appeared that most of the people who had been in line for the lunches had already left, and the volunteers had things well in hand. Polly was standing in the corner with several men, their new coats wrapped around them and their lunch bags in their hands. She recognized a few as regulars and hoped that if they were ill, they would meet with Polly inside the clinic.

Turning, she hurried out onto the sidewalk, her stomach doing cartwheels as she thought about her upcoming non-date lunch.

———

Back at his desk, Carter researched pharmaceutical companies and how their representatives worked while talking to Rachel on the phone. "Aren't you supposed to be on bed rest?"

"Where do you think I am? Anyway, I'm going to lose my mind if I don't do something. I've been home one day and even with a million TV channels, I have nothing to watch. So, tell me what you're finding out about the drug reps, Scout," she ordered.

He shook his head, wondering why he ever

mentioned he had been a Boy Scout when he was younger. She almost never used the nickname unless she was frustrated. A tenacious detective, it appeared that mandatory bed rest was not going to keep her down. "Okay, they're either seen as a necessary evil, drug hucksters, or an integral part of the pharmaceutical business depending on what you read. They're hired by pharmaceutical manufacturers to educate physicians about the different drugs in what's referred to as a *rapidly changing industry.* They provide doctors with samples of the drugs and the knowledge about those drugs. Some doctors run in the other direction when they see them coming, and some are glad to get the latest information on what's being available for their patients. From what I saw this morning, the Kilton rep had a trunk full of prescription drugs to give out."

"Honestly, Carter, I don't think that's so unusual. Every time I go to a doctor's office, I see reps traipsing through." She laughed, but it sounded more like a snort. "I swear, they all seem young, dressed to kill, wearing high heels and tight skirts."

"If I'd said that, it would have sounded sexist."

"Just calling it like I see it. But seriously, they're in competition with all the other drug companies who are out hocking their drugs to doctors."

Rubbing his chin, he thought about Beth handing the boxes to Polly. "Aren't they supposed to give the drugs to the doctor?"

"Nah, I've seen them give samples to the nurses or even the receptionists." She paused for a few seconds and then asked, "Do you want me to do some more digging on Kilton Pharmaceuticals? I'm stuck in bed but have my laptop."

Glancing at the time on his laptop, Carter said, "If you want to, I'm not going to argue, Rachel. Just take care of yourself first." Disconnecting, he stood and grabbed his jacket off the back of his chair. Hustling out of the headquarters building, he made his way down the street toward the deli—and lunch.

A few blocks later, he made it to Sherman's. Stepping inside, he spied Tara at a corner booth, just taking off her coat. He stalked toward her and lifted his hands to her coat. "Here, let me."

She looked over her shoulder and beamed. "Thank you, Detective Fiske."

They slid to opposite sides of the booth and ordered iced tea. Her attention focused on the menu, but he could not take his eyes off her. She looked the same as this morning with just a swipe of lip gloss added. Her gaze lifted and she nibbled on the side of her bottom lip.

Before she had a chance to speak again, he blurted, "Call me Carter, please." Her eyes widened slightly, and he rushed, "Detective Fiske sounds so stuffy."

Her lips curved upward. "Okay, Carter. And please, call me Tara."

Nodding, he smiled in return. "So, what's good here?"

"I know it's boring, but I almost always get their BLT. They put a ton of crispy fried bacon on it and use thick, butter-toasted bread." She glanced down at the menu, and before he had a chance to respond, her gaze jumped back to his and she added, "Oh, and you have to get their fries. Fresh-cut and seasoned with some kind of special salt."

Chuckling, he said, "You've sold me. Sounds like a perfect lunch. Good food and good company."

Cocking an eyebrow, she smiled. "You're assuming that I'm good company, Carter. For all you know, I'm a lousy lunch partner."

"Well, I eat with my fingers, use lots of ketchup on my fries, and sometimes knock my drink over. I might even have to borrow your napkins if I make too much of a mess."

She burst into laughter. "Then we'll be perfect lunch partners because that sounds just like my daughter."

At the mention of a daughter, his eyes dropped back to her ring finger, confirming that it was bare. He was glad she was staring down at her hands, giving him a few seconds to erase the shock from his face.

The server came over and they ordered the BLTs and fries. He refocused his attention back to her. "So, you have a daughter?"

She lifted her gaze and smiled. "She's in first grade and loves school. She actually didn't want to stay home today but woke up with a fever. I'm fortunate that my mom or sister can watch her when she can't go to school. That's why I was a little late to work today."

Seeing the obvious pride on her face, he met her smile with one of his own, although his stomach had dropped. "What's her name?" As soon as the question left his lips, he wondered why he asked. *It's not like I'm interested, I'd just like her help with the case.* He leaned forward, placing his forearms on the table, his gaze still on her. *Yeah, right. If I'm not interested, why do I hate finding out that she's married?*

Tara brightened and replied, "Colleen. She's the light of my life." Lifting her shoulders in a shrug, she added, "I confess, she's the only and best thing that came out of my disastrous marriage."

"Oh?"

"I'm sorry. I have no idea why I said that. That was so not appropriate for a working lunch."

He leaned forward a little more and shook his head. "No, Tara, that's fine. I mean, we're getting to know each other. Even if it is a... um... working lunch." For a reason he could not define and refused to spend time thinking about, he felt more relaxed finding out that she was single. Wanting to keep her from feeling self-conscious, he steered the conversation in a different direction. "So, how was the rest of your morning?"

She unrolled her napkin and fiddled with it before placing her silverware in front of her. "Well, busy, as usual. I guess actually a little more busy than usual."

"You didn't have any more problems with anyone, did you?"

Shaking her head, "No, that was well in hand by the time I left. We have a number of volunteers and a few staff members that always oversee the bag lunches." She looked down at the napkin that was now crinkled in her hands. "You probably want to know more about Rocky, don't you?"

He considered his response, then replied honestly. "When I asked you to lunch, yes. And that's still true, I do need to know what you can tell me. But I have to admit that I'm having a good time getting to know you."

Her smile brightened her already beautiful face. Tilting her head to the side, she asked, "Are you looking for anything in particular about him?"

"Honestly, anything you can think of. I know what you talked about privately with him or in counseling groups might be considered—"

"It's okay, Carter. With Rocky being deceased and the drugs he was carrying being investigated, I don't consider anything to be confidential." She cast her gaze back to the table and sighed. "He said he had been diagnosed with PTSD by the Army after he was treated for his injuries. He had been near an IED explosion and had several surgeries on his leg."

"Yes, his injuries were indicated in the autopsy."

A wince slashed crossed her face, and he hated that he reminded her. "Do you know how long he'd been homeless? We don't have an address for him since he was discharged from the VA hospital."

"I don't think he had a home. His father abandoned them early, and his mother was a substance abuser. He ended up in the foster system as a teenager and then joined the military as soon as he graduated high school. When he got out, he had some money he'd saved, but as you know, housing can be expensive. I first met him about six months ago when he came into the shelter. I put him on a list for a bed but went ahead and enrolled him in counseling. By the time the bed came available, he had been in and out of the center enough to see families in need. He told me that he was fine on his own and didn't want to take the bed away from someone else who needed it more."

She sucked in her lips for a minute, and Carter watched as she blinked as tears formed in her eyes. "I told him the bed was his and he deserved it as much as anyone." Shrugging again, she added, "But he came in for the lunches and counseling and got his meds at the clinic."

He reached across the table, his fingertips barely touching her hand in comfort when the server appeared with their plates. Startled, he jerked his hand back but not before seeing a flash of something in her eyes that looked very much like regret. Uncertain if he was reading her correctly, he turned his attention to his sandwich and they both began to eat.

After several minutes of eating and conversation centering around their food in the deli, she leaned back in her seat. "Can I ask you a question?"

"Absolutely."

"You said he had a plastic bag of prescription pills. Opioids, I believe. Was it the same type of plastic bag that the sandwich scraps were in?"

"Everything is still at the lab, but I can tell you that the only fingerprints on the bag of drugs were his. So, wherever he got them, someone was using gloves."

"Maybe he just had a few extra or saved them up if he didn't need them right away."

He battled the desire to reach across the table and smooth the wrinkle in her forehead, wiping the concern from her face. Instead, he pushed his now empty plate to the edge of the table so that he could lean forward, wanting to close as much distance between them as he could. "I think you know enough about substance abuse to know that's probably not true. And, Tara, I know enough about distribution to know that's not true either."

Her face fell, and he longed to see her smile again. She nodded slowly, and said, "You're right. I know you're right. Of course, the sandwiches would be bagged in all kinds of different ways by the many volunteers who are making them." She nibbled on the corner of her bottom lip, furrowing her brow again. Suddenly, eyes wide, she asked, "What about the other men? Were there similarities with their bags of drugs?"

Impressed with her analysis, he nodded. "Same kind of bags. No prints except for the men's."

"So, you're looking for the same person who's dealing drugs?"

"Not necessarily. It may be more than one person who's using the same method."

"Were they the same kind of drugs with each of the men?"

He hesitated, flipping his hands palm up on the table. "That's something I can't tell you right now."

"I understand, ongoing investigation, and all that."

He expected her to be angry or at least irritated that he was unable to give her more information. Before he had a chance to say anything else, the server dropped off the bill. Tara reached inside her purse, but he shook his head. "Lunch is on me, Tara." Seeing her about to protest, he added, "I'm the one who asked you. It was my idea, so my treat."

She lifted an eyebrow and her lips curved slightly. "So, by that logic, if I invite you out, then I get to pay?"

He grinned, her question surprising him. Of course, the idea that he would like to go out with her again was also surprising. "Absolutely. You can ask me out for coffee, and I'll let you pay. When I ask you out for dinner, that would be my treat again."

She opened and closed her mouth several times, then laughed aloud. Seeing her genuine smile, it struck him once again how beautiful she was.

"You said *when*," she said, tilting her head slightly.

"Well, there's no time like the present. Will you have dinner with me?"

She hesitated, but there was no artifice in her expression. Doubt. Confusion. Maybe even an inner battle. But he watched in fascination as these emotions moved over her face, and then she smiled again. "All right, Carter. I'd love to have dinner with you."

They stood and he helped her with her coat. Walking outside, she turned and looked up at him. "I know our schedules may be difficult to figure out. I'll certainly have to wait until I see if my daughter is well before I make dinner plans. I may have to take her to the doctor, even though one of my nursing friends at the clinic was offering me an antibiotic for Colleen to save me a doctor bill."

Her words hit his radar, but he adopted a casual pose. "Oh, really? I guess it's hard to find time to do everything you need to do with your job and being a mother."

"I refused, of course. Even though she's a nurse, I

wouldn't want to give my daughter anything that her pediatrician hasn't approved. Even taking an antibiotic if you don't really need one is not good."

"I met one of the nurses this morning. Kate, I believe was her name."

"Polly is the one who usually opens," Tara said. "She's the one that's been there the longest and offered to help Colleen. She also comes over and chats with some of our residents, making sure they make it into the clinic. She even volunteers her lunchtime to hand out bag lunches. She keeps her eye out for anyone who's sick and tries to get them to come to the clinic."

"Yes, I think I saw her going into the clinic when I was coming out. She looked familiar to me, but I couldn't think of her name."

"It's Starr, with two r's. Polly Starr."

Shaking his head slightly, he said, "No, doesn't sound familiar. She just must have that kind of face."

A strong breeze whipped a few tendrils of her dark hair, and she shivered. He reached out and draped her scarf over her shoulder. "So, Tara, what about this weekend? How about dinner?"

Nodding, she smiled her agreement. "I'd like that."

They traded cell phone numbers, and she stuck out her hand. He wrapped his fingers around hers, the warmth radiating from her to him. He watched as she hurried down the street before he turned in the opposite direction.

Scrubbing his hand over his face, he wondered what the hell he was doing. *Fucking taking advantage of her is what it's called.* It was one thing to use her to gain insight into the shelter, the area homeless, and the clinic. But now, he could not deny the pull of her as a woman he was interested in getting to know better. He may have been a Boy Scout, but this was one situation he was not prepared for. Blowing out his breath, he stalked toward headquarters.

## 1 0

Carter sat at his desk, surrounded by a few of the other detectives. Evan Barlow was at the opposite desk where Rachel usually sat. He had long hair, tats, a scruffy beard, and eyes that held a hundred secrets—the complete opposite of Carter and perfect for the job.

His head jerked around as his supervisor, Nancy Barker, walked out of her office and over to where they were meeting.

"You have the details ready?" she asked.

Carter nodded while turning toward Evan. "On Friday, he'll go to the Ever Hope Homeless Shelter for their bagged lunch program. It may take several visits, but he's gonna make contact with Polly Starr. Acting sick but not willing to go into the clinic, we're going to see if she offers him any prescription drugs."

"Keep me posted." Nancy turned and walked out of the room, leaving the others to finish their planning.

"I'll be nearby," Carter said to Evan.

"I got this." Evan stood and left the room just as Carter's phone rang. Looking down, he grinned. "Rachel, don't blame me if your husband leaves you because you can't stop working."

She laughed and said, "Actually, he's grateful. I'm in bed, off my feet, being a good little mommy-to-be. And, since I'm able to do a little computer research, he's got a happy little mommy-to-be."

"Okay, okay, whatever keeps you happy. What have you got for me?"

"Well, I know you're looking into Polly Starr, so you can fill me in on her in a minute. As far as Kilton Pharmaceuticals go, here's what I'm learning. We know from the lab that they identified the prescription pills in the bags that Carl, Jonathan, and Rocky were carrying. Almost all of them came from Kilton and were oxycodone. But there was also fentanyl not available in a prescription form. They were pills, but not legally produced and marked by a pharmaceutical company. Kilton does make a prescription fentanyl, but those pills don't match."

"So, with the oxycodone, is there identification on the pill so that we can trace exactly where they came from? I mean, doesn't Kilton keep up with where their drugs go?"

"Yes and no."

"Thanks for keeping it simple," he quipped, shaking his head.

Rachel laughed again. "Hell, Carter, you know nothing is simple in this line of work."

"Ain't it the truth!" He sighed heavily. "It's because they had been altered, right?"

"Yep, that's it. Whether someone had a shipment come in, and either with water or rough surface altered the pills slightly, or they came from someone inside of Kilton, we don't know."

"Okay, Rachel, that's it. No more research for you. You're officially on maternity leave, so I'll handle it from here. Your number one job is taking care of you and the little one."

"You know I'm here if you need me," she assured.

Disconnecting, he turned back to the open folders on his desk. He planned on being at the bag lunch give-away the next day, hoping to ask some of the regular volunteers if they had ever seen Carl or Jonathan. His phone vibrated an incoming text.

**She's fine. Back in school. Tara**

He had sent her a text that morning, letting her know that he made reservations at The Italian Garden. He had offered to pick her up, but she'd insisted on meeting him there. It was the smart play, but he'd miss the extra time going to and coming from the restaurant to get to know her. He had asked about Colleen, hoping she was better.

He leaned back in his seat and closed his eyes. *What the fuck am I doing?* There was something about her that called to him. Her calm voice. Her understanding. Her undemanding acceptance. *Yeah, but I just wanted to spend some time with her to find out more about the shelter in the clinic, not get fucking involved with her—or her daughter.*

*Jesus, I've never even dated someone who had a child.* But he could not deny the desire to get to know her better.

He squeezed the back of his neck, trying to ease the tension as he thought of what he had to do the next day. She had mentioned she generally did not get to help with the lunches and hoped he would be able to talk to some of the volunteers outside, staying out of her sight. The worry that she would blame him, thinking she was being used, stayed in the back of his mind. *No, she's practical. She knows that anything we talk about could be used.* Still, his gut churned.

---

Tara quietly shut Colleen's door after checking to make sure her daughter was cool and sleeping. Whatever she had must have been a twenty-four-hour bug because her daughter was back to her happy, bouncy self.

She enjoyed the quiet, never minding having a little time to herself. Settling on the sofa with a glass of wine, she felt restless. There was nothing on TV and she had no interest in starting a new book. When her phone rang, she grabbed it quickly, anxious for the distraction.

"Hey, Sis."

"Erin, how are you?"

"I'm good."

For her sister to call this late, she knew she must have something on her mind. Erin's twin, Rory, had immediately jumped into volunteering at one of the fire stations in Hope City and started paramedic training. He had reconnected with old friends and was quickly making new ones. Erin was still struggling in her effort to reacclimate into civilian life.

"What's on your mind?"

"I was wondering if you thought the clinic next to Ever Hope would be willing to take on a volunteer."

Tara leaned forward and set her wine glass onto the coffee table. A strange mixture of concern and excitement moved through her, but she wanted to make things easier on Erin to talk to her. "Uh… I'm not sure, although I think they do use volunteers. What exactly are you thinking, honey?"

"When I got out… out of the Army, I wasn't sure I wanted to use my medic training anymore. I just… I don't know… didn't feel like a healer. But I can't stay at Mom and Dad's and keep hiding out like I have been. I was thinking about finishing my nursing degree."

The warring inside shifted as excitement replaced some of the concern. "Oh, Erin, I think that would be a wonderful idea." The two were silent for a moment before she ventured further. "I know something happened over there. You've opened up a lot to me, but you still have your secrets. And that's fine. We all have those. I hope that in time you let me know more. But the fact that you're starting to look forward is really good."

A huge sigh of relief met her ears and Erin whispered, "Thanks. It feels good to finally make a decision. I've checked into the LPN program at Hope City Community College and they'll actually give me credit for my medic training, so it won't take as long for me to get through their program."

"Do you want me to check at the clinic for you? Obviously, you'll have to go in and talk to them and interview, but I can at least see what Dr. Tiller thinks."

"That would be amazing, Tara. Thank you so much." After a few seconds of hesitation, Erin added, "I love you, Sis."

Her throat closed as tears clogged her eyes. "I love you, too." Disconnecting, she leaned back against the sofa cushions and drained her glass of wine. The family had turned to her as a counselor to help Erin when she did not seem like herself. Erin had finally talked to her, but there were still secrets she kept deep. Secrets of things that happened in Afghanistan. And Tara knew that until her sister was ready to unburden herself completely, the secrets would remain hidden.

Exhausted, she headed to the kitchen and rinsed out her glass. Having already checked the downstairs security, she walked upstairs and into her bedroom. As soon as she was finished in the bathroom, she flipped off the light and slid between the soft sheets of her bed.

When Calvin left, she kept the furniture—except for their bed. She refused to sleep another night in the bed that she had shared with her husband. She had given him her love, her acceptance, and their child. When he turned his back on all that, she needed the furniture but wanted a new bed. She splurged on a king-sized, super supportive, and comfortable mattress. When it was delivered, she almost cheered when the delivery men carried away her old double mattress. It would have been nice if they could have carried away the bad memories as well.

She tossed from side to side, punching her pillow to find comfort, but her mind swirled. The residents of the homeless shelter. The needs of her job. The sack lunch giveaway the next day. Plastic sandwich bags. Bags with no fingerprints. Bags filled with opioids, with no reason other than to sell.

Rocky's face moved through her mind. She remembered the first time she met him, thinking his eyes were filled with a dark intensity, although he had a slight smile. "My name's Richard, Ma'am. Richard Stallone." His lips curved a little more and he added, "But everybody calls me Rocky."

Many of the veterans that the shelter served had taught her that their military nicknames meant more to them than their birth names. It seemed to give them an identity and a sense of pride.

*Oh, Rocky, what were you doing? Were you just looking to ease your pain?* She thought of Erin and wondered how she had eased her obvious pain when she was first discharged. Glad that her sister had a support system in place with family, she thought of Rocky's lack of resources. *What secrets did you have hidden? And if so, who gave you those pills? How did I miss all the signs?*

She remembered the times he did not show up for their group sessions. That was not uncommon with anyone but especially with a person who was homeless. When she first met him, he did not have a job, but that did not mean his time was his own. When someone's life is spent looking for the next place to sleep or the next meal to eat, where to find a toilet or shower, something as mundane as going to the doctor or coming for a group counseling session was not high on their priority list. She knew that. She accepted that. But now, her heart ached. *What more could I have done?*

Rolling onto her back, she stared up at the ceiling, knowing no answers were coming in the dark of the night.

---

Carter parked several blocks away from Ever Hope. As he approached the back door where deliveries were made and the bag lunches were distributed, it was easy to see he was in the right place. A long line had already formed, snaking down the sidewalk. His gaze searched the area to both identify the volunteer workers and to see if Tara was around. Not seeing her, he approached the long tables set up where several men and women were placing paper sacks.

It felt strange to be walking past the men and women standing in the line to get what might be their only meal of the day. The breakfast he had eaten at the coffee shop near his condo sat like a rock in his stomach. As a detective, it was not unusual to see people down on their luck. In fact, he dealt with it almost every day. But usually with individuals or families. Not in massive quantities all at once.

He passed by single men and women, couples, some with young children. Some appeared healthy, their clothes clean. Others were clothed in cast-offs, worn and dirty. Some sniffled, wiped their noses, coughed deep and hard. Many carried bags or knapsacks, and a few pushed small carts loaded with their possessions. Some looked eager, standing on their toes to peer over the crowd to see how close they were to the food. Others had eyes that were vacant or perhaps darting around nervously.

Several male volunteers with walkie talkies walked up and down the line, chatting in welcoming tones, encouraging everyone to wait their turn.

He moved to one of the men that was standing to the side, his gaze moving up and down the sidewalk. "Excuse me, sir. I'm Detective Fiske with the HCPD. I'd like to show you three pictures and see if you have ever seen any of these men here. I've spoken with the shelter and understand that these lunches are for anyone, not just residents."

"Sure, Detective. Let me take a look."

Carter handed the pictures of Carl, Jonathan, and Rocky to the man who perused them carefully before handing them back.

"Yep, I've seen all three. I haven't seen the first two in weeks, but that last boy was here about a week ago. All three of them used to come through the line regularly." His smile dropped as his brow scrunched. "They're not in trouble with the law, are they? They all seemed real nice."

"It's just a routine check," he lied. "Thank you for your help." He started to step back when he noticed Polly was standing near the tables, talking to the first group of people in line. She smiled warmly, pulling small packs of tissues from her bag and handing them to those who looked like they needed them. She chatted with the young mothers, offering a light tickle to the small children. And she wore bright blue rubber gloves. "Looks like this is a good program," he said, hoping to keep the conversation going.

"Oh, yes, my wife and I've been helping for the past several years ever since we retired. She spends hours making sandwiches. A lot of peanut butter, but sometimes we get a special deal on ham or turkey and we make those as well."

Smiling, he nodded. "That's nice of you."

"That's my Ruthie over there at the table," he said, nodding toward the front of the line.

"Oh, the one handing out tissues?"

"No, no. That's Polly, one of the nurses at the clinic here. That woman's a saint. I tell you, she's here for every lunch. Goes up and down the line and sees who's sick. Tries to make sure they come into the clinic, especially the ones who got little kids. Yep, a real saint. My Ruthie is the one behind the table, in the pink sweater."

Smiling, he shook the volunteer's hand. "Well, I thank you for what you're doing here and appreciate you confirming that these men had been here."

He stepped back and headed past the group again. He caught a glimpse of Evan appearing rough and ill. As he walked to his car, he was not sure if he hoped Polly took the bait and offered Evan prescription drugs. Knowing how upset Tara would be, he grimaced as he climbed behind the wheel.

That afternoon, he paced around their workroom, waiting to hear. Finally, Evan walked in, looking much cleaner than he had this morning. "What happened?"

"Jesus, man. Give me a chance to get a cup of coffee."

"Fuck the coffee," he barked. "You've already taken time to get cleaned up, so what happened?"

Evan once again settled into Rachael's empty chair. "You've got reason to be suspicious of Polly Starr. I made very little conversation with those around me, but from what I heard and could see, she's a nice lady who wants to help."

Carter's eyebrows jumped up as his eyes widened. "What?"

"I don't know if that's an act she puts on or if it's real. But the people in line seemed to really like her. I made sure when she got close, I sniffled and coughed. She came to me and asked how I was. I just mumbled that I was fine, then went into another coughing fit. She handed me tissues and cough drops and told me to come into the clinic. I told her I didn't trust clinics and didn't have any money anyway. She stood there for a second and I thought maybe she was going to offer me something else, but she didn't."

Leaning back in his chair, he kept his gaze pinned on Evan. "There must be something else. When you sat down you admitted that I've got a reason to be suspicious of her."

Evan nodded slowly, rubbing his fingers over his rough, unshaven chin. "She's got a bag that she wears across her body, and it seems to be filled with all kinds of stuff she was heading out. Tissues, lollipops, toothbrushes and toothpaste, cough drops." He leaned forward, his elbows on the desk, and added, "And unmarked bottles of pills."

"Shit."

Blinking in surprise, Evan asked, "Why do I get the feeling that wasn't the news you wanted to hear? I'm good to keep going back until she offers something to me. If this woman is giving out illegal prescription drugs, she needs to be out of that clinic and off the street."

"I know, I know. It's not that." He huffed, frustration pouring off him as he thought about Tara and how she would react if Polly was arrested. Looking back up at the evidence board, he thought about the bags of pills. "What does she have the pills in? Did you say bottles?"

Evan nodded. "It looked like the amber-colored plastic bottles that prescriptions come in when you get them from the drugstore. It happened very fast, but I don't think there was a label on it. I could be wrong. I won't know until she tries to give me something."

"That doesn't fit with the bags of opioids our guys had in their possession. Although, I did find out that all three used to go through the lunch line every time it was open. I just don't know that Polly was the one giving them the bags."

Pushing to a stand, Evan said, "She may not be the person you're looking for dealing opioids, but I think we're going to get her on illegal prescription drug dispensing. I'll be back in line on Monday." As he walked out of the workroom, he called over his shoulder, "Have a good weekend."

*A good weekend. A weekend that involved a dinner date with Tara, someone he was now wanting to spend more time with. And a weekend worrying about what the investigation was going to uncover next week that might affect her. A good weekend? Shit.*

---

"Dr. Tiller, thank you so much for giving me a minute," Tara said, sitting down in his office. "I'll make this quick, I promise."

Smiling, he waved his hand in dismissal. "We're always packed with patients, Tara, but I've been dying for a second cup of coffee so this gives me an excuse to get caffeinated while you tell me what you need."

"I wanted to find out if you ever use volunteers in the clinic for more than just reception work."

"Like nurses or techs?"

"To be honest, I'm not quite sure." Shaking her head slightly, she said, "I'm actually asking for my sister, Erin. She's recently out of the Army where she was a medic. She served in Afghanistan and is now back home in Hope City. She was uncertain what she wanted to do for the first couple of months but has now decided that she wants to pursue nursing. She's already checked with the university and they will offer her credits for some of her Army courses and experience. She should be able to get her LPN in a year but would really like to gain civilian experience and does not mind volunteering."

"I would be a fool to overlook free help. Of course, not everyone can handle working in a clinic like this. It takes a special person to be able to deal with the issues that we see on a daily basis with people who are very poor, often have neglected their health for years, or simply have never had the means to learn how to care for themselves." He tilted his head slightly, his elbows resting on the arms of his chair and his fingers steepled together. "And yet I can imagine that a military medic would have seen much worse. Tell you what, have your sister give me a call, and we'll meet."

Her breath left her lungs in a rush as she stood and extended her hand. "Dr. Tiller, thank you so much. I can vouch that Erin would be an excellent volunteer and can assure you that this would be very good for her, too."

Walking out of his office, she felt lighter and could not wait to call Erin. Digging into her purse, she rounded the corner and ran into someone. Jerking her head up, her gaze landed on Polly. "Oh, I'm so sorry."

Laughing, Polly said, "No worries." She glanced toward the doctor's office where Tara had just emerged. "Are you okay?"

"Yes, really good, actually. My sister is going to come in and talk to Dr. Tiller about being a volunteer here. She's going to finish the work necessary to become an LPN and would like to do some volunteering."

Polly's smile widened as she exclaimed, "Lovely! It would be so nice to have her here. Lord knows, we can always use an extra pair of hands!"

"I know the clinic is so busy, just like us."

"I'm always telling people in the lunch line that appear sick to please come in and see us. Occasionally they will, especially if they have little kids. But most of the others don't. I don't know if they don't have the required paperwork to be seen or if they're just suspicious. But I hate to see sick people not get the care they need."

Smiling, she patted Polly's arm. "Well, have a nice weekend. I'm getting ready to head home." With a wave, she hurried to her car. On the way to pick up Colleen from her after-school care, she called Erin to give her the good news. Her sister was happier than she had been in months with the news. Colleen barely stayed buckled as she bounced up and down telling her mother all about her day.

As she pulled into her driveway, Tara smiled. It was the start of a wonderful weekend.

Tara hated driving at night, even with GPS telling her step-by-step where to go. Finally, the sign for The Italian Garden came into view and she breathed a sigh of relief at not being late. *Maybe I should've had Carter just pick me up.* As appealing as that thought was, she did not want to expose Colleen to her going on a date—at least, not yet. Erin arrived that evening to babysit, and Colleen just knew that her mother was going out somewhere. A smile curved her lips as she thought of the first sign of true happiness on Erin's face at the decision to pursue nursing and her daughter's face, realizing her aunt was going to spend time with her.

She pulled into a parking spot, then looked into the mirror to touch up her lipstick. She stared at the close-up reflection of her face before offering a pep talk. *You've got this. It's just a date... Okay, a date with a gorgeous man. But it's been a while... Okay, it's been years. But it's just a date.* The encouraging words did little to still the flip-flops in her stomach.

Climbing from her car, she started to cross the parking lot when she observed Carter standing near the front door. He was looking in the other direction, giving her a chance to stare. Dark slacks paired with a white shirt. A black leather jacket. Clean-shaven with a strong, square jaw. Her stomach began to flip-flop again with each step that brought her closer to him. He must have heard her heeled boots as she neared, swinging his head around and pinning her with his gaze. And then, a wide, beautiful smile spread across his face. *Oh, hell, girl. Keep trying to remember, this is just a date.*

With his long legs, he reached her in a few steps, reaching out his hand. Uncertain of proper first date protocol, she was glad when he did not fumble with an awkward hug. Instead, his fingers wrapped around hers, keeping them warm as they walked to the door.

Once inside, she appreciated the welcoming interior of the family-owned Italian restaurant. It was decorated simply, with wooden floors and walls painted pale green. The cushions on the chairs and booths were dark burgundy with pale green stripes. The walls were adorned with pictures of Italian landscapes, interspersed with pictures of the owner's family through the years.

Carter gave his name for the reservation, and they followed the hostess to a corner booth near the back. Once again, he helped her with her coat and folded it neatly on the booth next to him. Sliding his leather jacket off his broad shoulders, he placed it on the booth as well.

"Tara, you look absolutely beautiful."

She smiled her thanks, adding, "You look very nice yourself." She cast her gaze out toward the restaurant, hearing soft music in the background. "I've never been here before. This is lovely."

"I discovered this place a couple of years ago. I was investigating a string of robberies in the area and had a chance to meet the owners. It quickly became one of my favorite places to come when I was in the mood for Italian. I confess, I'm not an overly picky eater, but everything here is fresh and homemade."

As though on cue, the server placed a bowl of hot, buttery garlic bread on the table. The delicious scent rising from the bread had Tara moaning. "I love bread. Especially homemade. We could probably forget the rest of the meal and I'd be happy with wine and bread."

"I'll keep that in mind as a future reference," he laughed. "But, for tonight, I hope you'll try more than just the bread."

They spent a moment perusing the menu before a man approached, round in the middle with a clean apron tied about his waist.

"Carter! I haven't seen you in a while! I was afraid you'd decided to find another place to eat."

Carter stood and the two men clasped hands in a hearty shake. "Lorenzo, it's good to see you." Turning to face Tara, he said, "Tara, I'd like you to meet Lorenzo, the owner and chef extraordinaire here at The Italian Garden. Lorenzo, this is the lovely Tara Wilson."

Before she had a chance to extend her hand,

Lorenzo grabbed both of her shoulders and kissed one cheek before moving to the other. Blinking in surprise, she laughed, uncertain what to say.

"Bella, I am so pleased to make your acquaintance. Carter never comes in here with a lady, so this is a treat. I will send my best wine, and please, let me offer you our special tonight. I'm doing manicotti just for you."

Carter held her gaze and lifted an eyebrow in silent question. She nodded and said, "That sounds absolutely delicious. Thank you." She watched as Lorenzo hustled away, and soon, a bottle of wine was brought to their table. Carter sampled it and nodded to the server, who then poured it in both their glasses.

The bread, wine, and Lorenzo's greeting had broken the ice, and conversation flowed.

"Have you lived in Hope City long?"

Her mouth full of buttery bread, she quickly chewed and swallowed as Carter laughed.

"Sorry, I didn't mean to make you choke."

Wiping her mouth with her napkin, she grinned. "I told you I love bread." Taking a sip of wine, she replied, "I've lived here all my life. My parents moved here right after my oldest brother was born and they bought a large house with the hopes that they wouldn't have to move. My siblings are all grown, but my parents still live in that house." Taking another sip of wine, she asked, "What about you?"

"I'm originally from Virginia. Baytown, a small town on the Eastern Shore. I did two years of college, playing football for a midsize university there." Shaking his head slightly, he added, "It just wasn't my thing. I think I was too young to know what my *thing* was."

"I'd say that makes you very normal. I don't think most eighteen-year-olds know what they want to do."

His blue eyes held hers and he nodded. "Exactly. So, I joined the Marines and decided on military police. I eventually did investigations and discovered that was something I truly enjoyed. After my tour was up, I went back to Virginia, finished a degree in Police Science, and worked for a small police department for a couple of years. I had a former buddy that lived in Hope City and when I visited, I fell in love with this place. Put it in an application and within six months I was living here full time and had a job as a detective."

"That sounds like all the pieces of the puzzle fit together." She leaned back and pushed the bread platter slightly away from her. "Ugh, keep that away from me or I'm going to completely fill up on his bread."

He laughed and slid the platter to the side before pouring more wine into her glass. "My parents still live in Baytown, and I try to see them a couple of times a year. I've got a sister who lives in Kansas City with her husband and kids. I generally only get to see them once a year."

Eyes wide, she shook her head slightly. "Wow! I know that's typical, but my whole family is still local. Some of my siblings joined the military, but they're all back now. We're a huge family, but we still manage to get together at least once a month at my parents' house for dinner."

Taking another sip of wine, she felt his eyes on her. Afraid she had spilled something on herself, she quickly wiped her lips, but he continued his perusal. "What are you looking at?"

"I'm sorry, I was just thinking about what you said. It fits you. I know that doesn't make any sense, but it's not hard imagining you having a close family. Where did you fit in birth order?"

Grinning, she leaned back in her seat. "Guess."

"Hmmm. Okay, I'm going to say you're either the oldest or the oldest girl in your family."

"Very good, Detective. How did you deduce that?"

"You're caring. I can see you caring for your other siblings. If you were the youngest, I'm not sure you would have that trait as strong as you do."

Nodding, she continued smiling. "I was the oldest girl. I have two older brothers, but three younger siblings."

He coughed, choking on his wine. Eyes wide, he sputtered, "Six? There are six kids in your family? And you're all still close?"

"Yes, and there's more. The family we grew up next to had five kids in their family, and I'm the oldest girl of all eleven of us. Lots of responsibility, but lots of fun."

"I can't even imagine. It's like having a whole sports team just between the two families."

"I'm surprised there was any grass that grew between our two houses." She shrugged, "But our parents didn't mind us running back and forth all the time."

Their conversation was interrupted when the server brought the plates. Steam rose from the melted cheese on top of the manicotti and the scent of tomatoes, basil, garlic, and fresh pasta had her mouth watering. The server placed another platter of bread between them and Tara's eyes bugged. "I'll need a doggy bag for sure, and it looks like this will be my lunch for the next couple of days."

For the next several minutes they ate, moans of appreciation taking the place of conversation. Finally slowing, she glanced at Carter's plate, surprised to see it was almost empty.

He caught her gaze and chuckled. "I like to eat, and Lorenzo knows how to cook."

"He certainly does. I don't often get out for an adult meal. I'm so glad you chose it."

"I'm glad you accepted my invitation," he said, his voice warm.

She could feel her face heat and could not remember the last time she blushed. The server came to take her plate away to box it up, and she was glad for the diversion. Taking another sip of wine, she looked across the table, finding his eyes on her.

"You keep staring at me," she said. "It makes me nervous."

He shook his head slowly back and forth. "It shouldn't make you nervous. I confess I've been admiring your beauty all evening, but it's getting to know you that makes this dinner more special." He continued to hold her gaze and said, "Tell me about social work. How did you get into it and what made you decide to work with the homeless?"

She opened her mouth to answer but was interrupted as Lorenzo appeared at their table, placing two servings of tiramisu in front of them.

"This is my daughter's specialty," he exclaimed, clapping his hands. "Eat, eat and enjoy!"

Her eyes widened as she stared at the delicate dessert tempting her beyond all reason. "I might explode, there's no way I can try that."

"I tell you what," Carter said. "Why don't we split one of these now, and you can box the other for later."

"It's a deal," she grinned and they both dipped their forks into the desert at the same time, moaning together as the flavors hit their tongues. She watched him close his eyes, pleasure moving across his face, and for an instant wondered what it would be like to see that face as he made love to her. She had not had a thought like that in years, but now that it had crept into her mind, she knew it would be impossible to forget.

After finishing her half, she said, "You asked about my work..."

Nodding, he swallowed. "Yes, please continue."

"My career path has not been nearly exciting as yours," she began, her fingers gently twirling her wine glass. "Growing up, I remember my parents relying on me to help with my siblings or neighbors. Not in a bad way, not like I had no choice or was put upon. I actually liked it. I liked helping my sisters get ready for school. I liked helping my mom fix dinner. I liked helping my dad in the yard. And as my siblings got older, I liked helping them with their problems. Even my friends used to tell me that it was easy to talk to me." Shrugging, she smiled. "By the time I got to college, I was taking psychology classes, counseling classes, and decided to go into social work for my Master's degree. I didn't really have to think about it—it was just who I was."

## 13

Carter had barely tasted the delicious dinner put in front of him, his mind and senses ensnared with the beautiful woman sitting across from him. She was so unlike any woman he had been with in many years. She exuded calm wisdom, and he could easily imagine a house full of children all relying on her. He never expected to take her to dinner, much less wanting to know so much more about her.

He reached his hand across the table and gave her fingers a little squeeze. Deciding to take the plunge, he asked, "And your marriage? It's okay if you don't want to talk about it. I mean, maybe it's too soon in us getting to know each other. It's just that I'd like to know more."

Her lips curved ever-so-slightly as she shook her head. "It's never too soon to find out about someone you're interested in."

He nodded his encouragement, and she took another sip of wine. He wondered if she needed the fortification or was just nervous.

"I'm afraid that when I met Calvin in college, we were a classic case of opposites attract. I was studious, and he preferred jamming sessions with some of his musician friends instead of going to class. I knew that I was going to need a Master's degree to have the career I wanted, and he was sure that he and his friends were going to hit the big time with their band. He dropped out of college so that they had more time to work on songs and some local touring."

Carter was not sure if she realized that her fingers were gently rubbing on his hand, but he loved the feel of her touch.

She suddenly looked up in haste, her blue eyes holding his. "The crazy thing, Carter, is that I never tried to hold him back. I didn't nag. I didn't beg him to get a paying job. I didn't belittle what he did." She lifted her shoulders in a shrug and sighed. "I believed in him... for a while. But three years later when we got married, I had my degree and a full-time job. And he was still essentially playing in a garage band. The original band members had left as their dreams changed, but Calvin hung on. I didn't mean to get pregnant when I did, but I was ecstatic to find out that I was going to have a baby. Unfortunately, Calvin didn't feel the same. Until I had a child, it hadn't hit me that Calvin was used to me taking care of him. In many ways, he was a child himself. By the time I had Colleen, I was no longer willing to take care of an adult child that should've been helping out."

"I really want to tell you that he sounds like an asshole, but I know I shouldn't." Carter slid his fingers between hers, linking their hands.

She laughed and said, "Oh, there's very little that you could say that I haven't said myself. And God knows, my family called him every name in the book." She sobered inside again. "One day, he simply announced that he no longer wanted to be married. He didn't want to be a father, and the baby was not something that interested him. So, he packed his bags and walked out."

"Holy shit. I confess I've dated a few losers myself, but he puts them to shame."

"You might think that I fell apart. But I knew my marriage had been over probably by the time it got started. So, the tears had already been shed. The screaming and ranting had already occurred. All that was truly left was wounded pride, bills that needed to be paid, a daughter that needed her mother, and a few regrets. Colleen and I moved in with my parents for a while until I could get everything taken care of and the divorce was final. The judge gave me full custody, and I got to keep all the furniture. All in all, it was the best thing. Calvin had spent more than he earned. He drank more than he should. And he became angry when success did not follow. Only his anger was turned outward, usually toward me."

Carter sucked in a quick breath, and his fingers clenched hers. "Did he ever—"

So focused on Tara, Carter jumped when a throat cleared nearby. Seeing the server with their check, he pulled out his card. Tara excused herself to the ladies' room while he paid.

He shrugged on his leather jacket, then picked up her wool coat from the booth. The delicate scent of her perfume wafted by, and he inhaled deeply. The idea that her ex-husband might have hurt her physically felt like a punch to his gut. He watched as she made her way back toward him, weaving between the tables. Understated beauty, class, intelligence, and caring. *Fuck, I'm so gone for her already.* He had never believed in anything more than instant lust. The idea that someone's heart could already be involved after only knowing someone for a short time wasn't a concept that he thought possible. As she reached his side, she held his gaze and her smile widened. *Yep. Gone.* Blowing out his breath, he held her coat while she slid her arms into the sleeves. He settled it onto her shoulders, squeezing before letting go.

With his hand on her back, he guided her out of the restaurant, calling out his appreciation and thanks to Lorenzo. Once outside, he reached down and linked fingers with her again as they slowly walked toward her car.

She turned and looked up at him, placing her palms flat on his chest. Even with the layers of a shirt and leather jacket, he felt her brand on his skin. Sliding his hands around her waist, he pulled her close.

"I had a wonderful time tonight," she said. "I honestly had no idea if I would. It's been a rather long time since I've gone out on a date."

He bent his head, stopping a whisper away from her mouth. "Would you be offended if I kissed you good night?"

Her lips curved and her eyes sparkled. "I'd be offended if you didn't."

He closed the scant distance and took her lips. Soft and gentle, not wanting to overwhelm her. She sighed gently, and as her lips opened, he angled his head a little more, sliding his tongue into her warm mouth. She tasted of sweet dessert and tart wine. He could not remember the last time he had kissed a woman, caring about the subtle movements of their tongues and wanting to bring pleasure to his partner with a simple kiss.

His cock stirred, and he knew he needed to step back. Tara was not a woman that he immediately assumed would take him to bed. And there was no way she would be a simple fuck. As the kiss continued, he wondered if that last thought would send him scurrying away. But the idea that she would be more than a simple fuck fueled his desire. Finally separating, he sucked in a ragged breath of cold air.

"Wow." She breathed the simple word and he chuckled.

"Yeah, wow."

Her tongue darted out and moistened her kiss-swollen lips, drawing his attention to them, once again. "Can I see you again?" he asked. "Not just for work, but I'd like to go out with you again."

She nodded, her smile even brighter. "I can't think of anything I'd like more." She glanced at her watch and sighed. "I hate for the evening to end," she said, her fingers giving a squeeze on his arms for emphasis. "But I really should get home to Colleen."

The mention of her daughter brought to mind that

they had been interrupted earlier. "Tara, before we go, I need to know. Please tell me your ex never got physical with you."

"Oh, no! He never did anything like that." A small chuckle slipped between her lips, and she added, "I would've never taken that. And, oh, my God, my brothers would have killed him!"

A sigh of relief left his lungs, and he smiled. "Good. It sounds like they're my kind of men."

She chuckled again and said, "I've never mentioned it. I truthfully wanted to get to know you first. But you probably know my brothers. And our neighbors, for that matter."

"Oh, yeah? Who are they?"

"My brothers are Detectives Sean and Kyle McBride. And you probably know my neighbors, Detective Brock and Sergeant Brody King, and their dad, Chauncey, the Hope City Police Commissioner."

Carter blinked, unable to believe his ears. *Gobsmacked.* That was the word his mother always used when she was completely shocked. And right now, he was completely gobsmacked. It hit him that both Sean and Kyle had started to tell him about their sister when both times they were interrupted. *Oh fuck, what are they going to say when they find out I'm dating their sister? And she's in the middle of my case?*

"Hey, are you all right?"

He jerked at the soft touch of her hand on his face and grinned widely to cover up his shock over her family revelation. "Absolutely."

She lifted on her toes and he readily accepted her invitation, taking her lips again. She melted in his arms and her acquiescence reverberated through him. From his perspective, the kiss became almost desperate. The wild tangling of lips and tongues as his cock stirred, the fear that he might not ever kiss her again hitting him in the gut. Or maybe, if he was honest, a little higher than his gut. Right in his heart.

They separated, and moving as one tightened their hold and pressed together. Her head was tucked under his chin, and his arms were bound around her. Unheeding the cold wind blowing, he closed his eyes and memorized the feel of her in his arms.

They slowly separated, and he opened her car door, assuring that she was buckled safely. "Tomorrow is Sunday. Would it be okay if I called?"

She smiled and nodded. "Colleen and I'll be at church in the morning, but we have no plans in the afternoon. Just a lazy Sunday at home."

He tapped the top of her car and stepped back, watching as she drove down the street. When her tail-lights were out of sight, he jogged over to his SUV and climbed in. He didn't bother blasting the heat, prefer-ring the cold to temper the heat moving through his body.

He wondered what was next in their relationship, and even that thought surprised him. Usually, by the end of the dinner date, he was either ready for a quick fuck if the woman was not giving off vibes of neediness or possessiveness or ready to go home alone if he felt no desire to continue the evening. Hell, at his age, either of those kinds of dinner dates had become fewer and farther between. His job allowed him little time to get to know someone. Even Allison had proven the difficulty of just having sex with no true relationship.

But Tara was different. Starting off as simply a person in his investigation to needing her insight and experience and to gain more information. Somewhere, in all of that, she became someone he wanted to know, and the more he learned about her, the pull to be with her was strong.

Starting his SUV, he drove home, his thoughts now on her family. *McBride. Fuckin' hell, McBride.* Her father had been with the FBI, now serving as a consultant. Sean and Kyle were fellow detectives and friends of his. *And the Kings as childhood neighbors. Jesus, could she be more untouchable?* He knew the Police Commissioner as Commissioner King. She knew him as Chauncey. If Sean and Kyle decided not to kick his ass, he had no doubt that Brock or Brody King would do so.

By the time he pulled into his condo parking space, he was almost convinced that Tara was not the person for him. Shutting down the engine, he sat in his vehicle and remembered the way she looked when sitting across from him. Her eyes sparkled in the candlelight. Her laughter was infectious, not affected. Her voice was warm, and her touch was soft. Open and honest. Loving and fiercely protective of those she loved. And her kiss —holy hell, her kiss. It had been a long time since he'd engaged in a kiss for the simple purpose of kissing. And now that he had tasted her lips, he wanted to taste them again.

Climbing from his vehicle, he slammed the door, beeping the locks. A grin spread over his face. *All right, boys, you might as well know. I'm going to keep on seeing Tara. So, if you don't like it... bring it on.*

## 14

"I never thought this would be us."

Tara looked at the couple sitting across the table from her. Both in their thirties, the woman's eyes were pleading as her hands clasped tightly together. Her husband's jaw was tight, and he gave off a vibe of wanting to be anywhere but there. Tara was used to that. People seeking a place at the shelter were often caught by surprise at the change in their circumstances.

A little girl wiggled on her dad's lap, and he leaned over to place a kiss on the top of her head. An older boy was standing in between his parents, leaning his weight against his dad.

"It was as though we got hit from all sides at once," the woman said. "Lonnie showed up for work one day and the hardware store was locked up with a note on the door saying that it was no longer in business. It took a while, but he found out that the owner had not been paying his bills and skipped out without letting anyone know or paying his employees. We lost our health insurance because of that, and I only work part-time as a clerk in a small store. Lonnie's been looking, but he can't find full-time work. He's a hard worker and doesn't mind doing whatever he can. He works two part-time jobs while still looking."

Tara's gaze scanned the forms in front of her. "I see you have no relatives in the area."

Shaking her head, the woman replied, "No. Both sets of parents have passed on, but we've tried to do everything we can to keep from coming here once we couldn't afford our rent. We've spent the last few months staying at some friends' houses, never more than a few nights at one place, not wanting to overstay our welcome. Even an apartment wants two months' rent and a security deposit, which is more than we can come up with at one time. Our boy here got sick and spent three nights in the hospital. Lord, Ms. Wilson, you can't imagine how much that cost. It wiped us out."

She smiled and nodded, knowing exactly how much it cost, both in money and in emotional energy. "Based on the information you've given us, you qualify for a place here at Ever Hope. You will have a small room that holds a double bed and two cots for your children. The room will include a sink, but there are men's and women's toilets and showers down the hall. We ask that you accompany your children to the bathrooms at all times. Breakfast and dinner are served here at the shelter, and a bag lunch is offered on Mondays, Wednesdays, and Fridays."

The woman nodded so quickly, Tara was afraid her head would bounce off.

"What about my children? They go to school, but—"

Waving her hand, Tara said, "Don't worry about your children. The law requires that their school system send a bus here to take them to their regular school. You'll find that we have other children catching the school buses as well."

The woman's eyes fluttered, and she pressed her hand against her chest. "Oh, thank you, Jesus."

"Please understand that this room is not yours forever. Your position is made much better because you're both working, and you'll be required to attend evening classes on money management, available housing, and work with a case manager on obtaining low-income health insurance. Our goal is to have you out of here in two months, less if possible."

For the first time since sitting down, the husband let out an audible sigh of relief. His wife continued nodding emphatically and said, "Oh, yes, Ma'am. We pray we can be out of here sooner. If we're not having to worry about food costs or rent for a month, we should be able to find a place to live."

"Well, having a case manager to help you through the process will be a big bonus." She looked up as the door opened and smiled. "This is Mr. Rogers and he'll be your case manager. He'll take over for now, showing you to your room and setting up your first meeting with him."

She walked to the door to say goodbye, not surprised when the woman threw her arms around her in a hug. She smiled at the two children who followed their mother.

The man stopped and thrust out his hand, shaking hers heartily. His wife and children were already in the hall, but he turned his attention to Tara. "It gets to a man when he's not able to take care of his family."

"What you're doing right now *is* taking care of your family. Staying in the shelter does not define you as a man. Making sure that your family is safe, warm, and fed is doing the best that you can do."

Tears shined in his eyes as he nodded, swallowing deeply. He turned and followed his family down the hall, leaving Tara getting ready for her next appointment. A movement across the hall in her office caught her eye, and she whipped around, surprised to see Carter standing there.

The sight of him caused her stomach to twitter and her heart to pound, both reactions seeming more adolescent than for a woman her age. Nonetheless, she could not have stopped the smile from spreading across her face if she tried. Arriving home from her date on Saturday night, she and Erin talked for an hour as she relived each moment of their dinner. That night, when she lay in bed, she thought about something her sister had said. *"Tara, this is the first time in a long time that I've heard you talk about something that you wanted. Not just trying to help someone else or solve someone else's problem. But the glow in your eyes tells me that Carter is someone really special. I hope he's deserving of you."*

For Tara, there was nothing more important in her life than being a good mom to Colleen. Next came being a good sister and daughter. After that came being a good counselor. But Erin was right, it had been a long time since Tara allowed herself to feel a tingle of excitement that came from a man's kiss. The *right* man. For the first time, she wondered if there was room in her and Colleen's life for someone else.

And now, he was standing in her office, smiling at her. "Hey, what are you doing here?"

He grabbed her hand and led her into her office, bending to place a kiss on her lips. "Had some business in the area, so I thought I'd stop and say hello."

Lifting an eyebrow, she laughed. "And do you say hello with a kiss to just everyone?"

"Only to the beautiful woman who I couldn't wait to see again." He kissed her lightly again and said, "I know we just talked yesterday, but we didn't set up a new date. And I couldn't wait."

She nibbled on her bottom lip in thought, jumping when he smoothed his thumb over the skin she had bitten.

"You're thinking hard about something," he said. "Care to share?"

She sighed, wondering if it was too early to broach the subject. *After all, we've known each other for such a short time.* "Okay, here's the thing. Other than a few work events, I haven't gone out on a date since my divorce. And I never introduced anyone to my daughter. I simply have not met anyone that I wanted to have a relationship with, and I was not about to confuse a young child with parading men in and out." She sighed again but forced her gaze to stay on his. "This is weird, because I haven't known you long at all, but I definitely want to see more of you."

MARYANN JORDAN

"And you're concerned about how Colleen will take you dating?"

Her brow furrowed as she considered her answer. "She's only six years old but quite mature for her age. I'm not afraid that she would suddenly see you as a daddy-substitute nor do I think she would pout about you taking up my time."

"Okay, that sounds good. So, what are you really worried about, Tara?"

She chuckled, but it came out more as a snort. Blushing, she shook her head. "My biggest problem is overthinking things, Carter."

He wrapped his arms around her and kissed her forehead. Pulling back, he held her gaze. "How about this? We go on a few more dates, whenever it's convenient to you and Colleen, and we'll have lunch together during the workday whenever we can. That way, we get to see each other, spend time together, get to know each other better without involving her. Then, when you're ready, I can meet her."

His words wrapped around her like a balm, and she smiled. "I think that sounds wonderful." Suddenly frowning, she said, "I'm booked today with intakes. The cold weather has brought more people in. But how about lunch tomorrow?"

"It's a date."

He bent and kissed her again, and she was glad her office door was closed, giving her the opportunity to press tightly against him. Finally separating, both sucking in ragged breaths, she grinned. "See you later."

She walked him toward the front, where Enrico had

her next appointment off to the side, talking in low voices. "That's my next appointment. I know he's a veteran and suffered major injuries in an IED blast."

The man appeared agitated, and Carter stepped closer to her. "Tara, I don't—"

She stilled his words when she placed her hand on his arm. "Carter, no. Just no. This is my job, and I'm good at what I do. That doesn't mean I'm not careful because I am. Please, go do your job, and let me do mine."

Frustration and uncertainty moved across his face as she stared up at him. Her breath caught in her throat as she waited to see what he would do. A flash of Calvin flew through her mind, his accusations that she cared more about others than his feelings.

Carter's gaze shifted from the man talking with Enrico back down to hers, and he offered a slight smile. Bending low so that only she would hear his voice, he said, "I know you're good at what you do, Tara. But I can't help but worry." His lips barely touched her ear, but she felt the sensation shoot through her as though he had taken her lips in a searing kiss.

Her breath left her lungs in a rush as he walked through the door of the shelter, and she smiled, her heart lighter with his support. Quickly turning her attention back to her next client, she rushed over toward Enrico.

"We can go back to the workroom to finish the paperwork," she said after introducing herself. Enrico followed along with the man, his silent support indicating that he was cautious for her safety. With almost a fourth of the homeless population having severe mental illness, Enrico always sat with or stayed nearby for the intakes of individuals.

Away from the crowded reception area, the man calmed. His medical history included prescription pain medicine, which had been downgraded to non-narcotic. He indicated his pain was manageable but still found sleep elusive. He had been in and out of VA hospitals for the past two years and unable to keep a job. He did not have a diagnosed mental illness, but that didn't mean he was not suffering. He rarely looked at her, keeping his gaze fixed on his clenched hands resting on the edge of the table.

She finished explaining the living quarters and meals provided and gave him a moment to peruse the papers he was signing. "Do you have any questions for me at this time?"

He barely shook his head, then lifted his gaze quickly, meeting her eyes for just a few seconds. "No, Ma'am. Thank you."

"Then welcome to Ever Hope. If you'll follow Enrico, he'll show you to your case manager who'll get you to your room."

Glancing at the clock, she could see why her stomach was growling. The bag lunch service should soon be ending, and she decided to check on them before having her own lunch. She walked through the empty dining hall and into the kitchen, stopping near the door that led outside. The tables set up had only a few bags on them, the volunteers already taking down the signs.

"Good crowd today, George?" she asked one of the men standing nearby.

"Oh, yes, Ma'am. I think the cold weather brings them out."

She looked down the sidewalk and caught sight of Polly standing with a man. He was hunched over, wearing a large coat and dirty jeans. His knit cap was pulled down over his ears, and he stared at the ground more than he looked up at Polly.

Glancing further down the street, she saw a man sitting in an SUV. He was too far away to see clearly, but he reminded her of Carter. Smiling, she turned and walked back into the shelter. *I must have it bad if I think I see him everywhere.*

## 15

---

"What happened today?" It was now the end of the week, and Carter had spent part of Monday, Wednesday, and Friday mornings sitting in his SUV down the street from the back of Ever Hope. He kept his eye on anyone Polly had talked to while Evan slowly started talking to the nurse, hoping to gain her acceptance. As soon as he finished, he hustled around to the front of the building to meet Tara for lunch. She knew nothing about his surveillance of Polly, and for the first time ever, he hated the subterfuge. *Hell, if Polly isn't giving out anything more than suckers and cough drops, it's time to pull the plug on this.*

Evan settled into Rachael's chair and scrubbed his hand through his beard. "I started talking to some of the people in line. The ones that spent more time with Polly Starr. I was coughing, snorting, hacking up a lung, and one of them told me I needed to see her. I told him I didn't like going to the doctor and they laughed, telling me that she could give me shit that would make me better."

Leaning forward, Carter kept his gaze pinned on Evan. "I saw you had a chance to talk to her by yourself. Anything?"

"She's still trying to get me to come into the clinic, but I refused. I think she's getting close to offering me something. Each day this week I've seen her giving things out. She must warn everyone to keep quiet because when I asked the guy this morning what she could give me, he just said he wasn't supposed to talk about it."

Scrubbing his hand over his face, Carter leaned back in his chair. "Maybe I'm chasing down the wrong fuckin' rabbit hole. If she's just giving out cold medicine, then I'm wasting our resources by going after her."

Evan shook his head in disagreement. "Look, maybe she's not the one giving out the narcotics, that doesn't mean what she's doing is right if it's prescription medicine. It sure as hell isn't legal."

He walked around his desk, leaning his ass against the edge as he stared at the board and the pictures of Carl, Jonathan, and Rocky. "All three had opioids in their systems, but there's no trace of them having a prescription or visiting a doctor recently. The only thing the ME could confirm was that it was oxycodone, but we've got no clue what brand. We can't find any link between the three other than they all went to the bag lunch distribution at the back of Ever Hope Homeless Shelter, where food is given out in paper sacks and sandwiches are in plastic baggies.

The same fuckin' kind of baggies that the drugs were in."

"Then I don't see how you can be wrong in what we're trying to find out. Maybe Polly isn't the end person, but just one of many. Maybe she starts giving out antibiotics and then works up to something else."

"What if we pull Polly in and spook whoever's doing the hard drugs?" he mused aloud.

"If somebody's getting these guys hooked on opioids, they're going to keep that pipeline going. With me on the inside doing some digging, we've got a lot better chance of finding out what the fuck is going on."

Looking at the clock on the wall, he sighed. "Okay. Monday you're back in there. For now, I'm heading home."

Evan stood and offered a chin lift as he walked past Carter and headed out of the workroom. Shutting down for the evening, Carter quickly followed him. Before Tara, he would have been tempted to stay at work longer or go to the Celtic Cock Pub for a drink. But tonight, he had a date—with Pirate Ship Pizza.

An hour later, he walked into chaos. Pure, unadulterated chaos. Children zipped between tables, some with parents dashing after them and others appearing unfettered in their quest to get to the games in the back. The scent of greasy pizza hit him, and for a second he wondered if he was crazy for venturing into this world. His gaze searched the crowd, landing on the dark-haired beauty standing to the side. Tara turned his way, and her smile lit her face. As though pulled by a magnetic beam, he dodged between the tables and the children on his way to her. *Oh yeah, I might be crazy, but she makes it worth it.*

As soon as he reached her side, he hesitated, uncertain of the proper protocol. For the past week he had greeted her with a kiss, both going and coming. Now, uncomfortably aware of their audience, he stood awkwardly with his hands jammed into his pockets. "Hey."

She laughed as though understanding his predicament and repeated his greeting. "Hey to you, too."

They had made a date for the next evening, but he hated not seeing her tonight. Tara had explained that Colleen was attending a birthday party at a children's pizza restaurant. She'd joked that he could come just to see what that part of her life was like. When he'd accepted, her mouth had hung open in surprise.

He glanced around the room, resisting the urge to scream over the cacophony, but he had no idea what Colleen looked like. "Where is she?"

As though able to keep up with her own child in the middle of the pandemonium, she pointed to a group of little girls. "Colleen is the one with a pink bow in her hair." She paused for a few seconds, then continued. "And the pink shirt, the pink leggings, and the pink sneakers." Drawing his attention to the coat in her arms, she laughed. "And yes, this pink coat is hers as well."

"I take it pink is her favorite color?"

"Yes, but I can say that purple is a very close second."

He stood next to Tara, and it didn't take long for him to ignore the noise and focus on her soft voice. He also found it strange, but it did not take him long to hone in on where Colleen was. When she darted from the table to the games toward the back, his eyes followed right along.

"I can't believe you actually came here."

His gaze left Colleen and moved back to Tara's face. Grinning, he shrugged. "What else was I gonna do on a Friday night?"

She tilted her head to the side and asked, "What do you normally do on a Friday night?"

"A lot of times I stop in at the Celtic Cock, a pub not too far from the headquarters—"

"Oh, believe me, I'm acquainted with the Celtic Cock. With two brothers in the police force and another brother working at a fire station, it's well known to me. I haven't gone very often, but I have popped in occasionally. Maeve Flanagan, one of the owners, is an old friend of mine." She suddenly snapped her mouth closed and shook her head. "I'm sorry, Carter. I asked you what you do on a Friday night and then I started talking again."

He chuckled at her embarrassment before casting his gaze around to find Colleen again. Looking back at Tara, he said, "There wasn't much else to tell. I might have a few drinks and talk to some friends that I don't get to see often. That's about it."

She lifted an eyebrow but remained quiet.

"I get the feeling you have something else you want to ask."

"I was going to imply that I doubted you often went home alone, but this is hardly the place to have that conversation."

"Aaargh, Maties! Having a good time?"

Jerking his head around at the feel of someone's hand on his arm, his gaze landed on a pirate captain—a person in a very bad pirate captain costume. The headgear completely covered their face, but before Carter had a chance to respond, the mascot moved over to a table full of children.

Tara laughed, lifting her hand to cover her mouth as she doubled over. "Oh, my God, Carter! If you could only see your face!"

"That thing gives me the creeps. I don't see how he doesn't give the kids nightmares. If he puts his hand on me again, I'm taking him out." Tara continued to laugh, but his gaze was pinned on the mascot moving toward the games where Colleen was. "He puts his fuckin' hand on Colleen, and he's gonna need a hook at the end of his other arm!"

By now, Tara was wiping tears from her eyes, and all he could do was glower. He refused to take his eyes off Colleen but jolted as the little girl with the big pink bow turned around to see her mother laughing. A smile spread across her face, and it hit him that she was a mini-Tara.

As Colleen began skipping across the floor toward them, he forgot about the mascot and was now full of terror at meeting her. Before he had a chance to prepare what he might say, Colleen stopped right in front of them and looked up at her mother.

"What's so funny, Mom?"

"My friend and I were just laughing at the pirate

captain," she said, bending to kiss her daughter's forehead. "Are you having fun?"

Nodding emphatically, Colleen's gaze moved up to his, and she tilted her head to the side in the exact same way Tara did. "Are you Mommy's friend?"

He smiled, but before he had a chance to speak, Tara said, "Sweetie, I'd like you to meet my friend, Mr.— "

"Carter. You can just call me Carter." He jerked his gaze to the side, now wide-eyed as he stared at Tara. "Um... if that's okay."

She smiled and nodded, placing her hand on his arm and giving a little squeeze. "Carter, this is my daughter, Colleen."

"Hi!" Colleen shouted, bouncing on her toes. "I'm six years old and in the first grade." She looked over her shoulder and pointed to a table several rows away. "My friend, Sally, is having a birthday today. She's already seven. I'll be seven on my next birthday."

He squatted so that he would be at face level with the excited little girl. "It's nice to meet you, Colleen. Are you going to have a birthday party here, too?"

Colleen crinkled her nose and looked around. "I don't know. I don't really like the pirate. He smells funny. Mom says we can have one in our backyard."

With a bark of laughter, he nodded. "I was just telling your mom that I'm not too crazy about the pirate, either."

Another little girl came over and shouted, "Colleen, come play!"

"Not too much longer, sweetie," Tara said. "You've

had pizza and birthday cake, and Sally has already opened her presents. How about five more minutes?"

"Okay, Mom!"

Watching her run off with her friends, Carter said, "She's cute, Tara. It's like looking at a miniature you."

She nodded, her eyes on Colleen for a moment before twisting around to look up at him. "Thank you. I have to admit that when I look at her, I see myself as well." She leaned forward and whispered, "I know this sounds bad, but I'm so glad she has more of the McBride genes than her father's!"

"Can't say that I blame you."

A few minutes later, Colleen came skipping back, stopping right in front of them. He watched as Tara bent and helped to zip her daughter's coat, adding a scarf around her neck, a cap on her head, and mittens on her hands. He started to laugh at how wrapped up the little girl was but remembered the blast of wind that had hit him as he walked into the building.

The three of them weaved through the tables as they headed toward the door. The pirate almost intercepted Colleen, but a growl from Carter had him backing off. Continuing forward, he heard Tara giggling behind him.

Stepping outside, he spied Tara's car, but before he could step off the curb, Colleen grabbed his hand. When he jerked his head down in surprise, she was looking up at him with a smile on her face.

"Mama says we have to hold hands when we cross the street."

His gaze shifted up to Tara, the smile on her face

chasing away the cool from the evening air. Looking back down at Colleen, he said, "She's absolutely right. Let's keep you safe and get you into your car where you'll be warm."

He stood back as Tara buckled Colleen into her car seat. When finished, she turned around and looked up at him.

"I still can't believe you spent your Friday evening at Pirate Ship Pizza when you could've been at a pub."

He reached out and linked fingers with hers, knowing that their hands were out of sight from Colleen. As with every time he touched her, the warmth traveled up his arm. "I don't want to rush things, Tara. But I really wanted to see you, and quite frankly, I really wanted to meet Colleen. She's a beautiful little girl, and you should be very proud of the job you're doing with her."

"Thank you. She is special, and believe me, it's not all from me. My family has pitched in and are the true definition of *'it takes a village to raise a child.'*" She glanced into the car before lifting her gaze back to his. "I know we said we'd go out tomorrow night, but I was wondering—"

"Tara, honey, if you need to be with Colleen, that's fine. I'll miss you, but I understand."

She sucked in her lips as though to still a grin. "What I was going to ask was if you'd like to come over for dinner."

"Seriously?" Seeing her nod, he let out a sigh of relief. "I'd love to. And we can play this however you want with Colleen."

Nibbling on her bottom lip, she said, "That would be good. I don't know that she understands dating anyway. But you can be a friend that comes for dinner."

"I can't think of anything I'd like more." Chuckling, he added, "Well, except to kiss you right now. But since I can't do that, I'll look forward to tomorrow night." He stepped back and allowed her to climb into the driver's seat. With a wave toward both, he grinned as Colleen returned his wave.

## 16

The hot dogs had been eaten along with the french fries, apple slices, salad, and homemade double chocolate brownies. The dinner certainly had not rivaled what Lorenzo would have prepared, but at least Tara was pleased that Colleen had eaten what was on her plate.

As soon as Carter had rung their doorbell, Colleen had screamed, "Mom, your friend is here!" Before Tara had made it to the door, Colleen had thrown it open, looked up at Carter, and shouted, "You can be my friend, too!" She then grabbed his hand and pulled him in, barely giving him a chance to take off his jacket before immediately launching into a tour of the downstairs, ending in the kitchen where she declared, "You're lucky! We get hot dogs tonight!"

Tara had wondered if it was a mistake inviting him over. *Was it fair to throw him into the lion's den with an excited six-year-old girl whose exuberance for life spilled over into every word and action?* On the other hand, she'd worried if it was fair for her daughter to become attached to someone who might not last. *But it's not like I've paraded men in and out of her life. Other than my brothers or the Kings, I've never had a man over.*

Her worries were laid to rest as the evening proceeded. Colleen appeared to charm Carter, and he did the same with her. She noticed how he would kneel so that he was on Colleen's level. He even joined in when she asked to play a board game after dinner. He didn't ignore Colleen, but neither did he act as though he were trying too hard to win her over. He just seemed natural, both for Colleen and her.

Now, he was downstairs in her living room, and she was just tucking a very sleepy Colleen into bed. "You've had a busy day. Was it fun?"

Her daughter's typical enthusiastic nod was slower as she yawned widely. "Uh-huh. I like our new friend, Mom. Can we keep him?"

A giggle slipped out at the thought of how much she would like to keep Carter. Clearing her throat, she said, "I hope so. But you never know, sweetheart. A few of the friends you had in kindergarten are in a different first-grade class, and you're not as close to them as you were last year. So, sometimes our friends change a bit. But when we make a friend, we always hope that they can stay our friend."

Colleen rolled to her side, her eyes closing as she tugged her favorite doll closer to her. "I hope he stays our friend. He's nice and he makes you smile."

"He makes me smile?"

Colleen yawned again and nodded. "You always smile a lot. But tonight, you smiled even more."

Bending, she tucked the covers tightly around Colleen's shoulders and kissed her cheek. Her lips lingered for a moment on the soft skin, and she inhaled the sweet scent that had filled her heart ever since she first held her baby girl. Standing, she tiptoed out of the room before shutting her door with a soft click.

She hurried across the hall through the master bedroom and into her bathroom. Looking into the mirror, she swiped underneath her eyes to take away the traces of smudged mascara. She reached for her lip gloss then hesitated. Pulling open one of the drawers, she fished around until she found the lip balm, gliding it across her mouth. *Better for kissing... if he kisses me. Oh, lordy, I really hope he kisses me.*

She had no perfume, finding that Colleen was allergic to many scents, so she sniffed under each arm to ensure that her deodorant was still effective. She hurriedly used the toilet, washed her hands, and ran a brush through her hair.

She stared at her reflection quickly, sucked in a deep breath, and tried to quell her nerves. So far, the evening had been perfect, but she had no idea what to expect now. She hastened to the top of the stairs then forced her steps to slow as she descended. It didn't matter how calm she appeared, the sight of Carter sitting in her living room, having poured two glasses of wine that were now resting on the coffee table, had her stomach flip-flopping again.

As soon as his gaze landed on her, he jumped to his feet and stalked toward her. She was struck once again with how his presence affected her. Unlike many women who panted after alpha men, she had never sought them out. Between her family and their neighbors, she grew up with plenty of alpha men. Maybe that's why she'd been attracted to Calvin in the first place. He was as unlike her brothers as possible. Handsome, but in a more *omega male* way. And now? She simply stared at the man who was now directly in front of her, exuding everything she found attractive.

"Breathe."

Blinking at his gentle command, air that she didn't realize she had been holding whooshed from her lungs. Her gaze moved over his face, settling on his lips. "I really want you to kiss me." The words came rushing out before she had a chance to pass them through her filter, but his reaction gave her no time for reversing.

His arms banded around her, pulling her tightly, his lips landing on hers. This kiss was not gentle but flamed white-hot immediately as they nipped, sucked, tangled tongues, tasted, and feasted on each other. Her hands were crushed between them, her palms flat on his chest. Not wanting to feel the impediment, she worked her hands around his waist. Now, with her breasts pressed against his chest, she only wished there were no clothes in the way.

Barely aware they were moving, she jumped as they halted when the back of his legs hit the sofa. She was stunned that he'd managed to maneuver them around the coffee table without knocking over the wine glasses. He sat and gently tugged her down. Her ass landed in his lap and when she attempted to wiggle to the side, his large hands clamped onto her hips.

His gaze on hers was intense, and he shook his head slowly. "Oh, no, babe. Your ass is right where I'd like it to be."

She grinned but had no time to respond as their lips met again and she wrapped her arms around his neck. She tangled her fingers through his thick hair, but her senses were filled with their kiss. His hands smoothed up and down her back from her shoulders to her ass, where he would squeeze before his hands repeated their journey.

Her nipples beaded and her sex tightened, electricity firing throughout her body. She could not remember the last time she felt so alive, so aware of her body, so needy. Wanting more of him, her fingers slid to the buttons on his shirt, fumbling to get them undone.

Suddenly, cold air rushed between them as he grabbed her hands and pushed her back ever-so-slightly. Groaning, she pressed forward, wanting to close the distance.

Sucking in a breath, he rasped, "Tara, babe, I'm sorry. This is my fault for letting it go too far, but I know we need to slow down."

Embarrassment slammed into her, and she felt heat fill her cheeks. She tried to scramble from his lap, but his hands held her in place once again.

"No, you're not getting me. I want this. I'm so fuckin' hard for you I can barely breathe. But Colleen is just upstairs. What if we don't hear her coming downstairs—"

"Her door is alarmed. If she opens it, we'll know."

Her hands slid up to cup his jaws and she leaned forward to kiss him lightly.

His fingers squeezed her hips again, and he repeated, "Her door is alarmed?"

Her top teeth landed on her bottom lip as she smiled slightly and nodded. "She sleepwalks. Ever since she could crawl out of bed, I would find her everywhere. Sometimes standing over me while I was sleeping, which would scare the hell out of me."

He chuckled, his face full of warmth. "I'll bet."

"One night, I got up to check on her, and she had only made it halfway down the stairs but had fallen asleep on one of the steps. She was old enough to unlatch the gate installed at the top of the stairs, but I didn't think she could do it when sleeping. I was wrong."

His eyes widened in surprise, and she nodded again. "Yep. Scared the hell out of me over that, too. So, even though I had a security system on the outside doors, my brothers came over and installed an alarm on her bedroom door. It beeps when it opens. Of course, that means I hear when she gets up to go to the bathroom at night, but that's much better than having her fall down the stairs."

"That's smart." He shook his head slowly. "I never even thought about a child sleepwalking."

She lifted her shoulders in a shrug, saying, "There're lots of things you don't think about until you're faced with it. Believe me, parenting is trial and error. Sometimes, the best you can hope for is to not screw them up too much before they're adults."

He lifted one hand, sliding his fingers around the back of her neck, sweeping his thumb over her cheek. She wanted to close her eyes and lean into the warmth of his palm but battled the desire because she wanted to keep her gaze on his crystal blue eyes.

"I think you're an amazing mother, Tara," he said. "You don't have to be around Colleen long to see that she's cherished and cared for, smart and funny, and a really sweet little girl."

His words washed over her, filling the cracks that sometimes appeared when she struggled being a single parent. She swallowed deeply, uncertain if she should bring Colleen's dad up when she and Carter had just been hot and heavy.

"I can see you thinking hard about something, babe. Whatever it is, just say it."

His gaze gave her courage, and she nodded. "It was Calvin's decision to walk away from us, but I know in my heart that I would have taken Colleen and left him if he hadn't made some serious changes in his life. I didn't want my daughter to be raised by a man that considered her to be an imposition—an inconvenience. So, while I worry if I'm doing enough for her, I know that alone I'm stronger than I would've been with his weaknesses pulling at both of us."

His smile curved his lips, and her heart felt lighter. "And that right there, Tara, is why you're a wonderful mother."

Sliding her arms around his neck again, she snuggled closer. She kissed the underside of his jaw and felt the quick intake of his breath. She continued to nibble little kisses until she met his lips.

As though his resolve snapped, he growled, banding his arms around her tightly, taking over the kiss. He fell back against the seat cushions, taking her with him. The two stretched out on the sofa, their bodies aligned perfectly—chest to chest, hip to hip, legs tangled together.

His weight was half on her, but she did not mind. Instead, her nipples ached, and her sex clenched as his pelvis pressed forward, the feel of his long, hard cock against her. She had not been with a man in over six years, but she could tell Carter's endowments were well beyond what her ex's had been. She had planned on taking things slow, but with the sexual electricity firing inside, all she wanted was to feel everything Carter could do for her. She pushed back on the idea that his previous partners would have more experience, refusing to give in to self-doubt. He was here, right now, with her, and he was not the kind of man to be where he did not want to be.

He thrust his tongue into her warm mouth, and she wondered if it was possible to spontaneously combust from just a kiss. His fingers slid under the bottom of her sweater and glided over her stomach, his palm resting just below her breast. If she thought his kisses inflamed her, nothing prepared her for the sweep of his thumb over her nipple. Her hips jerked as her sex weeped. He gently tugged the cup of her bra down, exposing the fullness of her breast. His lips left hers as he bent and sucked her nipple deeply into his mouth.

As he nipped and sucked, his hands slid down the front of her pants. When dressing for the evening, she had paired a pretty sweater with leggings, hoping for casual comfort as well as style. Now, she praised their easy access.

He moved slow, his deliberate movements driving her mad with want. When his fingers finally reached her slick folds, he moved his moistened finger over her swollen clit. Her body burned, but it was a fire she did not want to extinguish. She managed to jerk the tail of his shirt out of his jeans, running her hands along his bare back. Dipping her fingers underneath his belt, she delighted in the feel of his muscular ass.

When he inserted a thick finger into her sex, all rational thought fled as her entire being was centered on their touch. With his mouth working her nipple and his fingers scissoring inside, curling to hit the spot, she cried out her release as her body shuddered in his arms. Her first non-self-induced orgasm in years threatened to steal all rational thought as her body continued to tremor. Finally, when she was able to catch her breath, she lifted her head. Carter's gaze was locked onto her face, his smile beaming at her.

There was nothing in the world as beautiful to look at as her daughter but seeing Carter's smile after he made her come was a close second.

He slid his hand from the front of her pants and slowly licked his fingers, causing her sex to squeeze again.

"Oh, my," she said, barely able to whisper. "That was amazing."

He shook his head slowly, shifting upward slightly so that his lips could meet hers, and she tasted her essence on his tongue. Lifting his head, he peered down and said, "That was fuckin' beautiful. You're fuckin' beautiful."

They kissed again, long, languid strokes of their tongues and gentle murmurings as their lips moved over each other's. He shifted again, this time rising to sit, pulling her up with him. She thought about suggesting they go to her bedroom but hated to be across the hall from Colleen. While the couch did not offer them much room, she had no doubt they could make it work.

Much to her surprise, Carter stood with her in his arms, settling her feet onto the floor. He gently pulled her bra cups back into place and smoothed her sweater over her hips. He kissed her lightly, and before she could throw herself at him, he stepped back.

"I think it's time for me to go."

"Wh… what? Now? But, I… I…" she stammered, unable to hide her surprise. Dropping her gaze to his crotch, it was evident his erection was straining his jeans. She reached for him, but with his hands on her shoulders, he gave a little squeeze.

"Babe, all I want to do is strip you naked and bury myself inside you," he said, his voice ragged.

"So, what's stopping you? Are you afraid we won't hear Colleen if she gets up?"

"That's part of it, but honestly, Tara, I want to do this right. What we just did tonight shows we've got chemistry. If that's how you come apart with just my fingers,

I can't wait to see you come apart with my cock deep inside you. But we've got time. I want to do this right for you, and I want to do this right for Colleen."

As his words washed over her, she struggled to catch her breath, knowing he was right. Nodding slowly, she smiled. "I want to do this right, too." Daring to glance at his crotch again, she added, "I hate that you're leaving... um... unfulfilled."

Chuckling, he said, "Don't worry. I'll take care of myself when I get home. Just know I'll be dreaming about you when I do it."

She fought to remain standing as her knees threatened to give out at the vision of him jerking off to thoughts of her. Blowing out a deep breath, her fingers tightened on his biceps. "Wow, Carter. I don't even know what to say to that."

His low chuckle turned into laughter as he bent and kissed her again. "We do this right for all of us, and our time will come. Soon, I promise."

With arms wrapped around each other, they walked to the front door. He tucked the back of his shirt into his jeans and grabbed his jacket. Wrapping their arms around each other, they stood at the door and kissed like teenagers afraid their parents would stop them. Finally leaning back, he said, "Lock up after me, babe."

She did as he asked, setting the alarm after he left. She looked at the untouched wine glasses and grabbed them from the coffee table. Dumping the wine in the sink, she rinsed them before putting them in the dishwasher. Turning out all the lights, she went upstairs.

As always, she checked on Colleen, smiling at the

sight of her daughter fast asleep. With her door shut, she moved across the hall. After her nightly routine, she climbed into bed, her thoughts tumbling even if her body was well sated from the orgasm.

Carter put her and Colleen ahead of his own desires. He gave more than he took. There was no doubt he was an alpha, but so like her father, brother, and neighbors, he was strong without overusing his strength. He was caring without being overbearing. He was confident without being cocky. In truth, Carter was everything Calvin was not.

And his fingers on her clit were magic. Unable to keep the giggle from bubbling forth, she rolled to her side and fell asleep, anxious for when she could see him again.

Carter sat in his SUV a block away from the back entrance of Ever Hope. His mind was in turmoil, sure as hell not focused on just the case.

Saturday night at Tara's house had meant more to him than he thought possible. As soon as he pulled into her driveway and saw the quaint little suburban house, he had no problem seeing her living there. And entering, it was obvious she'd created a warm and loving home for Colleen. Dinner had been simple yet fun. Her daughter had been entertaining, and her enthusiasm for everything was contagious. And Tara—beautiful, sexy, confident—watching her come apart in his arms had been the sweetest thing he could remember feeling.

He wanted more—more Tara, more Colleen, more time at their house, more time getting to know them.

Glancing out the window at Evan talking to Polly, he sucked in a ragged breath, wondering if he was going to get more.

The lunch line had dwindled, leaving the volunteers

putting away the tables and Evan talking to Polly. Evan had managed to maneuver them down the sidewalk, out of sight from the others. Carter could see Evan coughing and wiping his nose but held his breath as Polly reached into her bag and pulled something out that she gave to Evan. Unable to see what it was, he waited.

It did not take long for Evan to give the silent signal, and Polly jumped in surprise as two officers approached. Normally, Carter would have approached as well, taking the evidence from Evan and gaining a statement from Polly. But his supervisor had insisted he let the officers carry out the arrest, both because of his involvement with the shelter and keeping a low profile if they needed to go back in for someone else in the clinic.

Even from a distance, he could see that Polly was crying as the two officers placed cuffs on her and started to assist her into the back of their patrol car. Movement near the back door of the shelter caught his eye. *Fuck no! Goddamnit!* Tara had rushed through the door, her eyes wide as she stared at the scene in front of her. She started toward the patrol car, but he could not hear what she was saying.

Jumping down from his SUV, he ran across the street and intercepted her. "Tara, you need to go back inside."

"No, no, no," she cried, fighting against the grip he had on her arms as her gaze shooting from Polly up to him. "What's happening? Why are they taking her? What's going on?"

He shifted them onto the sidewalk so that his body was blocking her view. Bending, he moved his face right in front of hers. "Tara. Listen to me, honey. Polly is being taken in for questioning. You need to go back inside and let us do our job."

She stared up at him, eyes wide, mouth open in shock. "J... job? Your job?"

Polly was not fully in the police car yet and turned to see Tara. "Tara!" she sobbed. "They're arresting me for distributing drugs. It was just the antibiotics! You know they need them! I'm just helping them!"

The police car door shut, silencing Polly's shouts. He felt Tara's knees buckle and held on tighter. He wrapped one arm around her back, but before he had a chance to move his other arm, she jerked backward, stepping away.

"Tara—"

"This is you. You did this. Oh, my God, I told you that she offered something to Colleen, and you decided to do this. Oh, God, how could you have done this?"

He lifted his arms to reach toward her, but she scuttled backward. He stepped forward to remain close but did not attempt to touch her again. "Tara, listen to me. Let me explain—"

She closed her eyes for a few seconds before snapping them open again. Agony was plastered on her face as she slowly shook her head. "You used me. You took something that I told you, and you used it. I thought... I thought I could trust you. Jesus, what a fool I am."

She whirled and ran back into the shelter, leaving him calling after her, fighting the desire to rush in, hold her tight, and make her listen to reason. Standing on the sidewalk, shaking with frustration and anger, he jerked his head around when Evan spoke through his earpiece.

"We need to go, Carter. I'm sorry, man. Really, I am. Give her time. She'll come around, I'm sure. She just needs some time."

He turned and looked at Evan standing off to the side away from the police but said nothing. As far as he knew, Evan did not have a wife or girlfriend. Evan was a good detective but shit with giving relationship advice. Without saying anything, he turned and walked toward his vehicle. Evan hurried across the street and into the park. Once he drove several streets away, he parked, allowing Evan to climb into the passenger side of Carter's SUV.

"I was closer today," Evan began. "I stayed near the end of the line, but there were several other people around me that were sick, and when Polly came by, I was able to see that she was handing them pills in a drugstore-type bottle. I hung back like I didn't want to be around anyone, and she stayed with me. I didn't have to ask for anything. I didn't even tell her I needed anything. I just coughed and sniffed like the flu or pneumonia was biting me in the ass. She reached in that bag of hers and pulled out a bottle." He held up the clear evidence bag containing the generic amber-colored plastic bottle that almost every drugstore uses to dispense prescriptions.

Carter glanced over at the evidence and asked, "Did she say what she was giving you?"

"Yep. Didn't hesitate. She said she gets free antibiotics from the drug manufacturers and passes them out to people who need them. I said I thought a doctor had to prescribe those, and she said that she couldn't see letting somebody stay sick if she could help them."

"Fuck," Carter sighed heavily. What Polly was doing was illegal, even if her motives were just to assist people.

"I tried to do it discreetly, but I couldn't see if the volunteers were close enough to see what was happening."

"I appreciate that, Evan."

Driving directly to the lab, the two detectives headed straight to one of the technicians that handled drug testing. "How long will it take you to tell us what this is?" Carter asked as Evan handed the evidence bag to the young man.

He opened the bag and pulled out the bottle, emptying several of the pills onto a sterile tray. "Give me just a minute." Typing in the color, shape, description, and identification numbers on the pill, the technician quickly found what they needed. "Azithromycin."

"Antibiotic?" Carter asked.

Nodding, the technician said, "Yeah. It's used to fight bacterial infections." He looked back down at his computer and began reading. "Can be used for respiratory infections, skin infections, ear or eye infections, and sexually-transmitted diseases. It's also for other infections, but those are the ones most listed. You should not use it if you have liver or kidney disease heart rhythm disorder, or low levels of potassium. Common side effects include diarrhea, stomach pain, fast heartbeat, shortness of breath, dizziness, and liver problems."

"Okay, thanks. If you get the report to us as soon as you can, we'd appreciate it." Offering chin lifts, Carter and Evan left the lab.

He spent the rest of the afternoon at his desk, writing up his report. He walked to the evidence board and re-drew a few lines, making new connections, talking out loud as he worked. Evan had plopped down at Rachel's desk, his attention focused on the board as well.

"Beth, the Kilton Pharmaceutical Rep, delivers samples of a variety of drugs to doctors' offices, including the free clinic. Like with most doctors' offices, she sometimes speaks to the doctor but often leaves the samples with nurses or receptionists. Polly reportedly hates to see homeless persons who are sick and yet won't come into the clinic. She takes the antibiotics and distributes them to those who won't see the doctor. So, we have her on illegal distribution of controlled substances."

He looked over at the pictures of Carl, Jonathan, and Rocky. Shaking his head, he added, "But there's not one damn thing that ties her to the opioids that are getting out. So, we took down one person who was doing something illegal, but we're no closer to solving the narcotic issue."

"Where do those bag lunches come from?"

"According to Tara, a bunch of different volunteers make them." He stared at Evan for a moment, then asked, "What are you thinking?"

"I dunno. I guess I just thought if they were all coming from the same place then maybe we're looking at another point in the pipeline." Standing, Evan said, "I'm heading out."

Before he made it out the door, their Lieutenant stepped out of her office and said, "My office, please." They followed her in and sat down, and in typical fashion, she got right to the point. "I talked to Rachel and warned her that she is not to continue assisting in any way, even if she's lying in bed with her feet up. As long as she's on bed rest, she's on medical leave. But that leaves you without a partner for several months." She speared Carter with her gaze before shifting over to Evan. "With the work you've just been doing on this case, I'm temporarily assigning the two of you together. Evan, the other case you're working on can take a backseat. Now that you're partnered with Carter, this opioid case is your first priority. That's all."

The two men stood and walked back out to the workroom. Evan glanced down at Rachel's desk and chuckled. "I guess you might as well get used to seeing me in the seat after all." Shifting his gaze back to Carter's, he asked, "You okay with this?"

"Yeah, it's fine with me." Stepping forward, he clapped Evan on the shoulder. "Glad to have you with me for the long haul on this."

"Good. I've got to go get my shit. You gonna call your woman?"

Sighing heavily, he nodded. After Evan left, he tried calling Tara's cell phone, but she never picked up. He left messages for her to please talk to him so that he could explain. She never called back.

---

"I feel so deceived." Tara wadded up the tissue in her hand, reaching over to snag another one from the box. She lifted her watery gaze to Erin sitting across from her at their parents' kitchen table. "I never meant for anything to happen to Polly. It never dawned on me when I said something the detective in him would take over. Jesus, she trusted me. I feel like I just handed her over to prison!"

Having left the shelter, she'd called her sister, desperate to have someone to talk to. Erin told her that their parents were out of the house, so she decided to meet her there. Now, with an unheeded cup of tea and a pile of wadded tissues in front of her on the table, she sighed heavily. "I'm glad I didn't tell anybody else in the family about seeing Carter. I can't stand the idea of everyone knowing what a fool I was."

"Honey, I know you don't want to hear this, but I have to say it."

She wiped her nose and stared at Erin. "Okay, go ahead and say it."

"Dad worked for the FBI and is now a consultant for them. Sean and Kyle are detectives. Hell, Chauncey is the Police Commissioner. On top of that, Brock and Brody are with the police. Tara, honey, you and I have been raised right smack in the middle of law enforcement."

Sniffing, she drew one leg up, wrapping her arms around her shin and resting her chin on her knee, still focused on Erin. "Okay…"

"These men don't just work in law enforcement. It's who they are. It's not a job they chose, it's part of their being. As betrayed as you feel, I'm not sure Carter had much choice."

She tossed another tissue onto the table and toyed with her mug before finally taking a sip. It had cooled slightly and the honey and lemon that Erin had added were soothing. Setting the mug back onto the table, she sighed. "Calvin was nothing like Dad. Nothing like our brothers. He was into music and freedom of expression. At one time, I liked the easy way he looked at life."

"I'm so sorry, Tara."

Lifting her gaze, she saw sympathy on Erin's face and snorted. "Don't be, Erin. I'm not. Even if I found out that Calvin wasn't all he was cracked up to be, I got Colleen out of the relationship."

Erin reached over and held her hand.

"You're right, you know," she admitted. "Carter is who he is. But that doesn't mean that I'm not hurt. And it sure as hell doesn't mean that I'm ready for a relationship with someone like my brothers and father. I guess maybe it really should just be me and Colleen." Holding her sister's gaze again, tears renewed as she said, "Thanks for listening."

"Honey, you've been here for me my whole life, but especially in the last couple of months as I've tried to make sense of what happened to me and where I want to go from here. Holding your hand while you cry is little repayment."

Heart still heavy, she sipped tea with her sister, filled with the familiarity and comfort of her parents' table.

Neither woman noticed Rory standing in the hall.

## 18

Carter sat at the bar of the Celtic Cock, nursing his second beer. The pub, located near headquarters and between two of the fire stations, was a favorite hangout for first responders. Being a Monday night, it was less crowded than the weekend, and that was just the way he wanted it. A chance to sit, drink, and feel sorry for himself.

Lifting his beer, a movement near the door caught his eye in the reflection of the mirror behind the bar. *Shit.* He watched as a group of tight-jawed, hard-eyed men stalked straight toward him. Sean, Kyle, and Rory McBride. Close behind were Brock and Brody King. *Fuckin' hell.*

Setting his mug back on the bar, he turned his stool and faced the firing squad. The five men circled around, giving him no room to move. It didn't matter. He had no plans of running anyway. He turned his gaze to Sean, figuring as the oldest McBride, he would be the first to speak. Until getting to know Tara, he only knew that

Sean and Kyle were brothers. Sean was quieter and known to analyze a situation or case carefully, usually dressed in button-down shirts and slacks in contrast to Kyle, who was always in jeans and boots. Kyle was quicker to temper, fast to action. Rory was the youngest brother, only known to Carter as a firefighter. And now that he understood the relationship between the McBrides and the Kings, he was not surprised to see Brock and Brody taking on a brotherly role as well.

"What the hell did you do to our sister?" Sean's calm voice belied the fire in his eyes.

He opened his mouth to defend himself, then snapped it closed again. Nothing he said was going to make a difference to these men who cared about Tara. Shaking his head, he admitted, "I fucked up."

"I'd say you did, asshole," Kyle growled, taking a step closer and halting only when Sean's hand snapped out and pressed against his chest.

He shifted his gaze around each of them, before coming back to Sean. "She was not part of my investigation. But she unwittingly gave me information about an illegal activity that was on the fringes of my investigation. I moved forward with my job but hoped it wouldn't affect her—"

"There's no way she would be unaffected by someone she knows getting arrested," Sean said.

"I didn't finish. I was going to say I hoped it wouldn't affect her until I had a chance to talk to her. To explain what was going on and what happened. This has nothing to do with that nurse offering Tara antibiotics without a doctor's prescription. We were already looking at the clinic and we were already looking at those employees. Somebody's getting opioids to people in that lunch line at the homeless shelter."

Sean remained quiet, but Carter had no doubt he was sifting through the situation. He glanced at Kyle, who appeared to be considering the investigation while still hanging on to his anger.

"That's not all, from what I heard."

He looked over at Rory, uncertain how to respond. Strangely, the thought ran through his mind that genetics ran strong with the McBride family. The three men looked so similar, no one would be surprised to discover they were brothers. The dark hair and intense expression in their blue eyes reminded him so much of Tara.

Rory continued, "Seems like you've been dating her, and no one knew about it. Why is that, Carter?"

"That's for Tara to say. You have to ask her."

"Hell, no. We're asking you," Rory growled.

"Tara's decision to tell you or not tell you who she's seeing is her business. From my point of view, we were never sneaking around, but I respected her wishes."

Kyle bit out, "She's got a daughter!"

His patience snapped and he crossed his arms over his chest, leveling his glare on them. "Yeah. Colleen. Her favorite color is pink, although purple is a close second. She likes birthday parties at Pirate Ship Pizza with her friends, doesn't mind crappy pizza as long as she's with those friends but thinks that the pirate captain mascot is weird. She likes hot dogs the way her mom fixes them but only wants ketchup and hates mustard. She'd rather have french fries than potato chips but wants ketchup on the side so that she can dip her fries and not get the ketchup on her fingers. She likes listening to bedtime stories but wants the reader to pretend that they're the characters. She likes school but wishes they would let her read bigger books. She loves her mom, her grandparents, her aunts, and believe it or not, she loves her uncles." He sucked in a breath and swung his gaze from the wide-eyed McBride's over to Brock and Brody. "She even considers you to be her uncles as well."

Focusing back on Sean and Kyle, he added, "So, yeah, I know she's got a daughter."

The five men staring at him were silent, their eyebrows raised, although Brock and Brody were fighting smiles as well.

"And Tara?"

This came from Sean, and Carter remained quiet for a moment. "She's beautiful, intelligent, and a fucking great mom. From all indications, she's also been a fuckin' great sister to all of you. She's spent her life helping others but never complained. She won't complain because she's happiest when she's responsible for people she cares about. The one time that responsibility bit her in the ass was when she fell for a man who didn't deserve her. Maybe she was just used to taking care of everybody else, and she figured she could take care of him, too."

He knew he had fired a shot straight to their hearts when all five men winced at his words. But too far gone to care, he continued. "A lot of women would've stuck that out and been miserable and made their child miserable, but not Tara. She put everything aside so that her daughter was raised with a sense of love and not guilt. I know you all helped with that. I know the whole family stepped in and helped. But that doesn't mean that she hasn't been very alone for a very long time."

Scrubbing his hand over his face, his shoulders slumped. "I was afraid falling for her might be a mistake. But it wasn't. The only mistake I made was not preparing her for fallout from my job. A job that every single one of you understand."

The noise of the bar fell away as the silence around him was deafening.

"You're in love with Tara."

The words coming from Sean were not a question but a statement. Nodding, he said, "Yeah. Yeah, I am."

Brock chuckled and slapped him on the shoulder while looking at the McBride brothers. "Well, hell, boys. Looks like you owe him a welcome instead of an ass-kicking." He and Brody continued to chuckle as they moved over to a nearby table.

"Are you really in love with Tara?" Kyle asked, his gaze less intense.

"Truthfully? The answer is yes. Does it make sense? Probably not. I wasn't looking for love. I wasn't even looking for a relationship. We met because of an investigation, but we spent time together because there was a spark. Something I haven't felt in a long time." Sighing, he reached to the back of his neck and squeezed the tight muscles. "But now, she won't even take my calls so that I can explain."

Sean's lips quirked. Kyle grinned. And Rory threw

his head back and laughed. Staring at the three, he wondered if he had missed the punchline to a joke.

"Let me tell you about McBride women," Sean said, clapping him on the shoulder. "Especially the oldest girl in an Irish family. Hurt or mad, you'll get the same fiery response. But if you get to the other side, you'll get loyalty like nothing you can imagine."

Kyle glanced behind him to the Celtic Cock's owner and bartender. "Torin, send a round over for all of us."

Torin offered a chin lift, mumbling, "Glad I didn't have to kick your asses outta here for fighting."

Carter followed the three McBrides over to the table where Brock and Brody had settled. After a few minutes of drinking, the youngest King brother, Blayze, walked in, and he and Rory joined other firefighters playing pool near the back. Brock soon left, wanting to get back to his woman, Kallie.

Sean finished his beer and stood, staring at Carter for a moment before extending his hand. "Gotta get to Harper, but I'll say this first. You're right about everything you said about Tara. And you're right about her deserving someone good. I'm glad it's you. You're going to have to work to get back into her good graces, but it'll be worth it."

Clasping Sean's hand, he shook it firmly. "Thank you. That means a lot coming from you."

Sean waved toward his brothers and friends and soon followed Brock out of the pub. Left with Kyle and Brody at the table, he wondered if he was going to take more heat about Tara.

"What have you got on Kilton Pharmaceuticals?"

The question from Kyle surprised him, but it was not unwelcome. "So far, I haven't done much with them. I've got my eye on one of their sales representatives who serves the clinic. I saw her give samples to the nurse that we just arrested. Why?"

"I'm working on a case that may indicate they have a security breach. So far, it doesn't look like anything that would directly affect your investigation, but I'll let you know if it does."

"I appreciate that. I'll do the same for you."

Brody asked, "Your partner is out now, isn't she?"

"Yeah. She's on medical leave until she has the baby, and then will be on maternity leave. At this point, she won't be back for four months. But my supervisor just handed me Evan, so he's shifting his other cases and coming over with me."

Kyle and Brody nodded in agreement. "He's a good man," Kyle acknowledged.

Shaking his head, he said, "Hell, if he was such a good partner, he should have been here taking my back when you all showed up."

Brody laughed, his eyes twinkling. "Not many people are brave enough to go up against the McBrides and Kings."

"Hell, you're brave just going up against Tara," Kyle added.

He sighed. "You're her brother. Got any words of wisdom for me?"

Kyle sobered and rubbed his hand over his chin. "Tara is tough. She's had to be. You were right—she was the responsible older sister, babysitter, counselor, and tried to take that role on with her loser husband. Up to now, the smartest thing she ever did was dump his ass."

Tilting his head to the side, he waited.

Kyle didn't make him wait long. "Now, the smartest thing she ever did was fall in love with someone who deserves her." Kyle drained his beer and slid off the stool. Glancing down at the table full of empty bottles, he said, "I've got this. It's on me." He started to walk away, then stopped and turned around, pinning Carter with his gaze. "We took care of that loser. Just make sure we don't have to take care of you." With a grin, he turned and walked out of the pub.

His brow furrowed as he swung around and caught Brody laughing. "What the hell did he mean by that?"

"It's part of Tara's story that she doesn't know." Brody chuckled some more, then continued. "Tara didn't walk away from her marriage easily, but she knew when Calvin said he didn't want to be a father, she had no choice but to let him walk away, which he did. But during the divorce, she knew he wasn't worth anything and would probably not pay child support, so she made sure to get the furniture, keep the money she had made, protect her savings, and get full custody. What none of us were expecting was that he tried to go after her money, claiming that since she made more than he did—hell, that wasn't hard since he practically never worked. So, Sean, Kyle, Rory, Brock, Blay, and I paid him a little visit."

Eyes wide, Carter reared back and stared. "No shit? Six against one?"

"No, no, we didn't kick his ass. But let's just say there

were a lot of implied threats. The asshole was pissing himself by the time we got through with him, and he promised he'd never go after her money."

Shaking his head, Carter grinned. "That's fuckin' brilliant, man. After what Tara's told me about him, I wanted to do the same. Since I wasn't around then, I'll just say thank you."

The two walked out of the pub, shaking hands as they each got ready to head to their vehicles. He felt better, having won the approval of Tara's brothers and friends. Checking his phone, he saw that she had not replied to any of his texts nor had she tried to return his calls. Sighing, he drove home, determined to give her only a few days more space before stepping up his game.

## 19

After a sleepless night, Carter walked into the clinic early the next morning. Part of him wanted to see Tara, but the other part desperately hoped that she stayed away. He needed to focus on the case and not her anger —at least for now. He arrived before they opened, and as before, Kate unlocked the door for him.

As soon as he walked into the office, the whisperings of the other employees quickly came to a halt. Eyes wide, they stared at him in unison. Behind him, Dr. Tiller and Robert were walking into the clinic as well. Before giving Dr. Tiller a chance to take charge, Carter said, "I'll be conducting interviews with each of you. Dr. Tiller, if you would designate a room that I can use."

Dr. Tiller opened and closed his mouth several times before finally sputtering, "Uh… Well, I guess you can use my office. I'll be seeing patients this morning."

After obtaining everyone's name, he decided to start with the nurses first. Once settled in Dr. Tiller's office, Kate knocked on the door. "I'll be first if you don't mind, Detective Fiske. Another nurse is going to cover for me, and then I'll cover for her."

It did not take long for Kate to answer all of his questions. She had no idea Polly had been squirreling away antibiotic samples. She had never seen Polly give them to a patient, although she admitted that if Polly was in an examining room with a patient, Kate would not have known what was happening behind closed doors.

The questions continued throughout the nurses, nursing aides, techs, and other staff. He discovered there was no accountability for the sample prescriptions that were given to them by the various pharmaceutical representatives that came by.

Taking a few minutes to review his notes before he interviewed the pharmacy staff at the clinic, he stayed seated at Dr. Tiller's desk.

"Oh, Doug, I'm so sorry to hear what happened to Polly—oh!"

He looked up as Beth came stuttering to a halt just inside Dr. Tiller's office. Her eyes were wide, and her mouth snapped shut. "Ms. Washington. How convenient for you to stop by. As you can see, I'm not Doug, but Detective Fiske, and I need to interview you."

"I... I... oh, yes... um... now?"

"Now is a perfect time."

She looked as though she were going to bolt but moved forward and perched on the edge of the chair. Composing her face, she clasped her hands in her lap and smiled. "Detective Fiske, I assure you I had no idea what Polly was doing with the samples."

"Before we get to that, I'd like you to explain your procedure, please."

"Procedure?"

"Yes. Your procedure from the moment you're given the drugs at Kilton Pharmaceuticals until they leave your possession."

"Oh, my, Detective. I assure you I follow every regulation—"

He had no doubt the smile on her face was a calculated attempt at either coercion or seduction. Maybe, even both. Shutting her down, he said, "The full procedure, please."

Her brows lowered as though confused as her smile drooped. "Oh. Okay. Um... I usually plan my next day the evening before. I get to about five or six locations each day and have about two hundred on my rotation in total. Sometimes, I just call the office to see if there's anything they need, but usually, I try to get in and see them in person."

"The drugs that you carry. What is the procedure for those?"

"Those are samples of drugs that Kilton produces. I have to learn all about the drugs and the diseases or conditions that they're for. Detective, you have to understand, this is a big, competitive business. The number one way to get a doctor to prescribe a certain drug is if they've received a sample. That's why my company continues to send out pharmaceutical representatives."

"When you get to a doctor's office, who do you give the samples to?"

Huffing, she squeezed her hands tighter together. "That depends on the office. Most of the time, the doctors can only see me for a few minutes, and they tell me to give the samples to whoever is available in the office. I've given them to receptionists, nurses, or even the doctors themselves."

"And this clinic. What is your procedure?"

"The same. When I drop by, this clinic is usually first on my rotation for the day. Sometimes, I bring coffee or doughnuts or bagels. I try to remember the long-time employees' birthdays. When I can see Dr. Tiller, I make sure to tell him what new drugs are available. As far as the samples, this is a clinic where I can leave them with whoever's available."

"The first time I visited the clinic, I saw you outside, Ms. Washington. Polly was just arriving, and you handed some to her straight from the back of your car and she placed them in her purse."

Gasping, Beth shook her head. "No! I mean, yes, I did, but it's not what you think. Polly was usually the person who opened early in the mornings. She was usually the person I handed the samples to. She was running late that day and stopped me on the street to say hello."

"Did she ask for samples?"

Beth opened her mouth, then hesitated, her brow furrowed again. "Yes, yes she did. I told her that I had left some inside, and she asked if there were more antibiotics that she could have. The samples are ours to give out, so I handed her some. She was going straight inside, so I didn't think anything about it."

"And just to clarify, you had no idea she was handing out medication that is supposed to be prescribed by a doctor."

Shaking her head furiously, she said, "Absolutely not. I had no idea she was doing anything with those drugs other than giving them to Dr. Tiller to distribute."

Thanking her, he sent her on her way. She had only taken a few steps out the door when he heard Dr. Tiller greeting her in hushed tones.

"Beth, I didn't know you were here."

"Doug, I went rushing into your office and was shocked when it wasn't you sitting behind the desk! He wanted to interview me."

"What did you tell him?"

"The truth. I told him the truth. I had no idea what Polly was doing."

"Damn Polly! The last thing this clinic needs is any reason for somebody to shut us down."

"I've got to go. I'm already running late."

He heard the sound of heels clicking down the hall and was not surprised when Dr. Tiller stepped inside the office. "Just in time, Dr. Tiller. Have a seat and I'll make this as quick as possible." Not giving the doctor a choice, he noted the man's grimace as he sat down.

"Dr. Tiller, let's talk about the opioid epidemic. It's now common knowledge that many doctors have over-prescribed painkillers to the extent that patients are addicted. There's kickbacks from pharmaceutical companies and, of course, the continuation of patients coming in, paying for office visits when they need more drugs."

Waving his hand as though swatting a fly, Dr. Tiller said, "Yes, yes. That's not the majority of doctors, but it does happen. I assure you it's not happening here."

"I'm not surprised," Carter said. "After all, unlike a private clinic, your salary is set. You aren't reliant on clients paying you."

"Exactly! It would make no sense for me to want the financially-needy patients to be hooked on narcotics. They can't afford the drugs. We wouldn't keep prescribing them. And it's not like I get paid for their office visits."

"Then do you have any idea where the drugs that Carl Burnley, Jonathan Rothberg, and Rocky Stallone were carrying came from?"

Rearing back, Dr. Tiller shook his head. "If you're implying that Polly was giving out more than antibiotics, well... I... Well..." He sighed heavily and said, "I was going to say that you're wrong. But honestly, I have no idea where they're getting the drugs."

"I assume you've put new measures in place for the handling of the drug samples that Ms. Washington delivers."

"Yes. I had a staff meeting yesterday and from now on, the samples are coming directly to me."

Brows lifted, Carter asked, "You? This clinic actually has a pharmacy, so I would have thought they would go there."

Shaking his head, Dr. Tiller said, "The pharmacy is regulated by our orders and laws. To add sample drugs would be confusing. I'm the one who sees the patients. I'm the one who knows what drugs they might need. If I determine that a sample would be worthwhile, then I'll give it to them."

Unable to argue with the doctor's logic, Carter simply thanked him for his time. His next interview with Robert yielded no surprises. Like the others in the clinic, he claimed to not know of Polly's quest to medicate the homeless who would not come into the clinic. But he complained that Dr. Tiller wanted the samples to come directly to him. Robert felt that they should go through the pharmacy, and Dr. Tiller insisted that he be the keeper of the samples.

By lunchtime, Carter was back at headquarters with Evan who had been talking with some of the homeless that wandered the park behind the shelter.

Shaking his head, Evan said, "I only found one guy that would talk to me. He said that he recognized Carl when I showed him the picture. When I asked him if he knew anything about Carl dealing drugs, he just laughed." Evan held Carter's gaze and grimaced. "Then he replied, 'Who the fuck doesn't? It's a way to make some fuckin' money.'"

Carter asked, "When you got to the table to pick up a bag lunch, did they hand one to you, or did you just grab one?"

"It seemed like they wanted to keep the line going quickly, so before you got to the table, they had someone ask if you had a peanut allergy. I noticed they had some bags with red PB on the outside, so I assume those had peanut butter. Other than that, all the bags looked the same. They had someone standing by the side of the table who had a bag and handed it to the next person in line. That way, no one was wasting time picking and choosing over the bags. The bag was handed to us and we walked a few steps more and were handed a water bottle. As we walked away, another person reminded us to throw our trash into the trash can."

"I've got no fuckin' proof other than a gut feeling that someone in that shelter line has added a bag of drugs to give out. Who, how, why, and when... Jesus, I've got no fuckin' clue."

Laughing, Evan said, "That's not much to go on, man. But I'll take gut instinct as something to go on any day."

"I also think there's a relationship going on between Dr. Tiller and Beth Washington. Again, no proof, but considering he's married with three kids, I would think he'd want to keep that well-hidden."

"You said he's now the one that will be getting all the sample drugs. But what would be the purpose in getting a homeless person hooked on opioids? Supposedly, they don't keep narcotics there. And the homeless have no money to come back and pay for anything."

"Selling? Besides the drugs that they're taking, are they selling them?" he wondered aloud. "When you were in the lunch line, was it the same volunteers each day?"

Evan shook his head. "I recognized a couple of repeat faces, but the others seemed new. One of them had a shelter badge on. Enrico was his name. He seemed to recognize and talk to quite a few of the people in line."

"I've met him. He works at the reception desk of the shelter." Lifting an eyebrow, he said, "Damn, I need to get back into the shelter and ask more questions."

Laughing, Evan said, "Oh, hell, Carter. You were in the Army, then a street cop, and now a detective. You can't possibly be afraid of Tara's wrath."

He dropped his chin and shook his head. "Man, you have no idea."

## 20

Tara leaned on her desk and rubbed her forehead, willing the headache to go away. It was now Friday afternoon, four days after Polly's arrest. Days of listening to her coworkers chirping and gossiping about what happened. Days of working with the volunteers giving out the bag lunches, explaining that everything was continuing as normal. Days of checking on the people receiving the lunches, making sure that they felt welcome while emphasizing that if they were ill, they needed to go into the clinic to get medication.

All of this on top of her regular duties at the shelter. Her head ached. Her body ached. But most of all, she tried to ignore the ache in her heart.

She had visited the clinic on Tuesday only to find the staff struggling with Polly's arrest. She was surprised to find that as upset as the other clinic employees were, most protesting that Polly just wanted to help, they were all equally upset that she had been dispensing medication illegally. Kate told her that Dr.

Tiller was furious and held a long staff meeting emphasizing the need to follow proper procedures to the letter.

If there was one good thing about the situation, it was that he wanted to hire Erin to assist in the clinic while she finished her nursing degree. She would not perform nursing duties, of course, but now that they were even more shorthanded, with her medic background they could use her for many of the procedures and assistance.

She leaned back in her chair and sighed, determining that nothing was going to take away her headache. Her phone vibrated for the millionth time that week. Never wanting to be out of touch from Colleen's school or her family, she had refused to silence her phone. Her gaze shot to the screen, and she was not surprised to see another text from Carter.

Her anger at him had abated, but she had not answered. For once, unwilling to analyze her feelings, she had simply remained distant. Colleen has asked when they would see him again, and she'd told her the truth—he was very busy, and she had no idea if he would be able to come over again.

She lifted her hand and pressed it against her left breast, wondering if she was too young to have a heart attack. She watched Michael and Bethany walk past her door on their way out of the building. Wanting to get home to Colleen much more than she wanted to stay at work and pretend to accomplish something when in reality she wasn't, she closed her laptop. Shoving her phone into her purse, she grabbed her coat and locked her office door as she left.

On the way to pick up Colleen, she tried to think of activities for the weekend that would make them both happy. Expecting her typically-bouncy daughter, she was concerned when Colleen remained quiet for most of the drive home.

Once inside, she asked, "How would you like to make some brownies with me?"

At first, Colleen shrugged, but after a moment she nodded. "Okay, I guess so."

"That doesn't sound very enthusiastic. Would you rather make cookies?"

"No, brownies are okay."

Concerned, she watched as Colleen climbed up onto the kitchen stool and leaned over the counter. They went through the movements of mixing the gooey, chocolate goodness, but Colleen continued to give simple answers to any of Tara's questions or suggestions. She reached across the counter and felt her daughter's head, wondering if she was ill. "You don't seem like yourself, sweetheart. Do you not feel well?"

Colleen scrunched her nose and shook her head. "What do you do when you don't like what somebody does?"

Her daughter's question caught her off guard, but she quickly answered, "Well, it depends on what they've done. We don't always like what other people do, but everyone has a right to make their own decisions." Sliding the pan of brownies into the oven, she set the timer before turning back to the counter. Colleen's bottom lip jutted out slightly, and it appeared her daughter was not satisfied with her answer. Probing further, she asked, "Can you tell me what they did that you didn't like?"

"They say mean things."

Whatever Colleen was talking about, it was much deeper than what she originally thought. She moved to the refrigerator and poured a glass of milk, then cut a banana into slices and grabbed the jar of peanut butter. "While we wait for the brownies to cook and then cool, why don't we have a healthy snack and we can talk."

Colleen's face brightened and she climbed down from the stool, moving to the kitchen table. Tara set the food in front of her daughter and watched as she munched on banana and peanut butter, her legs swinging back and forth. After drinking half her milk, Colleen looked up at her mom. "I was at the back of the line when we had our bathroom break. A girl came in and she was crying. I asked her what was wrong, and she said Vicki Burton called her fat. I told her she wasn't, but I didn't have time to stay in the bathroom because I didn't want to get in trouble with my teacher."

"That was sweet of you to say. I'm sure you made her feel better."

Colleen shook her head and said, "That's not the first time I've heard that about Vicki Burton. She was in my kindergarten class last year and she used to make lots of people cry." Her nose scrunched again, and she sighed. "I don't want to be a tattletale, but should I tell my teacher?"

"Oh, honey, I know that's a hard thing to understand, but if someone's doing something wrong, and we know about it, we need to do something. That's not being a tattletale. That's protecting others."

"I thought maybe that was the right thing. Grandpa's always saying we need to do the right thing, even if it's hard."

She smiled at the thought of Colleen piled up in Colm's lap as he would read fairy tales to her, then explain the morals of the stories. He had done the same thing for her when she was little. It hadn't always been easy being the daughter of an FBI investigator, but her parents instilled a strong sense of responsibility for others in each of their children. "Are you afraid of Vicki? Are you afraid that if you tell a teacher what she's saying about other children that she'll say things about you?"

Colleen's leg swung back and forth a little faster as she appeared to ponder her mom's question. "Not really. I guess if she was in my class this year, I might be. But I don't really see her. I just see the kids that she makes cry."

She held out her arms, and Colleen slid off her chair, crawling onto Tara's lap. The two snuggled together and Tara inhaled deeply, loving the scent of her little girl. "I'm very proud of you for wanting to help the kids who are being bullied by Vicki. It's not always easy to do the right thing, but you're very brave."

"I'm going to tell my teacher," Colleen declared. "And if that doesn't work, then I'm going to tell my uncles. If she's doing something wrong, then they can make her stop. That's what the police do, isn't it, Mom? They make people do the right thing."

Her breath caught in her throat as she listened to the words of her daughter. Swallowing deeply, she tried to steady the pounding of her heart. "I'm not sure that the police will keep Vicki from saying mean things. But you're right about the police. When someone breaks the law, they need to be involved."

Colleen hopped down after giving Tara a hug and ran into the den to turn on the TV. Tara remained at the kitchen table, her mind swirling with thoughts.

*Polly was engaged in illegal activities regardless of her desire to help. I knew Carter was working on an investigation that involved the clinic before I ever mentioned Polly offering antibiotics to me. He was doing the right thing, not me.*

She walked over to where her purse was lying on the counter and pulled out her phone. She started to call but chickened out. Blowing out her breath, she began to type a message. Before changing her mind, she quickly hit send.

**Making brownies with Colleen. Would you like one as a peace offering? T**

Immediately terrified, she wished she had a way to pull the text back. Before she could determine if there was a way to delete it, her phone vibrated.

**I'll be there in twenty minutes. C**

The air left her lungs in an audible whoosh. Glancing at her reflection in the window, she shot her gaze over to the oven, seeing that she had five minutes before the brownies were ready. "Sweetie, Carter is going to come have a brownie with us. I'm gonna run upstairs and brush my hair."

As she dashed down the hall, Colleen's joyful shout hit her ears. Running into her bathroom, she smiled. The first smile in five days.

---

Standing outside of Tara's door, Carter was nervous. When Evan had joked about being afraid of Tara's wrath, his partner had no idea how true those words were. He hesitated before ringing the doorbell, but just as he lifted his hand, he could hear Colleen shout from inside the house.

"Mom! I see Carter!"

"Colleen, come back. Let me open the door."

The door opened, and before Tara could greet him, Colleen rushed onto the stoop and looked up at him, a huge smile on her face. "Hi! I wasn't sure you were ever coming back to see us!"

"Colleen, honey, please use your soft voice," Tara begged.

His eyes devoured her, his gaze roving over her face. Offering her a smile, he turned his attention back to Colleen. He knelt in front of her, surprised when she threw her arms around his neck. He wrapped his arms around her and stood, his eyes now searching for Tara to see her reaction and take direction from her.

If the wide eyes and shocked expression were anything to go by, she was just as surprised as him. She stepped back and said, "Please, come in."

He carried Colleen over the threshold. Tara reached for her daughter and said, "Colleen, you can let go of him now."

"But, Mom, he's a policeman. I can tell him about the mean girl at school."

"Colleen, no. Let Carter—"

"It's okay, Tara," he said. "If she had a bad day, I'd like to hear about it." He observed warring emotions move over her face, noting her pale complexion and circles under her eyes. "And if her mom has had a bad day, I'd like to hear about it, also."

She stared at him for a moment, then blinked the moisture from her eyes. "Her mom has had a bad week."

"So, have I," he confessed, fighting the urge to reach out and pull her into his arms. "Maybe Colleen can tell me about her day over brownies. And then you can tell me about your week over a glass of wine."

Tara barked out a laugh, and it was the best sound he had heard since last weekend. Smiling, he said, "Now that's the sound I've missed."

He set Colleen's feet on the floor and watched as she darted into the kitchen, calling for him to follow since the brownies were now cool. He glanced at Tara and she smiled in return. "Come on back."

Once in the kitchen, he sat at the table with Colleen and listened to her tale of the first-grade bully. The strangest sensations moved through him, each unexpected but not unwelcome. He felt pride at her standing up for another person. Anger that someone who was only six years old was already a mean person. Frustrated knowing that Colleen had to fear what might happen if she told the teacher.

By the time Colleen had explained the situation, she was licking her fingers after having eaten a large brownie and drinking another glass of milk. She finished her story with her mom's words of wisdom.

Nodding, he said, "I think your mom is very smart. I think telling your teacher is the right thing to do. Standing up to bullies isn't easy, but we can't ignore when someone's doing something wrong."

Colleen brightened as she hopped down from her chair. "That's what mom said!" With everything right in her world for the moment, she ran off to play.

Tara had walked back to the kitchen sink, rinsing off the dishes. He walked toward her, leaning his hip against the counter. Close, but not crowding. Her hair was down, flowing about her shoulders, creating a curtain that hid her face. As much as he loved her hair, he wanted to see her. He lifted his hand, the silky strands feeling so familiar, and pushed it over her shoulder. She looked toward him, blinking back tears, her chest heaving.

All the things he had wanted to say flew from his mind as he lifted his other arm in invitation. She rushed toward him, leaning her weight into him as he wrapped her as tightly as he'd held Colleen earlier.

"I'm sorry," she whispered, her face squished against his chest. "I was wrong. I was angry, shocked, and just snapped. I'm so sorry."

The tight band that had encircled his heart for the past week released, and he felt as though he could breathe again. With one hand cupping the back of her head, holding her close against his heartbeat, the other arm encircled her back. He buried his nose in her hair, breathing in her scent. So familiar. So needed.

"I'm sorry, too, babe. Tara, I never meant to deceive you. I know you told me about Polly, but we were already looking at things going on at the clinic. I'm not always going to be able to tell you about my investigations, but I—"

He loosened his grip as she put pressure on his hand, lifting her face to stare at him. "Carter, I know. I of all people should understand. With my father's career and now my brothers' careers—I understand." She sucked in a ragged breath and let it out slowly. "I've never seen anyone that I've known be arrested. I was just so shocked. And when she yelled out about the antibiotics, all I could think of was that I'd told you she offered them to me for Colleen. It never dawned on me that she was doing that with someone else."

Cupping her face, rubbing his thumb over her smooth skin, he loved the feel of her touch. "I missed you so much, Tara. I missed you and Colleen." He bent and kissed her lightly, almost afraid that this was a dream and he would wake alone. But the feel of her lips moving against his convinced him it was real. Lifting his head, he stared into her blue eyes and asked, "Why now? Why the invitation for brownies?"

"Honestly? It was Colleen. I mean, she's been asking about you this week, but that wasn't it. I kept thinking about Rocky and wondering how I missed the signs of his addiction. But even that wasn't enough for me to call you. It was today. She was so upset about the bully at school, and when she asked me if she should do something, I told her that we always have to stand up for what's right. Even if that means confronting someone who's doing something wrong." Shaking her head slightly, she added, "As soon as those words came out of my mouth, I knew that I was wrong to blame you for something that Polly was doing." Nibbling on her bottom lip, she shrugged, then grinned. "Plus, I really thought you'd like my brownies."

Growling, he pulled her tighter as he kissed her deeply. His tongue thrust inside her mouth, the chocolate and essence of Tara combining in an unforgettable flavor. Remembering Colleen was in the house, he slowly eased the kiss, finally separating. "Yeah, babe. I like your brownies."

## 21

Tara stepped out of the shower, the water droplets still sliding over her body, the towel held in her hand. She stared at her reflection in the mirror, blowing out a deep breath. Her breasts were full. *But not very perky.* She definitely had tits and ass, and as she twisted back and forth, she could see the faint stretch marks on her abdomen.

Giving her head a shake, she stopped criticizing her body and dried off. *I counsel women on positive image and sure as hell need to heed my own words!*

As she dried her long hair and carefully applied her makeup, she tried to still her nerves. It was a date night. A real date night.

Carter had stayed for a while last evening, managing to sneak a few more brownies while they watched a Disney movie with Colleen. She was disappointed when he left, but he reminded her he wanted to do things right. When she told him that Colleen had a planned sleepover with her grandparents the next evening, she watched his eyes darken and his smile widen.

Now, with the house empty, she slipped into a matching panty and bra set, hoping that Carter would have a chance to see them and like them. *And I hope he has a chance to see me out of them.* On that thought, she glanced at the time and hurried to her closet. When he'd suggested they go to dinner, she'd counter-suggested they eat in. As soon as the words left her mouth, she had no doubt he was all for that idea, insisting he'd bring the food.

She chose a simple, long-sleeved, Jersey wrap dress. The emerald green color set off her blue eyes and dark hair. And the dress would make her body easy access for any plans he might have. *Oh Lordy, please let him have plans!*

With a last look in the mirror, she looked down at her feet. She chewed on the corner of her bottom lip, trying to decide what shoes to wear. Heels? *That seems like overkill in the house.* Low heeled pumps? *Jesus, I'm not going to work.*

The sound of the doorbell rang through the house, and making a last-minute decision for comfort, she grabbed her black satin slippers and tugged them on. Racing downstairs, she stopped at the door and sucked in a deep breath before throwing it open.

Her gaze landed on Carter and her breath left her in a rush. She barely registered that his hands were full of plastic bags and a cold wind was whipping at his jacket. All she could focus on was the tall, muscular body, square jaw, piercing blue eyes, and thick blonde hair that she wanted to get her fingers into.

"Babe? Can I come in?"

Blinking out of her Carter-induced stupor, she jumped back. "Yes, yes. Sorry, I know it's cold out there."

As soon as he stepped into her foyer, the scent of Chinese food wafted past. Glancing down at the bags, she saw the logo for The Golden Dragon. It was her favorite Chinese restaurant but was not close. Her gaze jumped back to his face as she exclaimed, "You went all the way to The Golden Dragon?"

Laughing, he bent to kiss her lips as he passed her on the way to the kitchen. "I asked Colleen last night what your favorite Chinese restaurant was."

She followed him into the kitchen and watched as he set the bags on her counter. Shrugging off his jacket, he turned around and stared at her, his blue eyes darkening.

"You opened the door and all I could see was a fuckin' vision of beauty. Jesus, Tara, you're gorgeous."

He opened his arms, but she hesitated, her gaze shooting to the bags of food on her counter before moving back to his face. "I know you're hungry and we need to eat. But I'm really nervous. I put on my best lingerie under this dress, hoping that you'd have a chance to see it. But if we eat first, I'm afraid I'll be too full from gorging on Golden Dragon goodness." As soon as she stopped blurting, she felt her neck and face burn with embarrassment. Before she had a chance to back-track, he stalked toward her.

"Good thing about Chinese takeout is that it's perfect when reheated," he said just before his lips met hers.

Their arms snaked around each other, pulling tightly so their bodies pressed from hip to chest. Noses bumped as their heads moved back and forth, searching for the best angle to drink each other in. Their tongues danced, tangled, thrust, and parried. She rose onto her toes, then was lifted in his arms.

He carried her easily through the hall to the stairs, where he halted at the bottom. She missed his lips when the kiss stopped, her gaze focused on his beautiful mouth. Wondering why he stopped, her eyes sought his.

"I want to do this right, Tara. You deserve everything that's good, and I don't want to take advantage of you."

"Honey, it may have been a long time since I've dated, but that was by choice. I wasn't willing to put Colleen through a revolving door of men. So, until I found one that was right, I wasn't going to go there. You're not taking advantage of me. This is me giving myself to you." She placed her hands on either side of his face, holding him close. "You, Carter, are my choice. You."

As soon as the words left her mouth, his eyes darkened more, and he started up the stairs. Moving swiftly into her bedroom, he kissed her again as he slowly lowered her feet to the floor. She kept her arms around his neck so that their lips would not separate, not willing to let him go.

His hands glided slowly down her back, cupping her ass before squeezing the globes gently. Her body responded, remembering the orgasm from the previous weekend. She pressed her sex against his jean-clad thigh, rubbing to ease the ache. A low growl sounded throughout the room, but she had no idea if it came from him or her.

His lips left hers but continued to kiss along her jaw and neck, sucking slightly at the pulse point. Swept away by the feel of his lips on her tender skin, she barely noticed his hand pulling her dress upward, his fingers now on her naked thigh.

His breath hitched. She was aware of the loss of his fingers on her skin, and she wanted to weep. Her hands pushed back on his shoulders to see why he'd stopped touching her, noticing his gaze as well as his hands were at the dress tie at her waist. Smiling in relief, she slid her hands down his torso, then helped to untie the belt that held her dress together. Once undone, she forced her gaze to remain on his face as he pushed the dress off her shoulders, letting it fall to the floor.

She shivered, uncertain if it was the cool air or his heated gaze now hitting her body. His hands were squeezing her hips as his eyes moved from her panties to her bra, then to her face.

"Perfect, babe. You are, without a doubt, the most beautiful woman."

His gaze moved back to her bra, searching and finding the closure when his hands slid over her breasts, unsnapping it from the front. As soon as the satin material was loose and falling from her body, his hands cupped her heavy breasts, his thumbs circling her nipples. She dropped her head back, sucking in a ragged breath as the electric sensation shot between her breasts and her core.

He bent, sucking a nipple deeply into his mouth while scooping her up into his arms. He placed a knee onto the bed and laid her back, his tongue still swirling around the swollen flesh. Moving between her breasts, he then kissed his way down over her stomach. A flash of awareness hit her, hoping he would not notice the roundness she had never managed to tighten after giving birth.

"Fuck, babe, you have the perfect body," he mumbled against her skin as he continued to kiss his way to her panties.

Her body warmed, both from his words and his lips. She lifted her hips as he slid her panties off, and she lay completely exposed to his perusal. He stood by the side of the bed, quickly divesting himself of his shirt and jeans. She leaned up on her elbows and stared at his perfection. His body was muscular without being overly bulky. His pecs and abs were clearly defined, leading down to a muscular V that disappeared into boxers tented with his impressive erection. His biceps and thighs were thick, and she could hardly wait to feel his body pressed on top of hers. Her gaze moved back to his face, and she grinned.

A touch of insecurity moved through his face, and he asked, "Do you like what you see?"

"Hmm, you'll do, I suppose." He threw his head back and laughed, and she loved the sound. "Talk about a perfect body, Carter. You look like you're sculpted out of marble."

He placed his thumbs into the waistband of his boxers, pulling them over his erection and down his legs, kicking them to the side. "Not cold marble, babe. All hot. All for you." Bending, he reached into his jeans and jerked out several packets of condoms, tossing them next to her on the bed.

Shooting a glance at the condom packets before looking up at him again, she lifted an eyebrow and laughed. "Prepared?"

He shook his head slowly, holding her gaze, and replied, "I was a Boy Scout. I was taught to be prepared."

She snorted and his eyes twinkled. "That did sound cheesy, didn't it?"

"Maybe, but the end result is the same." Lying back on the bed, she held up her arms, welcoming his body on hers as he answered her silent invitation. His weight was heavy, pressing her into the mattress even though he propped his upper body with his forearms planted on either side of her. It had been so long since she had felt the weight of a man covering her from breast to toes. She didn't want to give Calvin any space in her head, this bed, or with Carter, but for a flash, she could not help but compare.

Calvin had not started out as a selfish lover. He gave his body and his love to her, and she'd relished every joining. But over time, he acted resentful of any distraction that took her away from him, even though he was already distancing himself emotionally. She tried lingerie, introduced toys into the bedroom, different positions, but nothing seemed to help. Sex became perfunctory, more about his physical release than any pleasure for her. By the end, sex was rare, and one night, when he came home with someone else's perfume wafting from him, she no longer trusted that he was faithful to her.

"Hey, where'd you go?"

Guilt speared her that she had allowed her mind to wander. "I'm sorry. I was just... Well, it's been a long time..."

"Then we'll take it slow. I want to relish everything about your body in my time with you, so I'm in no rush."

His lips met hers and the kiss resumed, tasting and tempting as she gave herself over to the sensations coursing through her body. He kissed a wet trail down her chest to each breast, circling one tight nipple with his tongue while his hand molded the other breast. He continued kissing his way down until his hands pushed her thighs apart and he licked her slit. Her body jumped and she dug her fingers into his shoulders before sliding her hands into his thick hair.

Unable to keep her hips from undulating upward, she was so close to the edge. As his finger inserted into her warm sex, he sucked her clit, nipping it slightly. As her core tightened, she desperately wanted relief and cried out when it hit. Her body had a mind of its own, giving her no control over the rush of shudders and emotions. Lack of control usually terrified Tara, but in that moment, she gave herself willingly to Carter's gentle care.

Carter may have had his mouth between Tara's legs, but his eyes were pinned on her face. The taste of her was addictive, and he could not wait to get his next fix. Her body was so responsive, every touch he gave made him want to never break their connection. He closed his eyes for an instant and fought to dislodge the flash hitting him of Allison writhing on the bed in over-exaggerated movements and moaning.

He felt a touch on his shoulder and snapped his eyes open, smiling at the true beauty in front of him. With her essence still on his tongue, he kissed his way over her body, latching onto her lips so that she could share the taste.

Rising onto his knees, he reached for a foil packet, ripped it open, and rolled it onto his aching cock. Positioning his hips between her legs, he entered her slowly, wanting to savor every moment.

A slow smile spread across her face as her fingers gripped his biceps. "I'm not going to break, you know."

"And I'm not going to rush a moment of this." True to his words, he continued to enter slowly, pulling back and then pressing forward a little more, dragging his cock along her tight inner core. When at last he was fully seated, he groaned. "I said you were perfect earlier when I was just looking at you. But this, here, now, is truly perfect."

He began pumping, his forceful thrusts being met with her as she lifted her hips in rhythm. No longer slow and deliberate, the sounds of flesh on flesh filled the bedroom. Her full breasts bounced with each movement, their dark rosy nipples taunting him. Bending slightly, he captured one with his lips, sucking it deeply.

A tightness in his balls gave evidence to his impending orgasm, but he wanted her to come again. Leaning his weight on one arm, he slid his other hand down between them, pressing on her swollen clit. Much to his pleasure and relief, her fingers dug into his shoulders as she cried out. He felt her inner muscles clench, and losing all control, continued to thrust until the last drop had left his body.

He tried to drag in a breath, but it was hard to breathe over the pounding of his heart. His arms quivered and gave out, but he managed to shift just enough so that he didn't fall on top of her with his full weight. Uncertain he could move, he was thrilled when she rolled toward him, half draped on top of his body. Her breasts rested on his chest. Her legs tangled with his. Her arm draped across his waist. The top of her head tucked under his chin. But most importantly, their heartbeats pounded in unison.

He had no idea how long they remained, their breaths slowing and their hearts beating a normal rhythm. As though awareness overtook both of them at the same time, they opened their eyes and stared.

She smiled and chewed on her bottom lip. "I don't know what to say, honey. Part of me feels like I should say thank you for rocking my world. The other part of me wants to say that I hope this wasn't a one and done."

Barking out a laugh, he shook his head slowly. "Hell, no, Tara. That was not a one and done." Sobering, he cupped her face with his hand. "You gave me you, and that's so precious to me, babe. I just pray that I'll always be worthy of that gift."

They kissed lightly, this meeting of lips a celebration of shared emotions. He separated regretfully and said, "I hate to bring this up, but your brothers know about us."

She jolted, but he kept his arms banded tightly around her. "Tell me they didn't do the stupid man-talk to you!"

He opened his mouth to respond, then snapped it shut. "Uh... Man talk?"

"Threaten you. Warn you. Do the whole *'You better treat our sister right!'* bullshit!"

He now hated that he'd mentioned her brothers, considering her response. She wiggled to sit up, but he shushed her gently. "Come on, babe. It was nothing. You were upset and they were concerned. I get it."

She quieted, but he wasn't sure that was better. Leaning back so he could see her face, he gently smoothed his hand over her hair. "Honestly, Tara, that's all it was." She nodded slowly and he kissed her forehead, her body relaxing in his arms. "Anyway, now it's out in the open and it's all good between me and your brother and the King boys—"

"Kings?" she shouted, her body tight once more. "Don't tell me the Kings were there also?"

Chuckling, he kissed her forehead again and mumbled, "I've got to take care of this condom." Climbing off the bed, he continued to grin. *Let the McBride and King men feel her wrath for a change.* In truth, he'd pay to see that.

Coming back from the bathroom, he passed her as

she slid from the bed. Swatting her ass playfully, he reminded, "Don't forget, we've got Golden Dragon downstairs. If we're going to keep this up all night, we need a little sustenance."

Her beautiful blue eyes widened, and all irritation fled. "All night? You can go all night?"

Later, after delicious Chinese food, reheated and eaten with glasses of wine while standing at the kitchen counter, he took her back upstairs and had no problem backing up his claim—much to both of their pleasures.

## 2 2

"Are you nervous?"

Carter glanced to the passenger side of his SUV, annoyed to see Tara's wide grin. The answer to her question would have been 'no' if he was just meeting up with the McBride brothers for a drink. But considering they were on their way to her parents' house for a Sunday lunch and he'd been informed everyone would be there, the answer was a resounding 'yes'.

As he drove through the neighborhood, they passed large, old homes, built back in the time before McMansions when each house on the street was unique. With multiple cars parked in the driveway and on the street, it wasn't hard to see which house was the McBride's. As soon as he parked, he walked around and opened her door, offering a hand to assist her down.

She pulled her coat a little tighter to ward off the chill, and he wrapped his arm around her, offering his warmth. She twisted her head to look up and smiled.

"Do you think my family can tell that we had sex all night?"

Rolling his eyes, he squeezed her shoulder. "Jesus, Tara. I hope the fuck they don't know!"

Her laughter met his ears, and he loved the sound. Just as they reached the front door, it was thrown open and Colleen launched herself at him.

"You're here!" she yelled, giving him a hug before twisting and hugging her mom.

The three of them walked into the large entry foyer, but the space quickly filled. Colleen, still in his arms, began shouting introductions.

"This is my Uncle Sean and his girlfriend, Harper! This is my Aunt Erin and Aunt Caitlyn. This is my Uncle Kyle—"

"Colleen," Tara admonished. "I know you're excited, but use your inside voice. And give us a chance to take off our coats."

"Come on, squirt," Rory said, pulling Colleen out of Carter's arms.

Carter turned and helped Tara with her coat, handing it to Erin's outstretched hands. Shrugging off his own jacket, he thanked her as Erin took it also. Several of the others had moved down the hall toward the den and kitchen, but Harper stepped forward, hugging Tara. Sean's pretty girlfriend smiled up at him and said, "It's a little overwhelming, I know. This was me not too long ago."

He nodded his agreement and smiled as Sean threw his arm around Harper and they followed the others down the hall. Feeling a squeeze around his waist, he glanced down at Tara. He could see worry in her eyes and assured, "Don't worry, babe. I'm good."

They walked toward the back of the house, and when they entered the large open kitchen and den, they were met by an attractive woman, her silver hair neatly-trimmed and her blue eyes sparkling. He had no problem recognizing Tara's mother.

"Carter, welcome to our house. I'm Sharon."

He took her hand in his own and said, "I'm pleased to be here, Sharon. Thank you for having me."

It did not pass his notice that Sharon's gaze took him in before she bestowed her loving smile upon Tara. She leaned forward and kissed her daughter's cheek, saying softly, "Love you, sweetheart."

Sharon had barely stepped back before a booming voice came through the back door. He looked over and saw a tall, older man being dragged forward by Colleen.

"Missy, how can someone so little be so strong? I'm coming, I'm coming! I know we've got company."

Colleen did not stop pulling her grandfather's hand until they got right in front of Carter and Tara. She opened her mouth, then caught her mother's gaze and seemed to remember that she was supposed to use her indoor voice. "This is my grandpa," she said, struggling to whisper.

Carter thrust out his hand and said, "Thank you for having me, sir. I'm Carter Fiske."

"Good to meet you, son. I'm Colm McBride."

Colm's handshake was firm, and Carter watched as Tara's father greeted her much in the same way as her mother. Colm leaned forward and kissed her cheek, softly saying, "Good to see you, beautiful."

The family soon gathered around the largest table Carter had ever seen. His family certainly enjoyed getting together, and conversation had always been lively when he was growing up. But seeing the McBrides in action was nothing short of organized chaos. Food was passed around, conversation abounded, jokes were told, and stories were shared. By the end of the meal, he felt truly welcomed into their camaraderie.

After dessert, he learned that Colm led the clean-up crew since the women had cooked. Sharon disappeared into the den with Tara, Harper, Erin, Caitlyn, and Colleen. He joined the McBride men in clearing the table, rinsing dishes, and putting away the food.

Sean asked, "Anything new this week on your cases?"

"I interviewed everybody at the clinic but don't have anything definitive. My gut still tells me that whatever's happening, it involves someone there."

Colm leaned his hip against the counter and crossed his arms over his chest. "Is that the clinic that Erin is going to work at?"

"From what Tara has said, yes. But I don't think she's supposed to start for another month." Rory and Kyle swung their heads around, brows lowered.

"I need to talk to her. I don't think she should work there," Colm stated.

"Yeah, try telling her that," Rory said. "She's going to do what she wants to do."

Sean jumped in. "I'll see if Tara will talk to her. Get her to hold off."

Without hesitating to wade into the family discussion, he said, "Don't put Tara in the middle. If you've got something to say to Erin, say it yourself." The four McBride men were silent for a moment, and Carter wondered if he'd overstepped his bounds. Deciding it didn't matter, he knew Tara was his first priority.

With a chin lift, Colm agreed. "Carter's right. Tara has enough on her plate right now with the shelter and her dealings with the clinic. She can advise Erin in whatever way she feels is appropriate." Turning back to the sink, he finished rinsing out one of the pots.

Kyle moved next to Carter and asked, "Anything new on Kilton Pharma?"

"My money's on Beth Washington. I don't trust her. She's young and works her looks, which is no crime, but I think she's got something going on. For the life of me, though, I can't figure out what it is."

The sound of a phone ringing caught his attention, and he glanced toward the counter, seeing Tara's purse. He walked to the den with her phone in his hand. "Sorry, babe, it stopped ringing before I had a chance to get it to you."

She walked toward him, a smile on her face. Lifting on her toes, she offered him a quick kiss but was interrupted when her phone rang again. "Hello?" Her body stiffened, and her gaze jerked over toward Colleen.

Instantly on alert, he glanced around the room, seeing the other women's eyes on her. She swiftly walked out of the den, saying, "Calvin? Why are you calling?"

She was now within range of the kitchen, and Carter felt the temperature of the room drop as the McBride men moved closer, the hard set of their jaws matching the glacial glances they were giving each other.

He stepped next to her and placed his hand on her back for support. Her head was tipped down, her hair falling to create a curtain. She was quiet for a moment, then softly said, "I see. I'm very sorry. I'll tell her, but I won't bring her." Another pause was followed by, "Thank you for letting me know."

She lifted her head and it did not escape his notice that she looked to him first, bypassing her family. She glanced into the den, and he was sure she was checking on Colleen, who was working a puzzle with Harper. Erin, Caitlyn, and her mom had moved closer, but still ignoring her family, she looked up to Carter.

"Calvin wanted to let me know that his father had a heart attack and passed away two days ago. I don't think he was going to even tell me, but his mother wanted to know if Colleen was going to come to her grandfather's funeral."

If he had not known the dynamics before, there was no doubt how the McBride's felt about that news. Anger snapped about the room, but all he cared about was Tara. He slid his arm around her waist and pulled her in tightly

"God forgive me, but what a selfish cow," Sharon whispered. "They raised a selfish son and barely remembered their granddaughter at Christmas and on her birthday. And now she wants a six-year-old to go to the funeral of a man who hardly had time for her?"

"Sharon, sweetheart…" Colm said, his voice low, but Carter could hear the warning.

It was obvious Tara's family did not want to say anything that Colleen might overhear, but their anger had not abated. Letting the rest of the gathering fade away, he focused all his attention on Tara. "What do you need from me, babe?"

When she lifted her gaze to him, she shook her head slightly and replied, "I have no idea. After years of dating and being married, I barely knew his parents. Calvin wasn't close to them, and after the divorce, they only sent a Christmas and birthday card to Colleen but never asked to see her. I wouldn't have kept her from her grandparents, but neither was I going to force her on them."

"You're right about Colleen not going to the funeral. If she doesn't know these people, then there's no reason to overwhelm her with another grandmother at the funeral of a grandfather she's never met. If you feel like you need to go to pay your respects, I'll go with you."

She placed her hand on his chest and said, "Thank you. I'm a little shocked right now—and irritated at both Calvin and his mother." Her smile warmed his heart, and he bent to offer her a soft kiss.

As awareness that they had an audience settled in. It also struck him that the temperature in the room had thawed. Looking around, he was greeted with warm smiles from the women and chin lifts from the men.

Breaking the tension, Rory tossed the dish towel

onto the counter. "I'm getting ready to head out." Saying goodbye to his family, he shook hands with Carter. "Good to have you in the fold, man."

Harper walked over and gave Rory a hug. Smiling, she asked, "Are you heading to the Celtic Cock? I have it on good authority that a beautiful blonde you've had your eye on might be there."

Rolling his eyes, he quipped, "Aw, girl, you know there's too much of this awesomeness for just one beautiful blonde." As the girls groaned from the den, he tossed a wave before kissing his mother goodbye.

Tara asked, "Are you talking about your friend Sandy?"

Harper nodded. "You should see the two of them when they're together. She watches him, and when he looks, she turns away. Then he stares at her, and if she looks over, he turns away. They're worse than a couple of teenagers!"

Colleen wandered into the room, and Tara twisted her head around and up, catching Carter's eye. "Tomorrow is a school day, so we better be heading home."

He nodded and walked down the hall to collect their coats. As Tara bundled Colleen in hers, he moved over to Sharon to offer his thanks. She pulled him into a hug and patted his back, whispering, "Thank you for taking care of my girls."

"It's my pleasure." Making sure to thank Colm, he said goodbye to everyone else and waited while Colleen received goodbye hugs from the entire family. Finally, with her buckled safely in her car seat in the back of his SUV, he pulled onto the street.

"Are we going home now?" Colleen asked, yawning widely.

"Yeah, sweetheart, I'm taking you home." As the word 'home' left his mouth, it struck him how right it sounded. Not just for Tara and Colleen, but for him as well. For the first time, working on a relationship where he would share a home sounded good.

Tara smiled all through the morning with the memory of the perfect weekend lingering. Carter had sat with her as she talked to Colleen about her grandfather, but considering Colleen had no memories of the man, she was not upset. Carter had read to Colleen and tucked her in, then stayed the night again. Smiling, Tara felt the heat of blush move over her at the memory.

But it was now almost time for the bag lunches, and she wandered outside to watch. She couldn't define what she was looking for or suspected, but knowing something was happening, she didn't want to stick her head in the sand.

Leaving the kitchen through the back door where deliveries were made, she observed the tables already set up and volunteers placing bags onto the tables. A hand landed on her shoulder, and she jumped, whirling around. "Enrico, you scared me to death."

"Sorry, Tara. You're not usually out here so early."

"Well, I was finished with my intakes and thought I'd see how things were going."

He smiled and ambled over to the tables, greeting several of the volunteers. As usual, George had his walkie-talkie as he walked up and down the line making sure the people were staying orderly as well as chatting with many of them.

She heard a sound close by and turned to see who it was, not wanting to be surprised again. As Carter caught her eye, she smiled. "Hey, I didn't know you were going to be here." Her smile quickly dropped as her brow furrowed. "Oh, my God, is something wrong?"

He quickly shook his head. "No, no. Right now, I don't want to be out there where others can see me, but I'm hanging in here so that I can get a better view of how things are going."

They stood next to each other, close but not touching, watching the proceedings. Two church vans had delivered several hundred paper sacks of lunches for today's meal, and the volunteers were efficiently stacking them on the tables.

"How many churches and organizations help with this?" he asked.

"I'm not in charge of this project, but I know that there are close to thirty local churches, adult fraternities and sororities, and community service organizations that are on a regular rotation. Since there are only twelve days in a month that the lunches are needed, most only have to provide it once every quarter of the year."

She inclined her head toward the tables and said,

"Most of these people are volunteers who aren't here all the time. Enrico gets them organized. I know there are a couple of volunteers who are here often. The woman in the blue dress, Chelsea, is an employee of the shelter, and her job is to keep the organizations on schedule for their deliveries."

"Is Enrico always in charge of the bags with the 'PB' on them? The ones with peanut butter"

"I honestly don't know, Carter. I'm usually not out here, especially when it gets started. And when I am, well... I haven't been very observant." She peered up at him, noting his intense gaze as he watched everything going on around them. "You'd think with my father and brothers being in law enforcement, I'd have a better idea of how much observation you have to do in your job. It's not at all like on TV."

He spared a glance toward her and smiled. "A lot of my job is spent putting together pieces of an elaborate puzzle. Like with any puzzle, a lot of time is spent looking at one piece, turning it and twisting it until deciding exactly how it fits in the overall picture."

She nodded slowly, her gaze moving back over the hive of activity. "And this is one of the pieces."

Carter did not respond but instead moved closer. She had no doubt that he was carefully examining every aspect of the procedure. She tried to see it through his suspicious, analytical mind, but as she watched the people go by, taking their bag lunches, most grateful that they would not go hungry during the day, she could see nothing untoward happening.

"Ms. Wilson?"

She turned around and saw Bethany nearby. "Yes?"

"An emergency intake has come in. A woman with two children. She looks like she's had it rough. She may be better suited for the women's shelter, but I wanted to let you make that call."

Nodding toward Carter, she moved back inside, leaving him to do his job while she hurried inside to do hers.

---

He wanted to stalk over and demand to see inside each of the lunch bags, but with no evidence that drugs had ever been transported in them, he was stuck simply watching the procedure. Evan was outside today, not in line, but observing.

The procedure was quick, the volunteers hustling people through so that they got their bag lunch and moved on. He had to admit, for such a large endeavor, it was a smooth operation. His phone vibrated, and he looked to see Evan's name on the screen. "Yeah?"

"Watch for a man in a camo coat and jeans with a black cap pulled down low over his forehead. He's got long, dirty blond hair hanging down the back."

Considering Evan just described several of the people in line, he almost growled, but his partner continued, "He's coming up to the line right now."

His gaze latched onto the indicated person and saw someone greet the man before bending to snag one of the specially marked lunch bags.

"Follow him. He's seen me, so he'll know if I am. I'm moving closer to keep watch where you are," Evan announced.

Keeping his distance, Carter slid out of the doorway. A quick glance to the left showed the line to get lunches was nearly finished. To the right, he spied the ones with bags in their hands heading down the street or crossing the street to the park. Some alone and some congregating. Most had their bags open and were already eating the food.

He crossed the street, staying half a block behind the man he was following. The lunch bag was still clutched in his hand, although he pulled out the sandwich and ate while walking. He continued until they were blocks away from the center. An old, rundown apartment building filled the entire block. Several men lounged on the front steps, smoking and laughing, and the black-capped man walked past them. Even half a block away, Carter could see one of the men on the front steps immediately stand and fall into line behind the man with the bag. He was bundled in a heavy coat but wore no hat on his bald, tattooed head. Uncertain how the scenario was going to play out, Carter stopped when the bald man met up with his suspect.

Black-cap turned and opened the paper sack. Carter was unable to see a transaction clearly, but something was pulled from the sack and handed to Baldie, who in turn shoved it into his coat pocket. He then handed Black-cap something as well. Inwardly cursing that he was not hidden in his SUV and able to use binoculars, he moved to blend in with the other pedestrians on the sidewalk. He noted the apartment building that Baldie went into and stayed behind Black-cap for another block. Coming to a trash bin, Black-cap tossed the paper sack inside.

Once Black-cap had hurried on his way, Carter snapped on a pair of gloves and moved to the trash can. Ignoring the looks of bystanders, he picked up the paper sack, feeling its weight in his hand. He carefully unrolled the top and peered inside. There were three plastic sandwich bags: one with a partially eaten peanut butter sandwich on white bread, another with crushed chips, and another with a broken chocolate chip cookie. Reaching into his coat pocket, he pulled out a folded evidence bag. Placing the lunch sack inside, he sealed it. Calling Evan, he gave his location.

It only took a couple of minutes for Evan to pull up next to him, and he climbed into Evan's truck. "I checked inside after he disposed of this. He took something out and handed it to another man, getting something back. I wasn't close enough to see if it was a payoff. It doesn't look like much of the lunch was eaten."

Evan grinned. "So that means there was something else in that bag."

"Drop me off at the shelter, and I'm going to talk to the lady in charge and Enrico. Take this to the lab to see if they can pull anything off of it. I'll meet you back at the station."

Several minutes later, he knocked on a doorframe near the kitchen of Ever Hope. The nameplate said

Chelsea Davies, Volunteer Coordinator. He felt a sense of relief that this office was not close to Tara's. The woman sitting at the desk inside looked up and smiled. "May I help you?"

"Good morning. I'm Detective Fiske. I was told you were the person to talk to about the free lunch program here."

"Yes, I'm Chelsea. I organize the lunches, volunteers who assist, and the organizations that make the lunches. Please, come in."

He took a seat and pulled out his notebook. "Tell me about your program."

She reached behind her to a stack of folders and pulled out a sheet, handing it to him. "This is what we give to any of our churches or organizations who want to make lunches. It's very specific and they're told not to deviate from this. The bags include a sandwich, chips or crackers, and a cookie. When we get a new group that would like to help, before I put them on rotation, I meet with them to explain exactly what we need and obtain their agreement that they will follow our procedures."

He looked over the page of instructions and asked, "Can you explain why each bag must contain the same items?"

She offered a smile, but he noted it did not reach her eyes. Upon closer inspection, she was older than he originally assumed, gray beginning to streak through her hair and a few lines creasing her brow.

"Detective Fiske, I've worked with the homeless for many years. Like all people, and all groups, they represent a microcosm of our society. Some are hard-working and want to better their lives. Others are satisfied with where they are. Some are grateful for every offering of help, and others are demanding. Many are battling addictions or have varying degrees of mental illness. You may be wondering why I'm telling you this instead of explaining in simple terms what goes into a lunch bag."

His lips quirked. "Ms. Davies, I trust you to give me the information you think I need to have, however that information comes."

Her lips curved again slightly, and this time, the pleasure seemed true. "When we first started this program several years ago, it grew much quicker than we thought. The demand was larger than the supply. Several fights would break out as people were trying to get to the front of the line. We allowed people to pick up their own bag of food but found that the line got held up as they opened the bags and tried to see what was in them." She offered a rueful chuckle as she leaned forward and placed her arms on her desk, her gaze clear as she looked at him. "Some even complained. I don't like lettuce on my sandwich. I don't like mayonnaise or mustard. I got one cookie and they got two."

Understanding dawned, and he nodded. "Thus, standardized lunch bags."

"Quite so, Detective."

"A bag is handed to everyone who comes by?"

Nodding, she agreed. "Yes, that was part of our learning curve. It's not only best to keep them moving, but…" She hesitated, her lips pinched in a tight line. "I'm sure it's no surprise to you, Detective, but there are many who don't believe in offering a hand-out to those in need. Our program ran into many obstacles. Any large congregation of people, especially homeless or those in need, make people nervous. Even the police."

Carter did not need to respond. It was apparent she was very aware that others would be concerned or even downright hostile to the efforts of the shelter.

"We don't allow anyone to gather early. There's actually a police officer who walks behind the shelter to discourage people from coming too soon. Once the line forms, we have several volunteers with walkie-talkies who make sure everyone is where they need to be. But it is essential that the lunch line move as quickly as possible. We don't want loitering, and we don't want trash everywhere. So, we do what we can to make all of that happen."

"I notice Enrico is in charge of the bags with peanut butter."

"Yes. We want to keep those separate in case someone has a peanut allergy. If someone would like to request a peanut butter sandwich, they let the volunteer with the walkie-talkie know, and when they come up in line, Enrico or one of the other volunteers hands it to them."

"One last question, please. The ongoing volunteers who hand out the bags—how many of those are regular, here all the time?"

"Well, Enrico is an employee of the shelter but can't

be there every time. George loves to volunteer, and he's here most of the time. There's another man who's started volunteering each time. Lewis is his name. He helps hand out the bags."

"Do you know Lewis' last name?"

"Yes. It's Lewis Washington."

Stalking into the workroom, Carter headed straight to the evidence board. While Evan watched, he wrote 'Lewis Washington' on the board, drawing a line with a question mark between the new name and Beth. Turning, he said, "One of the volunteers that handed out the bag to the man I was following was Lewis Washington."

"Fuck, related to Beth?"

"Don't know yet. I wanted to interview Enrico again, but as soon as I heard about Lewis, I wanted to investigate." He plopped down in his chair at his desk, opening his laptop. Glancing up, he noted Evan's smirk. "What have you got?"

"Thought you were never going to ask." Leaning forward, he said, "I looked at the outside security camera of Ever Hope and managed to isolate a picture of the guy in the camo jacket. He never looked straight at the camera, but I got a good enough picture that I can circulate it."

"Got a hit?"

Chuckling, he said, "Looks like you can keep it all in the family. Your future brother-in-law, Kyle, is on his way over."

As if on cue, heavy steps were heard approaching, and Kyle rounded the corner coming into the room. Offering chin lifts, he got right to business.

"Evan sent a picture looking for information. I know we don't have a good facial, but from what I can tell, this guy is Levi Marks. Lives underneath the Thirty-first bridge, in the Cardboard Cottages."

The Cardboard Cottages was a moniker slapped onto a section under one of the bridges in town near the harbor warehouses. For several years, the homeless had been putting up cardboard boxes purloined from the warehouse dumps. It was not much, but the boxes created a small shelter from the outside elements.

Kyle stepped closer to the evidence board, staring at it before turning and looking back at the other detectives. "What's interesting is the last time I saw him, he was with this man right here."

Carter stared as Kyle pointed to the picture of Rocky Stallone. Jaw tight, he said, "Fuckin' puzzle pieces are starting to line up, but they're still not falling into place." Looking at Kyle, he said, "I need to find Levi."

Kyle grinned. "Considering I've been spending time with some of the residents of the Cardboard Cottages and know where a lot of them hang out during the day, you want to ride with me?"

Meeting Kyle's grin, he said, "Absolutely."

Thirty minutes later, Carter looked out over the cardboard city underneath the bridge. When he was a cop, this was not the section of the city he had been assigned to and had had no reason to be here in a couple of years. "It looks like a fuckin' war zone," he muttered. "No wonder Rocky found an empty row house to sleep in. It would have been a helluva lot safer than this place."

His gaze drifted over the cardboard structures that had been taped together, creating rooms. A few people were milling about, several standing next to fire pits, their hands extended as they tried to stay warm. Passing by the first couple of boxes, he could see others sleeping, or maybe strung out on whatever drug made their lives bearable.

Kyle walked straight to one of the barrels holding a fire. A few men backed away, but one man stayed, his gaze steady as the detectives approached.

"Looking for Levi Marks."

The man dropped his gaze to the fire, his fingers poking out through the ends of his gloves as he wiggled them closer to the flames. Carter remained quiet, not willing to interrupt Kyle's domain nor fuck up whatever relationship he had with the people here.

"Last I heard he had a woman. Shacking up at her place."

"You got a location for me?" Kyle asked.

Keeping his eyes on the fire, the man said, "You going to make it worth my while?"

"Don't I always?"

The silence stretched, and Carter wondered if the man was going to give.

"Somewhere on thirty-fifth near the harbor."

Kyle remained silent but reached his hand out and the two men shook. It was so smooth, even Carter almost missed the handoff. Following Kyle's initiative, he backed away and the two detectives headed away from the bridge.

Once inside Kyle's truck, he said, "Can't thank you enough. I owe you, man."

Kyle chuckled. "No marker. Hell, I'll do this just for you having Tara and Colleen's back."

Appreciating the assistance no matter how it came about, he nodded. "Drop me off at headquarters, and Evan and I'll head over to thirty-fifth."

Several hours later, he and Evan got a sighting of Levi walking out of an old brick apartment building near the warehouse district in one of the areas of Hope City that had seen better days and was nowhere near being on a renovation schedule.

They followed him as he walked down the street and disappeared into an alley at the side of a bar. Evan dropped Carter off, and he hustled into the alley. Levi stopped near the back door and leaned against the brick wall, pulling out a pack of cigarettes from his coat pocket. Carter was nearly on him when Levi jerked his head around, then took off running. Staying on his heels, Carter called out, "Police, stop!"

Levi ran around the corner, slamming into Evan. With Carter's hand planted in Levi's chest and pushing him against the brick wall, Levi began protesting.

"I haven't done anything! You got nothing on me!"

"You want to empty your pockets for me?" Carter asked.

Levi smirked. "Don't got nothin' illegal. Go ahead."

"Empty them." Carter kept his eyes on Levi as he barely loosened his hold. Levi stood fast for a moment, indecision passing through his eyes. He must have come to the realization that he could not get away from both of them, so he grumbled as he shoved his hands into his pockets.

Cigarettes. Keys. A prescription bottle with a few pills rattling in the bottom. And a wad of cash.

"Where'd you get the money?" Carter asked as he held up the bottle and read the label. It was made out to Levi Marks, filled a month ago at a local pharmacy, prescribed by Dr. Tiller, and was for oxycodone.

"Got me a job."

"Oh, yeah? Selling what?"

Shaking his head, Levi argued, "No, man. I'm not selling nothin'."

"So, you're just giving away bags of drugs."

Levi's dilated eyes widened, and he shook his head with more vigor. "Shit, those are my pills. I got 'em legit from a doctor."

"What for?" Evan asked, taking the prescription bottle from Carter and looking at it. "What do you need narcotics for?"

"I got a bad back. I was working construction up till six months ago. Making good money. Hurt my back and everything went to shit, man. Lost my job. Couldn't work. Someone told me the doc at the clinic could take care of me."

Carter leaned in, getting into Levi's face. "And does he? Just how does he take care of you?"

"I told him I couldn't afford physical therapy, and I ain't got no electricity, so I can't even use a heating pad. He gave me these stick-on pads to put on my back that have medication that's supposed to help take the pain away. And he gave me that prescription for pain as well. He says he can't give me many of those, so I take them only when absolutely need 'em."

Carter considered Levi's words, so far not giving him anything on Dr. Tiller that was not legitimate. Deciding to keep pushing to see if he could break Levi, he asked, "Are you telling me your fingerprints won't be on that bag of drugs we got off your customer this morning?" Carter hoped Levi had not been in further contact with Baldie to know he was lying.

Levi's face fell and his shoulders drooped. "Fuck, man."

Continuing to press his lie, Carter said, "We'll have your fingerprints off the lunch bag you threw away and bag of drugs you sold to your customer. Looks like you might not have to get your free lunch at the shelter anymore. City can give you free room and board with the conviction."

Levi opened his mouth, then snapped it shut, all bravado fled.

"I gotta tell you," Evan said, "I'd be more interested in what you have to say about where you got those pills than hauling your ass to jail."

"Shit, man, I can't do that."

Evan looked toward Carter and shrugged. "Guess he's not into a deal."

Carter grabbed Levi by the front of the shirt and jerked him forward before giving him a turn and pressing his front up against the brick wall. Pulling out his handcuffs, he got one snapped on before Levi began talking. "I don't know much. I just followed the directions I'm told."

"Yeah?" Carter chuckled. "I think I might need a little more than that."

"I was standing in the line for the lunches when one of the men came over and said he had a way for me to make some money and keep getting the pills I needed for my pain. I thought he was fucked in the head and asked him what he was talking about. He said he'd seen me in the clinic and knew I didn't have a job and overheard me talking to the pharmacist about why I had to go to a regular pharmacy to get the pills. I didn't remember seeing him, but that didn't mean nothin'. I asked him what I had to do."

"It didn't dawn on you that what he wanted you to do probably wasn't legal?" Evan growled.

Levi's jaw hardened and he shook his head. "You ever been hungry, Detective? You ever lose your place to sleep or your job? You ever been in so much pain you can't even sleep? I ain't never been homeless or unemployed in my life. I worked when I was in high school, did four years in the Air Force. Got back home and got a job. I did my time and paid my dues, and a fuckin' work accident took all that away. I'm standing in a fuckin' line 3 days a week to get a ham sandwich and a bag of chips. Someone offered me a way out of that, yeah, I was interested."

Easing the tone of his voice, Carter said, "Just keep talking, Levi. Tell us what you know."

Snorting, he said, "It was fuckin' easy. I go through the line and tell him I want the special peanut butter lunch. That's it."

"Just the peanut butter lunch?"

"Nah, it has to be the *special* peanut butter lunch. As soon as I got it, I hurried away and opened it up. Had a bag of some pills. It was more pain pills than what I could get the doc to prescribe. The next time I got in line, he came again and said that I'd be approached and paid for the pills."

"And the guy today?" Carter asked, his eyes narrowing.

"He's the one who approached me the first time. I give him the bag of pills and get paid." Levi licked his lips, his chest heaving. "This isn't the life I want," he whispered, his voice anguished.

Carter stared at Levi, watching as he blinked tears away. "What do you want?"

"I want to be out of pain. I want to be clean. Want a fuckin' job I can be proud of. I want to know that I can buy my own food and not have to sleep in a box under the bridge."

Levi's words scored straight through Carter. A good judge of character, he would swear that Levi was telling the truth.

"I heard there was a man at the shelter who can help veterans. His name is Enrico. I've seen him there but not talked to him. I got tangled up in this shit and don't know how to get out."

"Enrico?" Evan turned his gaze from Levi to Carter. "We wanted to talk to him anyway. Why don't we all take a trip?"

Nodding, Carter gripped the front of Levi's shirt and pulled him forward so that he was steady on his feet. "Sounds good to me. Let's see what Enrico has to say about all of this." Expecting Levi's gaze to turn wary or frightened, he was surprised. For the first time since they encountered Levi, his eyes looked hopeful.

## 25

Carter could not afford to let Levi go but didn't want him to remain in handcuffs as they walked into Ever Hope. Warning him, he gained Levi's agreement that he would not run. Now, if he could just talk to Enrico without having to involve Tara.

His luck was not holding as they ran into her as soon as they entered the reception area. Her gaze brightened when she saw him, then her forehead crinkled as she glanced between him, Evan, and Levi.

"Ms. Wilson, we need to speak to Enrico. Are you able to offer a private room where we can do so?" He held his breath as she glanced toward Enrico then back to him.

Inclining her head politely, she said, "Of course, Detective Fiske." She walked over to the reception desk and spoke quietly. "Sable, if you'll watch the desk alone for a few minutes, Enrico needs to follow me, please." She turned and walked down the hall past the dining area. Moving through a door, she stood to the side as the others moved into an empty classroom. "You're more than welcome to use this room as long as you need. There are no classes planned at this time."

As she was turning to leave, she offered a small smile toward Carter, and he breathed a sigh of relief.

"Actually, would it be okay if Ms. Wilson stayed?" Enrico asked.

At his words, Carter jerked his head around, his denial on his lips. "Absolutely not—"

"She needs to hear what's going on. She needs to hear what I've been doing." Enrico spoke to Carter, but his eyes were on Tara.

She glanced between Enrico and Carter, uncertainty written on her face, and Carter grimaced.

"If this is a private matter, then I should not be here," she said. She faced the group of men, her hands clasped in front of her, her demeanor calm. "On the other hand, if this involves the shelter in any way, I should be present."

The five occupants of the room remained perfectly still, and Carter finally released a held breath, giving a curt nod. At that, she stepped forward and waved her hand toward one of the tables, inviting them to sit.

Once seated, Tara immediately reached out her hand toward Levi. "Hello. I'm Tara Wilson, Lead Social Worker here at Ever Hope."

Levi hesitated before reaching his hand out. Snatching it back quickly, he wiped his palm on his jeans before taking her hand in his. Giving it a quick shake, he released her fingers, giving a slight nod. "Levi Marks, Ma'am."

Carter leveled his gaze on Enrico. "Detective Barlow and I were going to visit you today anyway, but our conversation with Levi has added a new level of interest. You already seem to know what that is. Care to elaborate?"

Enrico placed his forearms on the table, linking his fingers together. He sighed as he looked toward Tara, his expression unreadable. "I not only work at Ever Hope, but I also volunteer with several veteran organizations in the city. I spent twelve years in the Army, doing three tours in Afghanistan. I was one of the lucky ones. I saw action but was never injured. I came home to a wife, my kids, and found this job. Every person who walks into the shelter and needs a place to stay, I want to help. When that person is a veteran, it hits me right in the gut. We can't help everyone, but I try to discern those who need more than what we can give."

"What is it that you do?" Tara asked.

"Some studies say that ten percent of veterans have been diagnosed with a substance use disorder, which is higher than the general population. That's only those that have been actually diagnosed. We know that number has got to be more. In young male veterans, the rate is even higher, compounded by pain, suicide risk, trauma, and homelessness."

Carter leaned back in his seat and, glancing at Levi, noted the young man's intense gaze as he stared at Enrico.

"Recently, there's been a lot in the news about the amount of prescription pain medications for military personnel, especially between their treatment and medical discharge. And while doctors are starting to prescribe less, the opioid overdose rate for veterans is over twenty percent."

Tara exhaled audibly, seeming to deflate as she listened to the statistics. Shaking her head slightly, she shifted her gaze to Carter. He wanted to reach over and hold her hand, offer comfort, but maintained professionalism.

Enrico continued, "One of the organizations I volunteer with is Hope City Medical Group for Veterans. It's a small group of doctors who provide consultation and care for veterans who are fighting opioid addiction. They don't include alcohol abuse or other substance abuse at this time. They're focused on opioids, whether prescription or illegal. It's small, but they're starting to make an impact. It's a combination of nonprescription pain medicine, physical therapy, and counseling. Obviously, they can't help everyone and not everyone is ready to receive help. One of the things I do here is when I meet veterans, whether in the center or I start noticing who's going through the lunch line, if I feel like they might be a good fit, I can make a recommendation."

"Why did you not say anything?" Tara asked, leaning forward to place her hand on Enrico's arm. "This sounds wonderful."

Enrico shrugged as his lips tightened in a thin line. He looked over at Tara and said, "I didn't want it to be seen as a conflict with my job here. This is my job, my paycheck. I don't want to do anything to mess that up. But I spend time at the lunch line, chatting to see who is a veteran, do they look strung out, do they look like they want help. Once I make contact, I chat with them a little more, trying to discern if they might be a good candidate." He shifted his gaze and inclined his head toward Levi. "I've been chatting with Levi and finally told him that I thought he might be able to get clean so that he could get back to work. This morning, he disappeared before I had a chance to talk to him further."

Levi sagged in his chair, shaking his head slowly. "I'm sorry, man. I fucked it up."

Carter leaned forward, pinning Enrico with his hard stare. "What do you know about drugs in the lunch bags?"

Enrico blinked. His mouth dropped open, but no words came out. He snapped his mouth shut and blinked again, his gaze shooting around the table. His brow lowered as he shook his head slowly back and forth. Finally, as though just finding his voice, he said, "No. There's no drugs in the lunch bags. It's just food."

Carter heard Tara gasp and shot a glance her way. Her eyes were large, and she swallowed deeply but remained silent.

Evan said, "Someone's putting drugs in a few specially marked bags. It's someone's fucked up way of distributing. If the bag got into the wrong hands, it would be a fuckin' nightmare, but the system works."

"What do you know about Lewis Washington?"

Enrico stammered. "Uh... he's a volunteer. Uh... been working the lunches since last summer. I don't get a chance to talk to him much." He looked over at Tara, who was shaking her head as she lifted her shoulders in a slight shrug.

Levi shifted in his seat so that he was facing Carter. "Detective, what's gonna happen to me?"

Carter looked at Evan, understanding passing between them, and said, "Detective Barlow and I need to check out Enrico's story. If we find it's on the up and up, how interested are you in getting legitimate medical assistance?"

Levi's face scrunched as he burst into tears. Swiping at his eyes, he begged, "Yes, yes. I'll do anything you say to get out from under this shit and get clean."

"If you're serious about this, you're going to have to disappear," Evan added. "You can't go back to Cardboard Cottages. You can't go back into the lunch line here. You can't be seen here at Ever Hope."

Levi nodded, but his eyes registered fear. "What'll happen to me?"

"I'll ensure that you get a place at one of the other shelters."

All eyes at the table swung toward Tara at her announcement. "I'll make some calls, pull in some favors. That will give the detectives time to check out the clinic and if it all looks good, I can let them know where to take you."

Tears continued to slide down Levi's cheeks. "Thank you, Ms. Wilson. I don't know what I could ever do to repay you."

"Get help. Get clean. Then, figure out how you can help others."

Carter looked around the table. Enrico beamed. Levi

sighed in relief. Evan looked amused. And as his gaze landed on Tara, he could only imagine his expression holding awe. His lips quirked upward, and as they all walked out of the room, he held back just enough to quickly place a kiss on her smiling lips.

---

The sun had set hours ago, and Carter was still at headquarters. The afternoon had been busy, even if not in the way he originally planned. Evan stayed with Levi while Carter and Enrico went to the Hope City Medical Group. He talked to the director and discovered that what Enrico had told them about their mission was true.

A call to Evan brought him and Levi to the medical center. While Levi was undergoing an evaluation and intake process, Carter got the name of an accepting homeless shelter from Tara.

"Babe, I didn't expect any of this when we came in today," he began.

"Most of my days don't go the way I expected." She laughed and he loved the sound as it moved through him, settling deep inside.

"I'm going to be working late tonight, so I don't know when I'll get a chance to call. I wanted to touch base to let you know what's going on. Hell, I want to do more than touch base. This is a day I'd love to see you at the end of the day, talk about what's going on, find out how Colleen is, and pile up on the couch with a beer and you next to me watching TV."

She was quiet for a moment and he wondered if he had overstepped his bounds giving voice to the desire that he would like to be at her house. Just as he was beginning to backtrack, she eased his mind.

"I can't think of anything I'd like better," she said. "Are you sure you don't want to come over when work is finished? Colleen and I'll be there."

He opened his mouth to agree, then hesitated. *Am I ready for this?* It seemed like such an insignificant invitation— go to her house after work. See her and Colleen informally, not for a date. Eat something, share their day, everyone checking on each other. The answer to his question was abso-fucking-lutely yes. "If you don't mind, I'd love to stop by and see you two."

The relief in her voice was audible and he smiled. "Today we moved the investigation forward, Tara. I got to spend some time tying up some loose ends here. Plus, Evan and I need to figure out our next step."

"I can't believe that somebody's been dealing drugs through our lunch program." Tara's voice was tight as she continued. "I also can't believe that you won't let me shut it all down."

"Babe, you know this is the only lead we've got. It doesn't matter how many Levi's are out there, we've got to figure out where these drugs are coming from and shut down the pipeline. I'm not after the small fish, I want the fuckin' whale."

A snort came across the phone line, and he grinned wider. Evan walked into the room, and he halted his conversation but now knew they could continue it at her place. "Gotta go for now. See you tonight, babe."

Disconnecting, he turned his attention toward his partner.

Evan sat down and laughed. "Fuck, man. Weeks of this investigation like our feet are stuck in molasses. Suddenly, today, all hell breaks loose."

Chuckling, he nodded. Looking up at the board, he said, "So, now we know the use of the lunch line to get people down on their luck—especially someone who's already addicted—to carry and distribute. We spent today chasing down Levi and that line of questioning. I want to spend some time this evening digging into Lewis Washington. First thing in the morning, we're getting that fucker and see where that takes us."

## 26

Tara sat in her office, thinking about her call with Carter. Excited that he was coming over that evening, she knew it would not be early. Glancing at her clock, she saw that her workday was at an end. The events of the day had played heavily on her mind, not the least finding out from Levi about his opioid addiction.

Looking down at her phone messages from the day, she saw one from Kate. She hated that she had not seen the message earlier, being the kind of day that she could have shared with someone who understood. Knowing the clinic's phone would have already been shut down for the day, she wondered if Kate was still next door. Since Colleen was at a friend's house playing, she decided to run over to the clinic, hoping to see Kate before she left.

Tara grabbed her keys and walked down the hall in the opposite direction of the reception area. The little-used door that led from the shelter to the back of the clinic's supply area was kept locked to ensure that none of the shelter residents had access to the clinic that way.

She moved through the door and was just passing a supply closet when she heard sounds of panting and moaning. The instinct to rush through to see if someone needed help was halted at the sound of voices.

"Robert, Robert... hurry."

"Shift around a little bit, Beth. I can't get a condom on."

At that breathy declaration, Tara froze. The supply closet door was not shut completely, and she was afraid of moving for fear that they would know someone was there. The sounds of hushed moaning continued, and she couldn't imagine Robert having sex in the clinic. Granted, the clinic was officially closed by now, and much of the staff had probably left.

Her face burned at the fear of being branded a peeping Tom, even though there was no peeping to be had. Finally, after a long, low groan, she could eventually hear the sound of rustling clothes. Coming unfrozen, she tiptoed past, but not before she heard Robert tell Beth that she needed to stay quiet.

Continuing to tip-toe down the hall, she did not see any of the nurses or staff. Deciding she would come back tomorrow, she turned, then hesitated. *How the hell am I supposed to go back the way I came without running into Robert and Beth?* Skirting around the main reception area, she saw Dr. Tiller's door open. *If I talk to him for a few minutes, that will give the lovebirds a chance to pull themselves together.*

She knocked on the doorframe and he looked up in surprise.

"Tara? Is everything okay?"

Nodding, she said, "Yes. I actually came by to see Kate. She had called and left a message for me earlier today, but it was a crazy day."

He shook his head and sighed. "It makes me wonder if we're not having a full moon. The clinic was hopping today as well."

"Her message was that she desperately needed to talk to me, so I feel really bad that I didn't even get the note until she had left." She sighed heavily and offered a little smile that was more polite than happiness. "I had asked her to get some information on opioids to me."

His eyes widened. "Opioids?"

Nodding, she said, "Yes, but not just the prescribed ones. I'm also interested in the illegally manufactured drugs."

"Is there any special reason why?"

She lifted her shoulders in a slight shrug. "Let's just call it professional curiosity. We're seeing more and more of it, and I just want to be aware."

"I'm hoping we'll get to a point where we see a decline. Public awareness is now putting a lot of pressure on doctors to not over-prescribe, which I completely agree with." He shook his head and added, "I have no idea what information Kate felt like she needed to get to you. But you'll be able to see her tomorrow."

Turning to walk away, she looked over her shoulder and asked, "Do you know if Kate will be here in the morning? Her message was a little garbled, but she said something about a switch. It just dawned on me maybe she was talking about switching her schedule."

Brow lowered, he frowned. "I'm afraid I don't keep up with their schedules. Marsha, our office manager, handles that. But, as far as I know, Kate will be here tomorrow."

She stepped out of his office after saying goodbye and saw Robert going out the front door alone. *I guess Beth must have already snuck out.* Glad that she was not having to sneak, she walked toward the back. Suddenly remembering that she wanted to ask Dr. Tiller about Levi, she turned and started to head to his office again. A giggle from just inside his doorway caused her feet to stutter to a halt once again.

"Beth, keep your voice down. One of the shelter employees was just over here."

The sound of loud kissing was heard, and Tara backed around the corner, eyes wide.

"Wait, Doug. Let me get the buttons undone."

*Beth and Dr. Tiller? Oh, my God! She just screwed Robert, and now she's going after Dr. Tiller?* Tiptoeing backward, she retreated to the door leading to the shelter. Hurrying through, she locked it behind her, glad to be back on the shelter side. Leaning against the door, she allowed her breath to rush out of her lungs. Not usually one to give in to gossip, she grinned. *Looks like Kate and I'll have a few stories to share tomorrow.*

---

Carter was drowning. After a day spent hustling with

an investigation that was finally turning into some leads, he was now letting all that go and was drowning in Tara's arms. Neither needed an excuse for pushing the cares of their workday away, but making out was a good way to accomplish that task.

When he arrived at her house just in time for dinner, he felt guilty that she had not allowed him to pick up a pizza on the way. But then, he had to admit the juicy pork chops, scalloped potatoes, and buttered peas hit the spot.

Colleen had been full of tales of her afternoon spent with a friend, but fatigue settled in early and she went to bed with no complaints. Tara had insisted he take his beer into the den and relax while she got Colleen settled. Called upstairs for a good night hug, he sat on the floor next to Colleen's bed and read a story.

After weeks of waiting for the tight-noose feeling to hit when he was around Colleen, he was finally letting go of the fear. With her little girl arms around his neck, the cares of the day eased away. After Tara closed Colleen's door, he linked fingers with her and led her downstairs.

They had barely sat on the sofa when both twisted and looked at each other. Right now, the last thing he wanted to do was talk about the investigation. Tara held his gaze for a few seconds, then launched at him, taking him to his back, her lips landing on his. *Thank fuck!*

With his arms banded around her, he shifted so that he was partially on top, careful to keep them from rolling onto the floor. For several minutes, he reveled in the kiss. The softness of her lips. The silkiness of her cheek as his fingers drifted over her skin. The thick, sleek tresses of hair that fell back on the cushion. The scent of her floral shampoo and the taste of the wine on her tongue.

His cock was soon demanding attention, but he didn't want to rush one moment with her. While she had acted normal during dinner, he felt a heaviness about her. When he asked, she had simply smiled, gently touched his cheek, and murmured about the rough day. Now, he wanted to take away those worries, and from the moans coming from her lips and her fingertips gripping his shoulders, he hoped he was accomplishing his mission.

Her hands slid down his back, one hand cupping his ass and squeezing. Now it was his turn to groan as he lifted his head slightly and peered down. "Tara, babe, you can just relax. This doesn't have to go anywhere except right where we are. Let me take care of you."

Her other hand slid around to cup his jaw, her thumb sweeping over his slight stubble. "But what if I wanted it to go somewhere?"

"Are you sure? 'Cause as much as I'd like to sink into your sweet, soft body, I'm good with just making out on the couch. Being with you is all I need to do."

She pressed her hips against his erection and bit her bottom lip as she squeezed her eyes tight for a few seconds. Her breasts pressed against his chest as she sucked in a deep breath. His cock was straining against his zipper, but he remained still.

She opened her eyes slowly, and whispered, "Carter, honey, I want you. Yes, you can get me off right here on the sofa, and if that's all we can do, I'll take it. But I want more. I want more from you, and I want to give you more." She held his gaze and swept her thumb over his lips. "And I want it upstairs."

His breath halted in his lungs, his gaze searching hers. "Are you sure?"

She nodded, her lips curving into a soft smile. "I know we're not ready to take our relationship full force in front of Colleen, right now. And I sure as hell don't want to scare you away—"

"No chance of that, babe."

"Colleen is young, but children today seem so much more savvy than when we were children. She's asked me if you were my boyfriend, and I told her yes. She asked me if you were going to stay, and I was honest. I told her that we care about each other and that we both care about her."

Understanding moved over him and he sighed. "She's afraid of being left... like her dad did?"

Shaking her head slightly, she replied, "She's never known what it was like to have a dad. Calvin left right after she was born. But it's good that we're taking things slow with her. It's obvious she loves having you around. I just don't want to be too much for you."

He leaned forward and kissed her lightly again, his heart warmed by her love for her daughter and concern for him. "It's not too much, Tara. But you're right, we'll move slow in front of Colleen."

"Are you sure you're okay with that? I don't want you to feel hustled away or—"

He guided her hand so that her palm was flat against

his chest. "What I feel is in *here*. Believe me, I want you and Colleen in my life."

Her smile widened, and he met her grin as he pressed his erection against her belly. "And babe, what I feel just for you is *this...*"

Her eyes flared and she whispered, "Then let's take *this* upstairs."

He stood and bent to gently pull her to her feet. Leading her upstairs, they checked Colleen's door and then hurried into the bedroom. The moment had not been lost and they fell into each other's arms again.

Clothes quickly landed on the floor, and in less than a moment they were completely naked, standing next to her bed, their hands gliding over their bodies. He wanted to worship her body, but more than that, he wanted her to know he worshiped her. Everything about Tara called to him. Her caring concern for others. The love she had for her family. And now, the way she wanted to take care of him.

She suddenly stepped back, and his eyes snapped open at the separation. Staring up into his face, a grin curved her lips before she eased down on her knees. With one of her hands on the muscular globes of his ass, the other grasped his cock as she licked her lips then slid his erection into her mouth.

Caught by surprise, he almost dropped to his knees as well by the feel of her warm mouth sheathing him. She began working his cock, her tongue gliding along the ridges. His head dropped back and he groaned. His hands automatically moved to her head, his fingers threading through her hair. He clutched the silky threads, then forced his fingers to relax, not wanting to hurt her.

She continued to work her magic, but when he was close, he forced his body to step back. Not giving her a chance to protest, he reached down and grabbed her underneath her arms. With a deft maneuver, he tossed her onto the bed. She spread her legs wide, the evidence of her arousal glistening.

"I'm ready. Please don't make me wait, I need you now," she begged.

Snagging a condom from his pants pocket, he deftly rolled it on before looming over her. He guided the tip of his cock to her entrance, moving it through her slick folds. Her face held an expression of desperation, and he plunged inward, filling her. Her head fell back, and with her eyes tightly closed, she smiled.

He began thrusting, keeping his eyes pinned on her face, not disappointed when her eyes opened and she held his gaze. She lifted her hips in rhythm, meeting him thrust for thrust. He bent and took her lips in a searing kiss, then shifted so that he could pull a taut nipple into his mouth. His cock was ready to explode, and just when he thought he could not hold off any longer, her heels dug into his ass, her fingers dug into his shoulders, and she cried out her release.

With his head bent forward and the muscles of his neck tight, he poured his own release into her, muffling his roar with his face buried against the mattress next to her head. They lay, bodies pressed together, limbs tangled, as their ragged breathing slowly returned to normal.

He smoothed her hair away from her beautiful face and stared at her smile, knowing the one on his face was just as wide. "You okay, babe?"

She nodded slowly. "Yes, I'm perfect."

With another light kiss on her lips, he agreed. "Yeah, you are." Hating to leave her arms, he needed to deal with the condom. A moment later, he walked back from the bathroom and saw her leaning up on her elbows staring at him.

"You don't happen to have an extra set of clothes in your car, do you?"

Her question caught him off guard. He stopped at the side of the bed and asked, "Extra clothes?"

She blushed and dropped her eyes. Not wanting her to be embarrassed about anything, he crawled over her, forcing her gaze to meet his. "I hope you know you can say anything to me—ask me anything."

Her hand glided over his chest, her fingertips moving in small patterns on his shoulders. "I was just thinking that if you had a change of clothes, you could stay here tonight. Get up early and take a shower and be downstairs for breakfast when Colleen gets up. We can just say that you came over early for breakfast. But that's probably a stupid idea—"

"I always keep an extra set of clothes. I never know when I might need them at work or after the gym."

Her eyes widened and her kiss swollen lips opened slightly. Hoping she was not going to change her mind, he wanted to be sure. "Are you sure about this? You know I'd love to, but it won't hurt my feelings if you made the offer and then realized it's too soon."

Shaking her head, she smiled. "It's not too soon. Not for me. And while I'm not ready to explain an adult sleepover to Colleen, she would be thrilled to have you here for breakfast."

Breathing her in, he covered her with his body once more, his lips caressing hers. Right now, in this bed with Tara and Colleen safe across the hall, he could not imagine anywhere else he'd rather be.

---

## 27

"Colleen's school is on my way to the headquarters," Carter said.

Tara's head snapped up, uncertain what he meant by that statement. After a perfect night where they'd slept in each other's arms, he'd grabbed a gym bag from his SUV and taken an early morning shower. By the time she woke Colleen, he'd taken the bag back to his vehicle and was at the kitchen counter stirring oatmeal.

Colleen had bounded into the room, exclaiming her delight that he had come for breakfast. As she threw her arms around him for a hug, Tara saw him squeeze tight and loved seeing her daughter's enthusiasm. She also had to admit she loved seeing him in her kitchen fixing them breakfast. Such a simple act, and yet one she performed by herself every day. After being alone for so many years, it was also an act she didn't take for granted.

As Colleen ate, Tara reached over and squeezed his hand, mouthing '*thank you.*' He winked before giving

Colleen another squirt of maple syrup in her oatmeal. Her daughter squealed in delight at the extra sweetness, and Tara wanted to join her, his wink melting her heart.

After breakfast, Tara had hustled her daughter upstairs to brush her teeth while she rinsed out the breakfast dishes. Now, she stared at Carter, waiting to see what else he had to say.

"I can drop her off at school if that makes it easier on you."

She smiled. "That's sweet of you, honey, but I've got her car seat."

"Damn, sorry. I forgot all about that," he said, shaking his head.

She dried her hands then turned as he came up behind her. Placing her palms on his chest, she lifted on her toes and kissed the underside of his jaw. "Don't worry about it. Just the fact that you offered means more to me than you can possibly imagine."

A grimace crossed his face, and he leaned closer. "Babe, get ready to have a lot more offers. The fact that you had to do this all on your own for so long just shows how strong you are. But those days of going alone are over. I'm here. I'm staying. We're in this together."

His words washed over her and she wanted to leap into his arms, but the sound of Colleen rushing down the stairs meant that she could only send him what she hoped was a brilliant, heartfelt smile. He must have understood her message because he winked again.

Outside, she had Colleen buckled into her car seat and she turned to say goodbye. They settled for a quick kiss, and she was struck with something she'd meant to tell him. Whispering so that Colleen would not overhear, she said, "I can't believe I forgot to tell you this. I went to see Kate yesterday evening because she left a message that she needed to speak to me. When I went, I discovered Robert and Beth *getting it on* in a supply closet."

She watched as his brows lifted to his forehead, and she stifled a giggle. "And then, as I was leaving, I heard her *getting it on* with Dr. Tiller!" Seeing his eyes widen even more, she nodded. "Seriously! Two men—in the same office—one right after the other." Glancing into the car, seeing Colleen looking at a book, she added, "Okay, I gotta stop gossiping. I'll see you tonight." Lifting on her toes, she gave him another quick kiss.

His arms around her tightened, keeping her from stepping into her car. Twisting her head around, she looked up in question.

Leaning close, he said, "Be careful. I have no idea what's happening, but stay away from Beth Washington."

She swallowed deeply and nodded. "I'm never around her. I just happened to see her yesterday, that's all. I'll call Kate and see if she can come over to the shelter to tell me whatever was on her mind."

He offered a tight smile before stepping back and waving toward Colleen. Tara slid into the driver's seat and headed down the road. Glancing in the rearview mirror, she could see him standing by his SUV, staring after them. His words had surprised her, but his concern washed over her, chasing away any fears.

Thirty minutes later, she was at her desk, a cup of coffee in front of her, ready to start her day. The message light on her desk phone was blinking. *A message already today?* She took a sip of coffee and pressed the button to listen.

***Message received 8:07 p.m.*** *"Tara? This is Kate. I really wanted to talk to you today, but I know you were busy. I've been driving around trying to think of what to do and just got home. We need to talk when I get in tomorrow. I'll be there first thing in the morning. Please. I don't know what's going on, but meds are being switched... Shit... Sorry, someone's at my door. I'll call you right back."*

***That was your last message.***

"My last message?" she mused aloud, wondering why Kate didn't call back. Pressing the button again, she confirmed there was only the one message from Kate. *Meds are being switched?*

Picking up the phone, she dialed the clinic. As soon as the receptionist answered, she said, "Hello, this is Tara Wilson from next door at the shelter. I need to speak to Kate, please."

"I'm sorry, Ms. Wilson, but Kate isn't here yet."

Glancing at the time, she was surprised. "It's my understanding that Kate was working this morning."

"Yes, she's supposed to be here. But she's late and isn't answering her phone. We're concerned and will keep calling, but we're short-staffed today."

She almost disconnected but at the last second hastened to ask, "Do you happen to have her address? I must speak with her and if she's ill, I'd like to find out."

She heard the receptionist sigh and squeezed her

eyes tight, praying that they would give in to her request.

"Well, since it's you, I'm sure Kate won't mind. She lives in the Burlington apartment building. Um, let's see... It's apartment thirteen."

"Thank you so much. As soon as I find out what's happening, I'll make sure to let you know." She disconnected, a mission on her mind. Leaving her coffee to cool, she grabbed her coat and purse. As she passed Sable at the reception desk, she said, "I need to make a visit. Hopefully, I'll be back shortly."

Plugging in the address on her GPS, she was glad to see that Kate only lived about ten minutes away. *Meds are being switched. What did she mean?*

Calling Carter ran through her mind, but she dismissed the thought. *He's busy. Let me see what Kate is talking about first.*

When she arrived at the apartment building, she parked where visitors were indicated, seeing apartment numbers painted on most of the spaces. She found Kate's door easily since they all opened to a covered walkway, the appearance much like many hotels. Knocking on the door, she received no answer nor could she hear any noise coming from the inside. Glancing toward the parking lot, she could see that there was still a car in the space numbered thirteen.

Unease crept through her and she once again thought of calling Carter. She grimaced at her indecision, trying to figure out what to do. Knocking on the door again, louder this time, she still received no response. Starting to walk away, she passed by a window, the view to the inside of the apartment obscured with closed, vertical blinds. Her attention was snagged by a few of the slats that were separated as though someone had peeked out and the slats stayed in an open position.

Looking around but seeing no one, she leaned forward and pressed her face against the glass, peering inside. It took a moment for her eyes to adjust, the lights seeming to come from below instead of above. Searching closer, she could see that a lamp had been knocked over, the light still on but illuminating the room from the floor. A sofa was near the window, and a coffee table sat in front, a plate with a half-eaten sandwich and soda on it.

She was about to knock on the window, wondering if that would make a louder sound than the door, when her gaze dropped. Gasping, she blinked several times before cupping her hands around her face so that she could see clearly. The entire body was not exposed, but scrub-covered legs were visible from behind the sofa.

Stumbling back, she dialed 9-1-1, quickly reporting her location and what she was seeing. The operator wanted her to stay on the line, but she blurted, "No! My boyfriend's a detective, and I'm calling him." Without giving the operator a chance to speak again, she disconnected, then quickly called Carter.

He'd barely said hello when she interrupted. "I'm at Kate's apartment. Outside. Something happened to her. I can see a body inside—"

"Whoa, slow down, babe. What's happening?"

She heard him tell someone that she had found a

body when he called her name again. "Tara? Where are you?"

Forcing her voice to calm, she gave him her location and what she had seen. "I've already called 9-1-1."

"Get in your car and lock the doors," he ordered. "I'm on my way. Don't get out of your car until you see the ambulance and police arrive."

She nodded, then blurted, "Okay." Disconnecting, she rushed to her car and climbed inside, hitting the lock. Her heart pounded as fear snaked throughout her. Praying Kate would be okay, she sat and waited.

## 28

Carter ignored the squeal of his SUV's tires as he stopped on the street outside of the apartment building. He bolted from his vehicle, the flashing lights of two patrol cars and the ambulance barely registering as his gaze scanned the area for Tara. Catching a glimpse of her dark hair and pale face, he let out a breath that felt as if he'd been holding it since her phone call. Rushing forward, his gaze moved from her head to her feet, assuring him that she was all right. Her arms were clutched about her waist, but when she heard him running toward her, she flung them outward to hold him tightly as he grabbed her in his arms.

"I've got you, I've got you," he repeated, the feel of her safe in his arms followed by the shaking of her body. She nodded but for a moment said nothing as she clung to his neck.

He twisted slightly to speak to the officer but relaxed when he saw that Evan was already there.

"I'm Detective Barlow. This is Detective Fiske. We

received a call from Ms. Wilson. This might have bearing on a case we're investigating."

The officer nodded, replying, "The ME is on their way. Homicide has been called."

Carter gave Tara a squeeze. "Babe, I need to step inside to see what's happening. I'll be back in a minute." He felt her nod but leaned back to hold her gaze, ascertaining that she truly understood.

She swallowed deeply and nodded again. "It's okay." Letting out a shaky breath, she repeated, "Really, Carter. It's okay. You need to do whatever you can to um... Well, whatever."

A female officer was standing nearby, and he caught her eye. "Stay with her." The officer stepped forward and said, "Ms. Wilson, let's go stand over here so we're not in the way." Tara nodded again and moved with the officer to the side.

Careful not to contaminate the scene, he stepped inside, leaving Evan outside. His gaze swept the room. The living room opened to a small area with a dining table, and the kitchen only had a short counter separating the space. Other than a lamp knocked onto the floor, the room appeared normal. A plate with the remains of a sandwich sat next to a soda on the coffee table.

Looking down at the body, he could see it was Kate. Still wearing her light blue nursing scrubs, her feet were encased in thick socks. The prints around her neck indicated strangulation, but that was for the ME to determine and homicide to investigate.

After walking down the hall, he came back to the

living room and spoke to Evan, who was near the door. "One bedroom. One bathroom. No signs of injury. No signs of struggle. I'd say she knew who came in."

Hearing a noise outside, he looked past Evan's shoulder as Brock King walked in. His gaze swept the room, dropped to the body, and shot back up to Carter, offering a chin lift as his greeting.

"I saw Tara outside," Brock said. "She the one who called it in?"

"Yeah, it's a friend of hers."

"Fuck." Brock stood with his hands on his hips, looking down at the body.

"Upfront, Brock, this is your scene, but we're here not just because of Tara but because of the case we're on."

Brock's eyes shot up to his, and he nodded. "Got it. Can you give an ID, or do we need Tara in here?"

"Hell, no, I don't want Tara in here. She already had to ID another body, and I sure as shit don't want her to do that again. Her name is Kate Burks. She's a nurse at the free clinic that's next to Ever Hope. That's how Tara knew her."

"What was Tara doing here this morning?"

Just then one of the officers stuck his head in and said, "The ME is here."

Brock shifted to one side when Natalie walked in. She looked at them and asked, "You ready for me?" She came further into the room, and Carter stepped to the doorway, Brock next to him.

"We're working on the investigation involving the death of some homeless men carrying bags of opioids and the free clinic. Kate left a message for Tara yesterday saying she needed to speak to her. Yesterday was a shit-kicking day for all of us, and Tara was too late to talk to her. That's all I know right now. Tara ended up over here, peeked through the blinds, and thought she saw the body, so she called it in."

Both men looked at the slats in the blind that had been pulled slightly open. Carter said, "I took a look in the back. No signs of a struggle. I wondered if she peeked out the blinds, recognized who was there, and opened the door."

Brock pulled out his camera and began snapping pictures as Natalie continued to examine the body.

"You want to talk to Tara now?" he said. "I'll have Evan send you whatever we've got, and we can meet later."

Following him out of the apartment, Brock said, "Appreciate it, man." They both walked over to Tara. She opened her arms and slid straight into Carter's embrace, shifting her gaze from his face over to Brock's. "I'm real sorry, Tara," Brock said, sliding his hand to the back of her neck as he leaned over and kissed her forehead. "We'll find out who did this."

She offered a half-hearted smile. "Thanks, Brock." Carter sighed, drawing her attention back to him.

"Honey, I know the drill. You guys need to ask me questions."

Brock chuckled ruefully. "You can't be in the McBride family without knowing what we've gotta do."

Natalie came to the door and said to her crew, "Were

ready to take the body." Looking over at Brock, she said, "Tomorrow."

Carter felt Tara shift in his arms, and she said, "I don't want to watch this."

He escorted her down the walkway, finding a bench. Settling her so that she was facing away from Kate's doorway, he kept his arm around her as Brock settled in on the other side.

"Babe, tell us what happened this morning."

She went through the phone message she received from Kate the evening before and her efforts to see her at the clinic. "Kate and I were not close friends. I didn't even have her cell phone number." Then she told of the message she had received that morning and the events leading up to peeking through the window. Brock took notes throughout her explanation, giving her a chance to speak without interruption.

"Did you save the message on your phone at work?" Brock asked.

Nodding, she said, "Yes. I didn't erase it. The answering machine said that it came in a little after eight last night."

"I'll come by later and hear it. And you're sure it said the meds had been switched?"

She looked up at Carter and said, "I have no idea what she was talking about, but it has to be with what's been happening. It's all got to be related." Her brow scrunched and she nibbled on her bottom lip. Her gaze jumped back up to his. "Someone must know that she knows something. I mean, that she *knew* something."

Brock patted her leg before standing. "I'm going to

start processing the apartment. Carter, take care of our girl here."

With a chin lift, Carter acknowledged Brock as he walked away, then turned his attention back to Tara. "Babe, let me take you home. I'll drive your car and Evan can pick me up later. He can also send our reports to Brock."

She sucked in a deep breath and let it out slowly. Holding his gaze, she said, "Honestly, Carter, I don't need to go home. It was a shock, I admit, but I need to get to work and so do you. Me sitting at home wringing my hands isn't going to solve the crime. I have people that need me at the shelter, and while Brock is handling the homicide, I know you've got to work with him to figure out what she was talking about."

He stared at her for a moment, but she seemed steady. "You're fuckin' amazing, you know that?"

Snorting, she said, "I'm not sure about that." She reached up and touched his face and he leaned into her palm. "I do know that I'm better when I'm with you."

"Tell you what. I'll still drive you to work since I'm gonna need to talk to the people at the clinic. Evan can follow." She nodded her acquiescence, and he stood, pulling her up gently with him. He offered a chin lift to Brock as they passed by, and he escorted her to her car. Once she was settled in the passenger seat, he stood for a few seconds, his hands on his hips and his head tilted back, taking a moment to remind himself that she was fine. *Now, just to keep her that way.*

"So, you have no idea what she might have been referencing?"

Carter was sitting in Dr. Tiller's office, carefully observing him. After taking Tara back to her office at Ever Hope, he listened to the recorded message. He stayed while Tara told the other social workers what had happened, and once he was assured she was going to be okay, he headed to the clinic.

Not wanting to encroach on Brock's homicide investigation, he nonetheless wanted to question Dr. Tiller about the cryptic messages from Kate to Tara. The clinic had closed early and the staff was openly grieving.

Dr. Tiller had not been able to shed any light on Kate's personal life, but Carter accompanied him back to his office to continue questioning him about Kate's concern about switched meds.

"It's just all so bizarre. None of it makes sense," Dr. Tiller said, shaking his head slowly. He squeezed his eyes shut for a few seconds, his face scrunching.

Carter wondered if he was going to begin crying, but the doctor sucked in a ragged breath, cleared his throat, and reopened his eyes. "I'm afraid I honestly don't know my staff in any way beyond this clinic. We're so busy from the time we open until the time we close. After the patients are gone, I have reports to write, orders to sign—all the things necessary to keep the clinic going." He shook his head again and continued, "Even my evenings and weekends are sometimes spent making sure the clinic has funding." He lifted his hand weakly and waved toward the door. "I know the staff is closer to each other. They sometimes celebrate each other's birthdays. Perhaps one of them knows if she was dating someone or involved in something. I don't know."

"And what about here at the clinic? What kind of nurse was she?"

"I had no complaints about her at all. She was an efficient nurse. Very friendly. The patients seemed to respond to her, especially families with children. I know it was very difficult when Polly was... um... well, when Polly left. Kate stepped in to take more hours and take over some of that responsibility." His gaze shot up to Carter's, and he gasped. "Could this have anything to do with Polly?"

"What do you think, Dr. Tiller? You know the workings of the clinic better than anyone."

The doctor dropped his gaze to his hands resting on his desk. Sighing, he said, "No, I can't see how the two had anything to do with each other. Polly was just taking antibiotic samples that should have been dispensed only by me to patients that I saw and giving them to others. There was nothing that was switched." He lifted his palms up and shrugged. "I'm sorry, Detective Fiske. I just have no idea what Kate was referring to."

A knock sounded on the door and before Dr. Tiller could react, the door flung open and Robert hurried in.

"Oh, my God, Doug. What the hell? I mean, Katie? What the hell?" The words rushed from Robert, and Carter noted his deer-in-the-headlights expression. The pharmacist did a double-take when he saw Carter sitting in the office, and he began to blabber. "Oh, shit, I'm sorry. Uh... Detective?"

"Mr. Atkins. I have a few questions for you. I'll come to your office in a couple of minutes."

Still wide-eyed, Robert bobbed his head up and down, glancing between Dr. Tiller and Carter. "Sure, sure. Yeah... sure." He turned and hurried down the hall.

Carter shifted his gaze back to Dr. Tiller, finding the doctor's attention riveted to the now empty doorway before slowly moving back to him.

"Robert... I don't know how well he knew Kate, but he handles our medication." Dr. Tiller continued to shake his head and added, "Trust is a strange thing, Detective Fiske. When it's questioned, we're shaken, it's hard to get back. If he's got something to hide... Well, as head of the clinic, I've got some decisions to make."

After leaving Dr. Tiller's office, he glanced toward the front door where he spied Beth standing with one of the nurses. Not wanting her to leave before he had a chance to talk to her, he stalked toward her. "Ms. Washington?"

Her gaze shot up to him, and he could have sworn her eyes lit as she smiled widely. "Yes?" Her voice was breathy, and she immediately left the side of the tearful nurse and sidled up to him.

"I'd like to ask you a few questions."

"Of course. I'm all yours. But I assure you I know nothing about poor Kate's demise. It's just too, too horrible." She placed her hand on her chest, a maneuver he recognized as trying to draw eyes to her cleavage.

Refusing her invitation, he got right to the point. "Do you know Lewis Washington?"

Her face registered shock before she quickly adopted a blank expression. "I'm afraid the last name of *Washington* is very common. I certainly wouldn't know everyone who has that name."

"I didn't ask if you knew everyone who had that name. I asked if you knew Lewis Washington."

Blinking, her smile did not reach her eyes and her voice hardened. "No. I'm unacquainted with someone of that name. And since I had very little contact with Kate, I'm not sure there's anything else I can offer you. If you'll excuse me, I have a schedule to keep." She turned and stalked away, her heels clicking a rapid staccato down the hall.

He blew out his breath as he walked to the back where the pharmacy and Robert's office were located. Knocking on the doorframe, he found Robert sitting at his desk with his head in his hands. As he entered, Robert's head snapped up, his eyes still wide.

"This is crazy, Detective. I don't understand any of this."

"Do you have any idea why Kate would've told someone that she was concerned about meds being switched?"

Air rushed from Robert's lungs as he leaned heavily back in his chair. "Meds were being switched?" His mouth dropped open as he shook his head. "I... I don't even know what that means."

"If someone was going to switch medications here at the pharmacy, how would that work?"

Robert nearly leapt from his chair. "That doesn't happen! It can't! There's no way!"

Keeping his voice calm, Carter asked, "Then explain the process. Tell me how drugs cannot be switched here."

Slumping again, Robert said, "It's not just me that works here. I have a staff of two other pharmaceutical technicians that work on a rotating schedule. If one person was going to try to switch something, someone else would catch them. Plus, by law, we have to maintain a Controlled Drug Register, with running balances. Everything is computerized. Drugs dispensed. Drugs ordered. I don't even know what kind of meds could be switched. It doesn't make sense, Detective."

Robert reached to the side and grabbed a wad of tissues, dabbing his brow before scrunching them in his hand. "None of this makes sense."

Leaving the clinic, Carter felt the same, but that only served to make him angry.

## 29

Tara sat at her parents' kitchen table sipping a steaming mug of tea laced with honey. Her father had offered to dose it with whiskey, but she laughingly declined. After a harrowing day, she was desperate for normalcy, and when her mom invited her and Colleen over for dinner, she jumped at the opportunity.

She glanced toward the sliding glass door that led to her childhood backyard and smiled. *How many hours did we look at the stars with Dad as he showed us the constellations?* She had never asked her dad when his interest in astronomy began, but it was a shared hobby between him and Chauncey King. So much of a hobby that all eleven kids spent many hours staring through their telescopes as the dads pointed out stars, constellations, and even the stories behind the constellations. Now, her dad was doing the same with Colleen.

"I'm so sorry about your friend, sweetheart."

Turning her attention from the dark backyard to her mother sitting across the table from her, she nodded.

"Her memorial is tomorrow morning. The clinic is going to close for the whole day, but I'll be at the shelter in the afternoon." She sighed heavily. "Kate and I were not close friends by any stretch of the imagination. But she was someone I saw a couple of times a week, always smiling, always pleasant. And so young."

Her mom lifted an eyebrow, tilting her head to the side. "Oh, Tara, she couldn't have been much younger than you."

Thinking for a moment, she chuckled. "I guess you're right. Kate had been a nurse for several years, so she was at least in her mid-20s, probably only three or four years younger than me. Lordy, sometimes I feel old."

Inclining her head toward the backyard, her mom said, "You're not old, but being a mom can make you feel that way. Children have so much energy, and yet they still suck most of ours away."

Silent for a moment, Tara sipped her tea. Glancing up, she found her mother staring at her. "What is it?"

"I was just wondering about Carter," her mom said. "The two of you seem so… good together." She shook her head while rolling her eyes. "I guess what I meant to say is that seeing the way he was with you and Colleen made *me* feel really good. I've always been so proud of your strength. But it was nice to see someone who wanted to be a partner."

She closed her eyes and thought of Carter. His character. His strength. The way he wanted to step in and help with Colleen. Opening her eyes, she saw her mom smiling widely. "I really like him, Mom. And yet, that's a little scary. In the past few weeks, we've gotten closer. In fact, he's stayed over several nights. We're very careful around Colleen, and she doesn't know about that. But she loves having him around. Part of me was terrified to let him get close to Colleen in case something went wrong. I've never wanted her to have the feeling that there was a revolving door of *dads*."

Her mom scoffed. "Tara, you never had her around another man other than family." Reaching over, she closed her fingers around Tara's hand. "I've never thought you needed a man to be a complete person. And you're certainly raising Colleen beautifully. But I've always worried about you being lonely, and since Carter's been in your life, you seem happy."

Squeezing her mom's hand in return, she smiled. "I am."

The back door opened, and Colleen came flying in. Bundled in her coat, scarf, and hat, her cheeks were rosy, and her eyes were bright. "Grandpa showed me the North Star! I finally saw it! I used to look and look and look and never saw it, but I did tonight!"

While Tara wrapped her arms around her daughter, pulling her in for a hug, Sharon moved to the counter to retrieve a mug of now-cooling hot chocolate. Tara glanced over Colleen's head, smiling as her dad came into the room, stamping his feet and rubbing his hands together.

"It was a perfect night to watch the stars," Colm exclaimed, bending to kiss Colleen's head. He walked into the kitchen, accepting a mug of hot chocolate from

Sharon. "Oh, thank you, darling. This is going to hit the spot."

As they sat around the table, Colleen continued to bounce as she exclaimed over the stars they had looked at. "Grandpa says that because the Earth turns, it sometimes looks like the stars are moving, too. And they looked different at different times. Right, Grandpa?"

Tara smiled as she took a napkin and wiped the hot chocolate mustache off Colleen's face.

"That's right," he agreed. "Sometimes, the stars are in different places, and we have to search for them. Sometimes, they're right under our nose, but because a position is a little different, we have to search to find them. It's like they're hiding in plain sight."

Glancing at the clock, Tara said, "Colleen, honey, we need to head home." Soon they were bundled up again, and goodbyes were said.

---

That night, lying in bed with Carter's arms around her, she shivered.

"You cold, babe?"

Snuggling deeper into his embrace, she said, "No. I guess I was just thinking about Kate. The memorial is tomorrow morning. How short life could be. We never know what's going to happen to us. Make the most of each day... you know... all those thoughts that sometimes hit us."

He pressed his lips to the side of her head and tightened his arms. "Damn, sweetheart. What can I do to take some of that away?"

His words soothed over her, and she smiled. "You already are. Just by being in my life. Just by caring."

The cloudless night allowed the moonlight to shine through the slats of the blinds, casting a soft illumination over them. They lay facing each other, their gazes fixed.

"I wanted to hold back," he said.

She leaned back slightly to get a better view of his face, his words confusing.

He reached up and slid her thick tresses off her shoulder, cupping her cheek with his hand. "I wasn't looking for a relationship when we met. But I've found one. You've come to mean the world to me, Tara. And so has Colleen."

Swallowing deeply, she blinked at the growing moisture in her eyes. "Thinking about Kate has made me realize that I don't want to hide anymore just to protect myself from hurt. I'm falling in love with you, Carter."

He leaned forward and placed a gentle kiss on her lips. "That's good to hear, babe, because I'm already in love with you."

"We're a lot to take on."

"I'm a man who knows what I want when I find it. I'm not worried about trying to chase a dream when all I want is right in front of me. You. That little girl across the hall. The *us* we're becoming, and the *us* we're going to be. I love you."

"I love you, too," she whispered, giving in to the desire to kiss him again. Their lips moved slow and gently, reverently. Separating, she said, "We still need to go slow for Colleen. She knows we're dating, and she adores you. But I just want to..."

"We both want to protect her."

"Yes," she nodded, a tremulous smile on her face. A tear escaped as her heart warmed.

Tara sat at her desk, the desire to do any work low. She had attended the memorial service that morning but found herself uneasy. Her attention had been riveted on the mourners from the clinic. As far as she could see, everyone was there, most visibly upset. Dr. Tiller sat with his wife. The other nurses and staff sat together. Robert came alone and so did Beth. She surreptitiously watched, but they barely looked at each other and did not sit together.

Michael and Bethany stopped by to check on her, which she appreciated. Sable and Enrico had offered heartfelt hugs, also appreciated. She had checked on some of the residents, completed two new intakes, closed out a few reports, and now was at loose ends, sitting at her desk.

Glancing at her phone, she reached over and pressed the message button again, knowing she was a glutton for punishment.

**Message received 8:07 p.m.** *"Tara? This is Kate. I really* *wanted to talk to you today, but I know you were busy. I've been driving around trying to think of what to do and just got home. We need to talk when I get in tomorrow. I'll be there first thing in the morning. Please. I don't know what's going on, but meds are being switched... Shit... Sorry, someone's at my door. I'll call you right back."*

Sighing, she played it two more times. Hearing Kate's voice made her sad. It was obvious something was happening at the clinic. She knew Carter had been over there several times but was limited in the scope of his investigation.

She played the message one more time, but this time, anger fired her blood. Anger that something was happening. Something at the clinic. *Whatever Kate discovered, she didn't feel that she could call the police. Why? Was it dangerous? Hard to prove? Easily covered up?*

She stood and grabbed her keys from her purse. Stepping into the hall, she spied Michael. "I'm going next door to the clinic."

"I thought they were closed today."

"They are, but I had something that I wanted to check on. I didn't want to leave this building without letting someone know where I was."

He nodded and she hurried down the hall to the door that connected the shelter with the clinic. Unlocking it, she peered in, but all was quiet. Flipping on a light in the back area, she moved to the pharmacy. It was eerie being in the clinic when no one else was around, but she was determined to take advantage of the opportunity. *Snooping might be considered illegal, but I want to know what Kate discovered.*

Glancing through the door into the pharmacy, she knew there was no way inside with its added security. But unless the pharmacy techs and Robert were all in on something, she doubted whatever was happening was inside the pharmacy room.

Glancing to the side, she saw Robert's office. *Anyone with a private office could have the ability to do something they shouldn't or hide something.* With her hand stuck in her sweater pocket to obscure fingerprints, she tried his doorknob and was surprised when it opened. A box of surgical gloves was on his desk and she snagged two, pulling them on. Uncertain if she watched too much TV or had simply been raised in a law enforcement family, she at least wanted to keep her fingerprints off anything she touched. She sucked in a quick breath at the thought of her family—and Carter, who would have a conniption fit if they knew what she was doing. Pushing that from her mind, she flipped on the light switch in Robert's office and looked around.

There were no boxes of medication visible. His desk was messy, strewn with papers surrounding his computer. His desk drawers held nothing but office supplies. The filing cabinet only contained files. Thinking back to a time when she had been in this room, there was virtually nothing changed. *If Kate had found anything about Robert, it didn't come from his office.*

Flipping off the light, she closed the door as she reentered the hall. Walking around the clinic, there were examining rooms, supply closets, the nurses' station, the staff workroom, the reception area. Lots of nooks and crannies, but nowhere for someone to keep something secret from everyone else. With emptied trash cans, it was obvious the cleaning night crew had come through.

The only other office was Dr. Tiller's and she was certain it would be locked. A jiggle on the doorknob proved her right. She felt her key in her pocket and it struck her that she assumed it would only work on the door between the shelter and clinic. *But what if it was a master key?* The key slid into the lock in his doorknob, and she was stunned when it turned. Opening the door gently, she flipped on the light.

His desk was much neater than Robert's. All papers were filed neatly, and the files were stacked precisely on one corner. A small table sat behind the door, piled high with the sample boxes of medication that Beth delivered. A quick check of his desk and filing cabinet yielded the same results as Robert's. Nothing but files and office supplies.

She sighed, frustrated that her flight of fancy at being able to find something pertaining to Kate's message was not coming to fruition. She turned back to the table of sample boxes, curious as to what drugs a pharmaceutical company handed out. Knowing the costs of medication, the practice seemed excessive but very standard.

She recognized a few names on the medical labels. Common antibiotics. Picking up one of the small boxes, she was reminded of Polly. She had not asked Carter about Polly recently but knew she was out on bail, obviously no longer working at the clinic. *Or probably anywhere right now.* She had never questioned the practice of pharmaceutical companies supplying drugs to doctors' offices and clinics until Polly's situation. It came down to a simple marketing strategy of spending money to make money. She had read that doctors who received drugs from pharmaceutical companies were more likely to recommend and prescribe those drugs.

Replacing the antibiotic box back onto the table, her attention snagged on the clear, round plastic seal. Lifting the box again, she could see that the seal had been slit open. Carefully lifting the flap, she took out a plastic pill bottle. Opening the top, she peered at the pills inside. Blinking, she stepped backward to allow the overhead light to illuminate what she was seeing. Inside was a combination of different pills. There was no way these were the same antibiotics that were listed on the label. *I've got to tell Carter!*

Indecision struck as she tried to figure out the best course of action. If she took the whole bottle, would Dr. Tiller see an empty box? If she took the whole box, would Dr. Tiller notice it was missing?

Checking several other boxes, she discovered almost all were still sealed, indicating whatever type of drug was on the outside must be what was on the inside. Besides the bottle in her hand, she found two others that were unsealed. Observation concluded they were also filled with a variety of pills.

Pulling her phone from her pocket, she snapped pictures. The table. The boxes. The broken seals. The pill bottles. She even dumped some of the pill varieties on the table, taking pictures of those as well. As she replaced the pills inside the bottle, she held out three.

All different shapes, colors, and sizes. Wrapping those in a tissue, she shoved it into her pocket. Carefully placing everything back exactly the way she found it, she stepped backward and looked around the office. Assured it was just as she found it, she went into the hall, relocked his door, and scurried back to the shelter.

Her hands shook as she pulled her phone back out of her pocket and called Carter. *Oh, lordy.*

---

"Are you crazy? Seriously fuckin' crazy? Jesus, Tara, where was your head?"

Carter was livid. His hands clenched around his steering wheel so tight he was surprised it didn't crack. Glancing to the side, he saw her open her mouth to respond, but he wasn't finished.

"You sneaked into the clinic when you had no idea if someone could be there. Knowing that Kate had suspicions that probably got her killed. Someone who, like you, figured no one would be there since the clinic was closed and decided they wanted to keep doing whatever it was that she discovered!"

"I know, I know! But, Carter, I had to do something. It was a calculated risk—"

"You think?"

"Okay, it was a risk. But I kept playing Kate's message over and over and all I could think of was that she had something she wanted to tell me. Something important. I felt like I had to do anything to figure out what it was."

Pulling into the parking lot of the lab, he shut the engine down and unbuckled his seatbelt but made no movement to get out. His body was strung tight as fear threatened to choke him. Fear of what could have happened if Tara had been discovered. The silence in the cab of his SUV was thick with emotion. "She was strangled."

He felt Tara's gaze boring into the side of his head, but he kept staring straight ahead, afraid that if he looked at her, he would never be able to get the words out. "Still in her nursing scrubs. Halfway through dinner. In her apartment, in a place she felt safe. And she opened the door to someone who walked into her safe place, put their hands to her neck, and choked the life out of her."

Tara's hand flew to her mouth and the sound of the sudden intake of her breath resounded. "Oh, my God."

"I know you want to help. I know you're involved. But you've got to stop and back away. No one," he said, now turning to stare at her, "no one can know what you've done."

Her head jerked, nodding up and down, her fingers still pressed against her lips.

"If that happened to you... If anything happened to you..." He swallowed deeply, his chest depressed as he sighed heavily. "Now that I've found you, I can't lose you." He knew he was going for the jugular when he added, "Colleen can't lose you."

Tears began sliding over Tara's cheeks as she sucked in her lips and just nodded. Moving swiftly, he jerked her closer to him, kissing away her tears before taking her mouth. The kiss was hot and wild and yet achingly desperate. They clutched each other's faces as they drank each other in. Giving and taking, reminding them both of the preciousness of life. Her tears, now on his face, finally had him pull back.

She held his gaze, then rasped, "I'm sorry. I never wanted to put myself in danger. I wanted to help, but I know it wasn't the right thing to do. I'm sorry. Please, don't be mad at me."

His fingers slid to the sides of her head, smoothing the tresses away from her face. "I'm over being mad, babe. Still scared. I want to keep you safe, but you're going to have to help me do that."

She nodded her acquiescence, and he kissed her lightly again.

"I'm going to take the pills you gave me and get them inside to the lab. You stay here and I'll be back as soon as I can. It may take a little while unless they can get to me right away."

"I'll be here, I promise."

With a final kiss, he headed into the lab, the tissue with the pills tucked inside an evidence bag. Once inside, he headed straight to the lab set up for drug testing. Seeing a familiar tech, he stalked over to her station.

"Hey, what have you got for me?"

"I need testing on these pills. I need to know what they are. They were found in a bottle labeled antibiotics, so I need to—"

"I can tell you right now those aren't antibiotics." She

took the clear plastic evidence bag from him, holding it up to the light.

"Right, I figured as much. How long will it take you to let me know what they are?"

"I should be able to let you know by the end of today. I'm not terribly backed up and can go ahead and do the presumptive tests on them. The easiest thing I could do is a color test. That'll let me know what type of substance they are, but not identify the exact drug. It might be tomorrow morning before I can do a gas chromatography mass spectrometry on them. That will let me know exactly what we're dealing with."

"Rosemary, you're the best. Get the results to me as soon as you can."

She smiled and nodded, then tilted her head to the side. "Rumor has it that you're dating Sean McBride's sister."

Standing with his hands on his hips, he dropped his chin and stared at his boots for a moment. "Please tell me this isn't high school."

She threw her head back and laughed. "Nah. Just jerking your chain." As he lifted his head and looked at her obviously-pleased expression, she continued, "I'm real glad for you, Carter."

Chuckling, he started to walk away, calling over his shoulder, "Thanks. Me too."

"I know you're pissed as fuck, man, but Tara may have just moved this case forward in ways that we could not."

Carter sat at his desk after dropping Tara back at the shelter. He shot a glare toward Evan. "Seriously? Somehow thinking about my girlfriend putting herself in danger because we, the professionals, can't nail down where these drugs are coming from does not make me happy."

"I didn't say it was going to make you happy. I just stated a fact."

"Yeah, I hear you." His phone rang and he snatched it up. "Fiske. I'm gonna put you on speaker, Rosemary. You've got me and Evan."

"Okay, boys. I did a Marquis Color Test, indicating two of the pills are possibly some kind of opium-based drug. I was almost certain the third one was synthetic. But you guys are absolutely in luck. I moved up in the queue of the GCMS so I've got a definitive, and you sure as heck aren't looking at an antibiotic."

The air rushed from his lungs as another break in the case hit him. "Hit us with that, Rosemary."

"I ran all three through the chromatograph and spectrometer. The first two were oxycodone. The last one was synthetic fentanyl."

"Fuckin' bingo," Evan breathed.

Carter interrupted, "Can you tell the maker of the oxycodone?"

"Kilton Pharmaceutical."

Carter smiled, sharing a look with Evan. "Thanks, Rosemary. You just won free drinks at the Celtic Cock from us for a month."

She barked out a laugh. "I'll hold you to that. I'll fax a report over to you as soon as I get it finished."

Disconnecting, he held Evan's gaze. "Looks like you're right. Tara has just moved this forward. Now, we plan."

An hour later, he looked up as Kyle walked into the room. Seeing the look on Tara's brother's face, he sighed. "Shit."

Kyle stood with his hands on his hips, nostrils flaring and his hard stare pinned on Carter. "Tara? Are you fuckin' serious? Tara broke in and *stole* drugs?"

"Technically, she didn't break in since she had a key," Evan stated.

Carter knew Kyle wasn't satisfied when he jerked his head around and pinned Evan with a death glare. He recognized it, considering he'd hit Tara with the same stare earlier.

"When I get hold of my sister—"

"Don't go there." Carter threw his hand up toward

Kyle. "I've been over it with her, and she gets it. She's scared. Terrified she did something wrong but trying to balance that with wanting to help. She and I've already had it out this morning and come to peace with where we are right now. She doesn't need you coming down on her, fuckin' with her head. Not happening."

Evan tried to stifle a chuckle, but Carter was too focused on Kyle to care what his partner was doing. He and Kyle stared at each other for a long, tense moment.

Kyle slowly shook his head from side to side, his gaze never leaving Carter's face. "So, this is it for you."

"Yeah, this is it for me."

"And Colleen?"

"Absolutely Colleen. She's not just collateral with Tara. I've got them both."

Kyle sucked in a deep breath through his nose, then let it out in a long sigh. "All right, Brother. Let's get this done."

---

The next day, Carter sat next to Kyle in an interrogation room. Across the table sat Lewis Washington, a bag of drugs on the table in front of them. They had laid out their evidence and the charges they were ready to file against him. Possession of controlled substance. Possession with intent to distribute. Distribution of controlled substance. The list went on.

Kyle leaned forward, his arms on the table, his voice harsh but controlled. "You do this for us, and we reduce the charges. If you agree to this, then you follow the instructions to the letter. You fuck up even one little bit... You step one toe out of line and these charges are slapped right back on you."

Lewis lifted his hand and rubbed it over his head. "Yeah, I hear you. Shit, man, it ain't like I got a choice."

"You've always got a choice. Let's just see if you know how to make the right one."

Lewis shifted his gaze over to Carter, seeming to ponder his words. Leaning back in his chair, he nodded. "Fine. I've got no loyalty to them. I'll do it."

———

"Just checking on you, babe."

"I'm at work, busy as ever," Tara replied. "How about you?"

"Are you in your office?"

"Yes, I just finished an intake with Bethany. I checked to make sure everything was going okay with the lunches, and I've got a class later this afternoon. For now, I'm waiting on my next residence counseling session." There was a slight pause, and then she asked, "Any special reason you asked if I'm in my office?"

Chuckling, he was not surprised how intuitive she was. "I want to make sure that you stay out of the clinic today."

"Okay," she said, drawing the word out. "I had no plans of going over there, but now I'm worried. I'm assuming something's happening, isn't it?"

He had not confided to her the results of the lab test, determined to keep the investigation as far away from her as he could. Sighing, he considered his words carefully. "I just need you to make sure you're at the shelter."

Another pause moved between them, this time a little longer. Just when he was about to speak, she said, "It's okay, Carter. I know you can't talk about it. Please, be safe."

"Babe, it's not me I'm worried about."

"Don't worry, I'm safely tucked away in my office."

He glanced toward the passenger seat where Evan sat, then decided he did not give a fuck what his partner heard. "How about tonight I take you and Colleen out for dinner?"

"Oh, sounds good! Hopefully, we're not going to Pirate Ship Pizza!" she said, her laughter filling his ears.

He chuckled, loving the sound of her laughter. "Nope, no pirate pizza. No scary pirate captain mascot. How about we go to the Inner Harbor, have dinner somewhere Colleen will like, and then take a boat ride."

"We'll need to bundle up since it's so cold, but that won't matter to her. She will love that!" Her voice softened as she continued. "Is there a special occasion?"

"We'll talk about that later." Evan looked over and sent him a signal. "Okay, Tara, I've gotta go. Stay safe in your office, and I'll see you tonight." Disconnecting, he looked at Evan.

"They're in. Lewis has been seen by Dr. Tiller, and Kyle's up next."

Kyle had a credit-card-sized voice recorder and audio transmitter attached to his phone. They had already been warned by Lewis that Dr. Tiller would insist on his phone being turned off. He would also insist on a full physical examination, probably to assure that there was no recording device evident on his body.

When Kyle showed up, Carter almost had not recognized him. His long hair was unwashed, and his clothes were worn, oversized, and grungy. His beard was scruffy, and his hands and fingernails looked as though he had been digging in the dirt.

Lewis had already set the stage by telling Dr. Tiller that he met Kyle in the free lunch line. He had also told Dr. Tiller that Kyle had been one of his customers but was looking to make some money.

Listening in, Carter prayed that Dr. Tiller would take the bait. Glancing to the side at his partner, he knew Evan was doing the same thing. Kyle had been in Dr. Tiller's exam room for almost 15 minutes, and Carter was beginning to lose hope. Kyle had played the role perfectly. A down and out veteran, homeless, in a lot of back pain, swearing the pills that Lewis had given him were the only way he could get any relief. But Kyle also had not gone overboard, not alerting Dr. Tiller's suspicions.

"Get dressed and meet me in my office across the hall," Dr. Tiller instructed.

Carter did not hear a response, assuming Kyle had simply nodded. A rustling sound could be heard, and then came Kyle's quiet voice. "Audio check. Getting dressed, now. Hopefully whatever he's going to give me will come from inside his office."

Responding, Carter said, "Audio check, affirmative."

"This could be it," Evan said.

A flash of red walked by and pulled open the front

door of the clinic. "God dammit!" Carter growled when he saw Beth heading inside. "She's a fuckin' distraction for the doctor." There was nothing he could do about her now, so they refocused on listening to Kyle and Dr. Tiller.

Talking to Kyle, Dr. Tiller paid lip service to the benefits of painkillers being used sporadically. Kyle, frustration lacing his voice, growled, "Lewis said you could help me. If you ain't gonna help me, then what the fuck am I doing here?"

The radio waves grew silent, and Carter held his breath, waiting to see if their plan was going to work. He wished that he had a way to see what was going on in Dr. Tiller's office and not just listen.

Finally, Dr. Tiller said, "I have something that I can *give* you to take away your pain."

"Give me? I don't gotta pay Lewis anymore?" Kyle asked.

"Well, you will be expected to make contacts and *help* others."

"Okay, that's it?"

"Take this bottle with you. No more than one a day, and your pain will ease and you will be able to sleep," Dr. Tiller instructed.

"And what do I gotta do?"

"Lewis will give you all the instructions you need. You'll be available certain days of the week to get an extra something in the bag lunch."

"What? At the shelter? Them bag lunches we get at the shelter?" Kyle asked.

"Well, I can hardly have everyone come to the clinic

to get help with their pain, now can I? Now, shut up and listen. Once you get the extra something, then you're free to sell it to whoever you can. Lewis is your contact. You get the money to him and he pays you a percentage."

Kyle said, "Says on the outside of this that it's antibiotics. I'm not stupid. That's not going to do shit for pain."

"I think when you look inside, you'll find exactly what you need. The same thing will end up in your lunch bag. Plenty to use. Plenty to sell. Just keep in mind to do exactly what Lewis says or you won't live to see another day."

Carter did not need to look at Evan to know that they were ready to enter the clinic. Both men climbed from the SUV at the same time, heading for the front door. Throwing it open, they walked inside. Flashing badges, Carter ordered, "We're here to see Dr. Tiller."

"Don't worry. We don't need appointments," Evan threw out.

They stalked straight to Dr. Tiller's office, opening the door. Kyle was clicking the handcuffs on the doctor, whose grim face and wide eyes glared daggers.

"I was just reading him his rights," Kyle said. Moving so the doctor was facing the two detectives, Kyle started over, quoting the rights to Dr. Tiller. Kyle nodded to the table behind the door and said, "There's the evidence."

"I'll start bagging," Evan said.

Carter stepped out into the hall, motioning for the staff to stand back as Kyle walked Dr. Tiller out of his office. Immediately, the gasps and murmurs began, several staring with open mouths, shaking their heads. He waved to three police officers who had entered after them and said, "Keep the staff together for questioning."

"Holy shit, I can't believe it," came a voice from behind Carter. He jerked around, seeing Robert standing in the hall, adjusting his pants. The two pharmacy techs were next to him, and just like the others, their eyes were wide as they gaped at the scene unfolding in front of them.

The flash of red darted from Robert's office toward the back, and Carter realized he hadn't seen Beth. She disappeared from sight, and he rushed after her. Pushing his way past Robert and the others, he turned a corner and saw her disappear through a door.

He grabbed the knob on the door, finding it locked. Looking over his shoulder, he yelled, "Who's got a key for this?"

Robert leapt out of his stupor, running toward him with his keys in his hand.

"Where does this go?"

"It's a door that goes between the clinic and the shelter," Robert explained, his hand shaking as he shoved the key in the lock.

Carter threw the door open but barely made it three steps inside the shelter when his feet stumbled to a halt. Toward the end of the hall stood Beth. One of her hands was gripping Tara's upper arm and the other held a gun to Tara's head.

Tara didn't move a muscle. In fact, she wasn't sure she was breathing. Having heard a noise coming from the door down the hall that led to the clinic and the rapid sound of stilettos on tile, she stepped out of her office to see what was happening. She recognized the pharmaceutical representative, but before she had a chance to ask what she was doing, she was staring at the barrel of a gun pointed straight at her.

Before she could do anything other than gasp, the door opened again and Carter's eyes landed on her, a flash of anguish moving through them before it morphed into pure, white rage.

Robert was holding the door open, his eyes wide in what appeared to be shock. Finding his voice, he shouted, "Beth! What the hell are you doing? Oh, Jesus, you can't do this!"

Bethany and Michael came out of their offices, looking first toward the clinic door where Robert was shouting, and then swinging their heads at the same time to peer down the hall at her. Both gasping, they froze in place.

Afraid to look at the woman next to her, Tara kept her eyes on Carter, drawing strength from him. Tremors moved through her body, and she locked her knees in place to keep from falling. Swallowing, she tried to steady her breathing as images of Colleen drifted in front of her.

"You two," Carter said, gaining Bethany and Michael's attention. "Step back into your offices and stay there. Make a call to reception that no one is to come down this hall." They immediately jumped to follow his orders, disappearing inside their offices.

Directing his attention back to Beth, he said, "Ms. Washington, there's nowhere for you to go. Nothing you can do to make this any better other than give yourself up."

Tara could feel the woman's hand shaking on her arm. Or maybe it was her own body shaking. At this point, she couldn't tell.

"I'm the one with the gun, Detective. Me. I think that means I'm in charge, not you."

Someone came up behind Robert and whispered to him, and Tara watched as Robert gave a quick nod. He moved slowly back into the clinic and Tara recognized Evan who replaced him at the door. She wanted Carter to give her some kind of sign, tell her what to do, but his gaze stayed centered on the woman with the gun.

Afraid to speak, and yet afraid to stay silent, Tara finally whispered, "Beth?"

Her arm jerked in Beth's grip. "Shut up. I need to think."

"Put the gun down, Beth," Carter's voice rang out again. "You're only making this worse for yourself."

Snorting, Beth said, "Worse? How much worse can this get?"

"We know that you're only part of the pipeline. You put the gun down and talk to us, and the DA will take that into consideration."

"Oh, really? So, I'll just get ten years instead of twenty!"

"Right now, every minute that ticks by that you've got that gun on an innocent woman, you're coming under the Federal Hostage Taking Act. That can carry a death sentence."

Beth gasped, and Tara felt the jerk on her arm again.

Keeping up the pressure, Carter said, "You can put down that gun. You can let Ms. Wilson go and come with me. We'll talk. We'll find out what you know. You'll help us. Ms. Washington, that's the only way this is going to end successfully. Anything else is not going to go well for you."

Tara, keeping her voice low and soft, said, "Beth, please listen to him. This is all bad enough. Please don't make this worse on yourself."

"They took Doug. He's the one who killed Kate. He's the one you want."

It took a second for Tara to register that Doug was Dr. Tiller, having always addressed him formally. Uncertain what had taken place in the clinic before

331

Beth ran through to the shelter, she could only imagine that Beth had witnessed Dr. Tiller's arrest.

"That's right, Beth," Carter interjected. "I have no doubt he's going to start talking. He's going to fill us in on the pharmaceutical pipeline. If we get everything we need from him, no one's going to want to make a deal with you. It'll be too late."

Beth suddenly jumped, twisting around so that she was in the doorway of Tara's office, giving Tara a visual in the other direction of the hall toward reception. There was Kyle, his face ravaged as he stood with his gun in his hand. His clothes, hands, and face were dirty. She recognized the tic in his jaw and prayed he maintained his cool. A flash of her childhood rushed to her mind. Sean, so calm. Rory, so funny. And Kyle, so intense.

Afraid to move her head, she shifted only her eyes so that she could gaze at the other end of the hall, focusing once more on Carter. While Beth had looked at Kyle, Carter had moved closer. Tara could now see how clear his blue eyes were. It was one of the first things she ever noticed about him, even though their meeting was not the friendliest.

His gaze had settled on her, and she mouthed *I love you*, wanting him to know that no matter what happened. His blue eyes flashed and then his jaw tightened just like Kyle's.

"Beth, I wasn't kidding when I told you that time is running out. You keep this up, you're fucked. You lower that gun and let Ms. Wilson go, we've got a chance of working some kind of deal."

"I had everything," Beth whispered, her voice now sounding defeated. "Money, a penthouse, clothes, jewelry… I had everything."

Tara racked her brain for something to say but came up empty. Her mouth opened, but with her eyes still on Carter, she saw him give a slight shake of his head. Interpreting that to mean he wanted her to remain quiet, she sucked in her lips, attempting to cease the quivering.

"This is it, Beth," Carter stated. "This is our last offer."

As though in anguish, she tightened her grip on Tara's arm before suddenly letting it go and dropping her arm with the gun. The next few seconds were a blur as Kyle rushed forward, grabbing Beth and pressing her up against the wall, snapping handcuffs on her wrists while Carter scooped up Tara, whose legs were no longer supporting her.

Evan rushed past, aiding Kyle while belting out orders to more policemen who came from the clinic and through the front door of the shelter.

Carter stood with Tara in his arms and pushed his way into the workroom down the hall. Michael popped his head in and asked how he could help. "Get some water and a coat."

Tara kept her arms around Carter, pressed tightly, holding on as though she was afraid he might disappear. She felt his arms band just as tightly around her and wondered if he had the same fear. "I'm okay, I'm okay," she assured even as her body shook.

Kyle rushed in, encircling her as well. "Fuckin' hell,

fuckin' hell, Tara. I never get scared, and I was fuckin' scared out of my fuckin' mind."

Unable to keep a nervous laugh from slipping out, she reached out to touch his face. "Mom would be so mad if she heard your language."

Kyle leaned back and speared her with a glare, shaking his head. Finally, his lips relaxed slightly, and one side quirked up. "Jesus, Tara. Only you could fuss about my cursing after something like this." He stood and kissed the top of her head, then looked down at Carter. "I guess I really do have to welcome you to the McBrides now."

He reached out and clasped Carter on the shoulder. "I'm heading to the station with Beth and the doc. Evan's going to finish interviewing the staff next door, and I've got officers bagging up all the evidence. I'll see you later." He started to walk out then looked back at Tara. "Just so you know, Sis, I'm not keeping my mouth shut so you can expect mom and dad to descend on you." He winked before walking out of the room.

Michael came in with her coat and handed it to Carter. He wrapped it around her, enclosing her in its warmth.

She turned her gaze back to Carter, clutching his face with her hands. His eyes were still tortured, so she pulled him in for a kiss. A kiss of need and promise.

"I gotta agree with your brother. Scared me shitless." He shook his head, his eyes once more filled with anguish. "God, this was my fault."

"Your fault?"

"I should have had you go home, be far away from the center—"

She shushed him with her fingers on his lips. "Carter, if I hadn't been here, she would have grabbed someone else. I was scared, too, but I was able to remain calm. Mostly out of fear, but calm. Bethany would've freaked and Beth might have killed her. I have no idea how Michael would have reacted, but it doesn't matter. This was nobody's fault but Dr. Tiller and Beth."

She watched as his face finally relaxed, and he leaned in, kissing her once more. She breathed him in, pressing tightly against him, feeling their hearts beating together.

---

Night had fallen over Hope City by the time Carter left headquarters. While everything with the investigation had been processed, the emotions running deep inside had not. He had talked to Tara a few hours earlier, needing to hear her voice and be assured that she was safely ensconced at home. Her family had descended as Kyle predicted, and she had spent the rest of the day surrounded with love and care.

Now, instead of driving straight there, he found himself standing in his condo looking out the large picture window facing the Inner Harbor. The city below twinkled with lights and their reflection on the water created a beauty that could hide the dark ugliness that existed in the corners of society. Those with no home, no bed to sleep in. Those without warm clothes to protect them when the winter wind howled. Those in pain, desperate for any pill that would offer relief. Those who called the Cardboard Cottages home.

He sucked in a ragged breath and turned from the window, looking over the clean, modern lines of his condo. What had once given him order now stood in stark contrast to the warm home that Tara had created. A knock on the door jolted him from his confused musings.

Throwing it open, he was surprised to see Sean standing in the hall. "Tara? Is something wrong with Tara?" His heart pounded, fearful for the response.

Sean threw his hands up, quickly assuring, "No, no, she's fine. Everybody's checked on her, and she's fine. Colleen got home from school and Mom made sure everybody had dinner. Honest, man, she's good."

Stepping back, he allowed Sean into the condo. He had no idea why Sean was there but figured the man would tell him when he was ready. He grabbed two glasses from the cabinet and poured a finger of whiskey in both, handing one to Sean.

Sean took a sip and nodded appreciatively. The two men walked back to the window, both staring out over the night skyline. "I've been where you are. I know the shit going through your mind right now."

It was on the tip of his tongue to deny what Sean was saying, but the words would not come. Swallowing heavily, he waited to see what else Sean had to say.

"I stood on the sidewalk surrounded by firefighters and watched as black smoke boiled out of one of Harper's windows. I watched my brother lift her body out of the third-floor window, not knowing if she was alive or not."

Carter turned to look at Sean, not only hearing the words but feeling the impact of them in his gut. "Jesus, Sean."

Sean twisted his head and held Carter's gaze. "I figured you'd come here before going to Tara's. You'd need a chance to wrap your head around everything that happened today. Kyle filled me in, and he's battling his own demons while seeing Tara held hostage. I figure you are, too."

"How do we do it?" He watched as Sean tilted his head to the side in silent question and worked to pull his churning emotions into coherent thoughts. "We go out every day and deal with people who have no problem putting a gun to someone else's head. How do we do that job and then at the end of the day go home to beauty and not contaminate it? My job—my investigation—brought that to Tara. How is that fair to her?"

Sean turned his body fully toward Carter and growled, "You want to know what wasn't fair to Tara? Her ex-husband. He was a weak-ass man who never could figure out how to stand on his own. He whined and bitched and moaned every time life didn't give him exactly what he thought he should have at the age of twenty-four. Tara. Smart, giving, tough, hard-working, fuckin' beautiful... everything she had to give, including a perfect daughter, was offered on a silver platter to that man, and he walked away. A man worthy of her would've taken those precious gifts, appreciated them, and vowed to hold them in his heart. Not try to keep her safe from all harm, because none of us can make that promise. But a real man, worthy of her, would promise to hold all that is her precious. And that, my friend, would keep the demons at bay." He stepped closer and leaned in. "What you've gotta decide—are you that man? 'Cause if you're not, then stay away from her. It'll break her heart because I know she loves you, but it would go better as a clean break now."

Carter reared back, his heart threatening to pound out of his chest at Sean's words. The idea of not having Tara and Colleen in his life cut like a bitch straight to his heart.

Sean leaned back, and his lips quirked upward on one side. "I see I got through." He tossed back the last dregs of whiskey and walked over to the counter, setting his glass down. With his hand on the doorknob, he looked over his shoulder and added, "Nice condo you've got here. But I know someone who's got a warm house and a warm heart waiting for you." With that, he walked out, shutting the door behind him.

Carter stood unmoving for several minutes, Sean's words passing through his mind, sinking in and replacing all his doubts and fears. He walked swiftly to the kitchen and poured the rest of his whiskey down the sink and headed to the bedroom. Grabbing a bag from the closet, he began filling it with some clothes and toiletries.

Traffic was light and it only took fifteen minutes for

him to pull into Tara's driveway. The upstairs window in Colleen's bedroom was dark, but a faint glow from behind the curtains in the living room gave evidence that someone was waiting. *Home. This feels like coming home.*

## 3 3

A buzzer sounded, jarring Carter from a deep sleep. His eyes jerked open and it was evident the sun was up as it streamed between the slats in the blinds. The warm body next to him grunted before setting up quickly.

"Oh, God, we slept late," Tara groaned, pushing the covers off her legs.

Unable to ascertain the buzzing sound, he looked over and could not help but smile. Tara's thick hair was sleep-tousled, and her lips were still kiss-swollen. He wanted to pull her back into bed and continue making love to her the way they had late into the night. The investigation faded away the moment he took her in his arms, and words of love and commitment were the only ones spoken long into the night.

"Get up, get up, get up," she whispered loudly.

His foggy brain finally caught up to her sense of urgency and his gaze shot over to the bedroom door, relieved that it was locked. He jumped from the bed and managed to pull on his sweatpants as Tara jerked on a robe. She was just tying it about her waist when the sound of little hands banging on the door rang out.

"Mom! Can we have pancakes?"

Tara glanced at him, a flash of indecision passing through her eyes before she straightened, squared her shoulders, and smiled. Throwing open the door, she wrapped her arms around Colleen, saying, "And good morning to you."

Colleen laughed and murmured, "Good morning," before looking past her mom, staring wide-eyed up at Carter.

He was sure his eyes were just as wide, but before he had a chance to think what to say, Colleen's smile brightened. She left her mom's side and rushed toward him, her arms thrown up in the air.

"Carter! I didn't know you were here, too! You can have pancakes with us!"

He snatched her up off the ground as her arms wound around his neck. Tara walked forward, and still holding Colleen with one arm, he banded his other arm around Tara, embracing them both. After breakfast, he headed back to headquarters but promised their dinner out and boat ride that evening.

---

Sitting in his supervisor's office with Evan, he smiled when they received the news that Rachel had had her baby boy, and all were fine. "The two of you will continue to partner until Rachel returns," the supervisor said.

Nodding, he looked over as Kyle walked into the office and joined them. He offered a chin lift in greeting and began. "We know it's not the whole pipeline, but what we've got so far is that Kilton Pharmaceuticals has security breaches that they've tried to keep hidden. Beth managed to get extra drug samples from one of the men at the warehouse that she was sleeping with. So far, it looks like what she delivered to other clinics and doctors' offices was correct. It was Doug Tiller that was organizing the setup, although we still don't have who was supplying the fentanyl. The pharmacist, Robert Atkins, was not part of the organization, but she slept with him, keeping him from asking too many questions."

"What is Dr. Tiller's game?" their supervisor asked.

"There's still a lot that we're untangling, but essentially, he was the conduit for illegal fentanyl and other opioid sales and distribution. The free clinic gave him the perfect market. Someone who's homeless, can't afford medical care, in pain and desperate is the perfect person to get hooked on opioids and then control. With the extra opioids that Beth was supplying him, it wasn't hard for him to get them reliant on the drugs he was giving them. The next logical step was for them to have the offer of making money by selling the drugs. Not wanting them to be seen too often coming into the clinic, they used the free lunch line next door at the clinic as a way to distribute the drugs."

Evan shook his head and said, "That's the part I struggle with. That was so fuckin' risky."

"Desperate people take desperate risks," Kyle grunted.

"They only distributed through the lunch line on certain days, making sure that Lewis was there. A code word was given, and he would hand them a marked bag that had the drugs inside." Carter shook his head slowly and sighed. "Their instructions were to sell the drugs immediately so they wouldn't be found. Carl obviously didn't do that before the freezing cold struck that night and he died in his sleep with the drug still on him. Same went for Rocky. He probably thought he'd found the perfect place to spend the night out of the elements and by pure bad luck died of smoke inhalation when the arsonist set fire to the townhouse next door. Their bad luck was the dumb luck that gave us a starting point on the investigation."

"Never discount dumb luck," their supervisor said. "Good work, gentlemen."

They filed out of his office, and Evan headed back to his desk. Kyle clapped Carter on the back and said, "See you at the next family dinner." He offered a chin lift and watched as Kyle headed out of the workroom. Glancing over at Evan, he said, "I'm heading home."

"Got big plans tonight?"

Grinning, he said, "Best plans ever—dinner with my girls."

---

Kyle stood in his superior's office, staring out the window, his hands on his hips.

"You want it?"

Kyle turned and looked at him. "Yeah, I want it. I've got contacts at the Cottages that can get me closer to whoever's making the fentanyl." Kyle held his gaze as the silence stretched between them.

Finally, he nodded. "All right. Consider that your next assignment."

<br>

## Four Months Later

<br>

The summer day was perfect. Blue skies with only a few white clouds passing overhead. Sunshine warming their faces. The clear water of the Hope City harbor reflected the light as the water-taxi moved from one side to the other. Sitting in the very front so their view was unobscured, Colleen spread her arms out wide to catch the breeze, laughing as her hair was tossed about her face.

Carter grinned at her obvious excitement before shifting his gaze to Tara. Her dark hair was pulled in a ponytail, keeping the wind from blowing it into a tangled mess like her daughter's, but her smile was just as wide.

"Baby, stay close," Tara warned.

As she reached out to place a calming hand on Colleen's shoulder, the rings on her finger sparkled in the sunlight, catching his eye. Colleen turned around and grinned, and he caught a glimpse of the gold necklace with a small diamond solitaire hanging around her neck. Both represented his promises to them.

When he'd asked Tara to marry him, he had also asked Colleen if he could be her dad. Her response was to scream while jumping up and down before throwing herself into his arms. Tara had cried, and he was sure that a few tears came from him as well.

He wanted Tara to have the wedding of her dreams, but she confessed that the wedding she had when she was in her twenties was no longer important to her. "All I want is family and a few friends. Something small... maybe in my parents' backyard." Laughing, she had added, "If I know Mom and Hannah King, they'll make it beautiful."

He agreed, and the wedding had taken place two weeks ago. And, just like Tara had predicted, the McBrides and Kings together had created a memorable celebration. Their honeymoon had been a long weekend on the Eastern Shore of Virginia, staying at a lovely inn in Baytown. Befriending the owners, Tori and Mitch Wilder—who also happened to be the Police Chief of Baytown—gave them an excuse to plan another trip to the little town before Colleen had to go back to school in the fall.

Leaning back in his seat with one arm around his wife and an eye on his daughter, he knew that Sean had been right all those months ago.

All that Tara was and everything she had to give, including Colleen, was offered on a silver platter to him. And he took those precious gifts, appreciated them, and held them close in his heart.

For the next Hope City books, click below!
Brody book 3 by Kris Michaels
Kyle book 4 by Maryann Jordan
Ryker book 5 by Kris Michaels

Continue on for the sneak peek at Brody, Chapter 1, by
Kris Michaels!

## SNEAK PEEK AT BRODY, THE NEXT BOOK IN HOPE CITY!

### BY KRIS MICHAELS

Detective Sergeant Brody King stared down a Hope City back alley at the dented steel exterior door that wore the scars of collisions it had survived. He and two of his men were assigned to cover this entryway. He listened intently to police comms via an earwig. Thanks to an undercover agent wearing a wire, the conversation inside the building was being broadcast to his team. Twenty-two men and women, permanently assigned to the Hope City's Joint Drug Enforcement Team, or JDET, waited in position for the undercover DEA agent to give the signal. At the undercover agent's predetermined code words, they would storm the building and take down the participants, including the undercover officer. His arrest would keep the man's identity from the rest of the scum currently exchanging cash for a shipment of drugs. His team was highly trained, briefed with the latest available intel, and ready to take down a major conduit of cocaine into the city.

"Standby, we may have new players inbound."

Through the comms, DEA Agent Amber Swanson's voice slapped his ears in a hard, professional clip; gone was the soft, quiet voice he remembered.

*A lot of shit has changed in the last ten years.* The ten years since she walked away... and left him down on one knee holding a diamond engagement ring in his hand. Brody's muscles tightened with anger, confusion, and embarrassment—emotions he'd thought he'd put behind him. He drew a steadying breath. His past had nothing to do with this moment, and his focus needed to be on his team, this raid, and the takedown of a major player in Hope City's drug scene.

Brody held still while listening to the drug deal going down inside. Colt Rayburn nudged him and motioned down the alleyway. A blacked-out SUV drove into the tight alley. As one man, he, Colt, and Derek Watson, slid back behind a dumpster. The smell coming from the industrial sized garbage bin could choke a maggot, but it was the only place they could still see the doorway and be shielded from the SUV's direct line of vision.

"Juliet Three. Black SUV. Unknown occupants pulling up to the back door." He whispered the license plate number and shut up when the doors opened. *Wonderful.* The bastards were carrying Uzis.

He keyed his mic and barely breathed, "Four. Armed. Heavy."

"Are you in position to take them?"

He clicked the mic twice. It was their team's way to confirm without talking. Once for no, twice for yes. They'd be able to flank the bastards.

"The deal is almost done. On my count, move in." His captain's voice cracked over the comms. He motioned to Derek to go to the front of the vehicle. Colt nodded to the rear. He agreed with a slight movement of his head.

When they were ready, he keyed the mic three times, giving his captain the signal they were ready. It was a dance the team had done too many times to count.

"On one." Captain Terrell counted down. "Three... two... one!"

Colt and Derek sprinted at the same time he did, except he didn't round the vehicle. He sprinted to the hood, used the bumper as a step and launched onto it. The sound of his weight landing on the hood swung all four men to his position. Derek and Colt yelled, "Police!"

"Drop your weapons!" His Desert Eagle Mark XIX leveled on the man closest to him. Looking down the barrel of the massive handgun would clench anyone's ass, and it worked almost every time. Their free hands went up, and all four leaned down and placed their weapons by their feet. Derek kicked the guns away as Colt spun the gunmen and zip tied their wrists.

"Clear!"

"Get down!"

"Police!"

"We got a runner!"

A door slammed; in the distance, he heard Amber's voice yell, "Halt, DEA!"

"You got this?" Brody jumped down from the newly dented hood of the SUV.

"Go!" Derek dropped one of the restrained men to his knees.

"Runner heading down Marlin Avenue!" Amber yelled into her open mic.

Brody sprinted through the alley and across the street, running full tilt down an alley the next block over. Marlin Avenue curved, and if the runner didn't duck into a building, he'd be coming around right where Brody would exit the alley.

Pounding against the asphalt, he saw the man flash by the alley entrance. He sped up and flew around the corner. He launched at the guy's knees and tackled the man as he ran full speed. The cement sidewalk stopped their fall.

Brody scrambled on top of the bastard and had him cuffed before Amber made it to their location. She glanced at the man and panted into her radio, "We need an ambulance at Marlin and..." She glanced around.

He keyed his mic. "Marlin and Pier Drive. Perp has abrasions, needs to be cleared by medical before we transport."

She nodded and dropped her hands to her knees, her service weapon still grasped in one hand. "Damn, he's a fast son of a bitch."

Brody stood and glanced at the perp. They both were going to be sore, but they'd both okay. He wished he was as resilient as the suspect appeared to be. Guess the cement wasn't very forgiving today. He pointed to the man and for the first time looked at Amber. "You got this?"

"Yeah. Thanks." She stood up and holstered her weapon. "Look, Brody, we should probably talk."

Wisps of her long red-gold hair fell from the ponytail she'd cinched it into, and the strands perched against her high cheekbone. Her face was flushed and her eyes, damn those blue-green eyes of hers, threw him right back to the moment he'd last seen her. She was still as beautiful as he remembered, perhaps more so now. The confidence she was rocking looked damn good on her. He shook his head. "Little late for that."

She flipped her ponytail to her back and put her hands on her hips. "We're going to need to talk eventually. I'm permanently assigned to this team, and there are things I need to say, that I should've told you--"

"Let's cut through the shit. You're a member of my team. We work together. Nothing more. I'm your sergeant and in your chain of command. If you can't deal with that because of our past, you can report directly to Lt. Anderson or Captain Terrell." He turned as the ambulance rounded the corner on Marlin with a black and white behind it. He looked back at her. "Your refusal ten years ago said more than enough. I wasn't what you wanted."

"I was scared! I didn't want my life to pass me by!" she hissed as the ambulance stopped at their position.

He pointed at the man. "Deal with him. Radio in when you're clear."

He spun on his heel and headed back down the alley. The road rash and ache in his shoulder from tackling the suspect was nothing compared to the pain her words recalled. *She didn't want her life to pass her by. As if he was going to weigh her down and stop her from living.* He'd loved her with every cell of his being. She was *the one* for him. She always would be.

He'd almost died when she'd fled from him. Literally. No, he hadn't been willing to let her go without a fight. When he'd recovered from the shock of her refusal, he'd driven to her sister's house. On the way there, he'd been t-boned by a delivery truck. The accident had put him in a coma for two weeks and then shit got tough. Surgeries and physical therapy distracted him from the rejection that caused more pain than any doctor could inflict. When he came out of the coma, he realized that while he'd gone after her initially, he wasn't going to beg her to love him. As he crossed the street, Colt shouted down the alley, "Brody, Captain wants to see you inside!"

Colt was obviously in charge of processing the SUV. All the doors stood open, and the forensics team assigned to their department was digging into their kits.

"Roger that. Derek and the perps?"

"Perps are in the wagon. Derek's heading down to the precinct with them. He'll sit on them until we get there."

Making sure their perps weren't "accidentally" released wasn't a joke. His father, the Hope City Police Commissioner, had made huge strides in rooting out the systemic corruption which had riddled the department as few as five years ago, but there were still those who "lost" paperwork for a few hundred dollars.

He made for the first door and entered the skanky smelling bar. His eyes adjusted to the darkened interior, and he headed toward the sound of voices. He entered the main seating area of the bar in time to hear his captain.

"What did you say?"

Oh hell, that couldn't be good. When Captain Terrell's voice got low and growled like that, he was one step away from flaying someone alive.

"What's up, Cap? You wanted to see me?"

His boss turned. Oh, hell yeah, he was pissed. The man's face was lobster red, and his jaw was tightly clenched.

"It seems the DEA is declining to share the bust even though my team effected the apprehension and saved their undercover agent's ass."

He walked forward, planted his feet shoulder width apart, and crossed his arms, as he glanced at the smug DEA agent who was pointedly ignoring his captain. "That so? Well, hell, if they don't want to share the collar, let's call off our team. Let DEA process the scene."

He turned his back on the agent and lowered his voice. "We've got the four perps from the alley. They were loaded with Uzis. This was a hit. They will have intel. If the DEA bastard wants to play it that way, let's take the ancillary busts which have nothing to do with the drug deal. We can push this up the chain. The DEA will be persona non grata for years."

His captain released a huff of air. "Still stuck with one of the sons of bitches on my team. She'll feed info to her agency."

"Not if she doesn't have access to it. She can earn her wings and our trust like everyone else on the team."

"You know her. Do you trust her? She seemed to have her shit together in the van. Tore out of it when the runner darted." The captain turned his head and stared at him.

He sighed. "I don't know. Haven't seen her for ten years. I have no idea if I can trust her or not. The person I used to know? Yeah, I'd trust her, but..." He wasn't going to sell Amber down the river because of their personal relationship. He wasn't that type of person.

"But, like you said, you don't know her now."

He nodded.

"Follow me." His captain glowered at the DEA Agent. "Degrassi, you've got the scene."

The DEA agent whipped his head around to gape at them. "What?"

"Your scene. We're taking the four men we arrested. They aren't a part of this bust."

"No, they're mine." Degrassi put his hands on his hips.

"What are you charging them with?" He angled his head back to his boss.

"Whatever charges you've booked them on." Degrassi's forehead furrowed. The man resembled a Shar Pei dog with all the folds smooshed together.

Captain looked at him. "Are we charging them?"

"Nope." Brody rocked back on the heels of his well broken in combat boots. "They were in the wrong place at the wrong time."

"Bullshit." Degrassi shook his head. "You're working an angle. I can feel it."

Captain Terrell lifted his radio and said, "Juliet One to all Juliet teams. DEA has the primary scene. Let's go home."

All movement around them ceased. "Your police commissioner guaranteed your assistance."

His captain shrugged, "You guaranteed him we'd be credited with a portion of the bust."

"That's fiction." Degrassi sneered.

"Really? That's not what the Commissioner told me when I saw him," Brody sneered right back.

"Right, the Police Commissioner happened to have the time to talk to a piece of shit sergeant."

Brody shoved his hands in his pockets so he wouldn't be inclined to deck the son of a bitch and let loose with a fake laugh. "That is so funny! Damn, I'll make sure to tell my dad you think I'm a piece of shit sergeant, and he can't trust the DEA."

The man looked from the captain to him, confused.

"Oh, sorry, I was late to the briefing, and we weren't introduced. King. Brody King." He saw the moment the DEA agent put two and two together.

Amber strolled into the bar, brushing off her black jeans. She stopped short and glanced between the three of them. "Degrassi, what's going on?"

The man didn't acknowledge her. The DEA agent's stare still focused on him.

"Degrassi here is saying the DEA will take full credit for the bust," Captain Terrell said, but didn't move.

"For this collar? Nope. It's fifty-fifty. That's what we

were briefed at DEA headquarters, and that's what was relayed to your Police Commissioner." Amber glanced from Terrell to him to Degrassi.

"Oh, for fuck's sake, were you making a grab here, Degrassi?" Amber raised her phone and waved it at the man. "One call and you're doing support work on the coast of the Bering Sea. You've been warned about this shit before."

"There's no problem here. We're sharing credit." The man spun on his heel and stalked to the back of the room where three members of the JDET team and two of the DEA's people were certifying a count of money.

"He'll be arresting polar bears for smoking pot if he keeps this shit up. I'm sorry about him. I'll include his actions in my report to my superiors. It will be the last report from me they'll get until I'm released from this task force, by the way. If I work for you, my loyalty is to you and only you." She slid her phone back into her pocket. "I'd like to debrief our undercover agent with Degrassi, in case he has anything we can work from a Hope City level. Has the cocaine been tested?"

Captain Terrell held up a small ampule. The light blue color of the tube testified to the content of the packaged white powder. "It's legit according to the street kits. We'll have it tested in the lab." He crossed his arms and rocked back on his heels before he spoke. "We have Jorgenson and Estrada for conspiracy to distribute. First count on the cash was fifty thousand. They are doing a second and third count to validate the first pass. Weapons charges are in line for the muscle inside with Jorgenson and Estrada. We'll be able to roll some of them."

She nodded and turned to Brody. "Do you have any intel on the four you arrested outside?"

Brody kept his gaze focused on the count going on at the back of the room. "Not yet."

"King, you and Swanson head to the precinct. I need you to make sure the team gets their shit done. Go through the reports, and then we'll start with the suspects. Having them sit and wait until our interview specialists go after them won't harm anything. I'm not leaving until *that* asshole is gone." Terrell nodded toward Degrassi.

He nodded his understanding while he watched the people counting the money. "Derek is sitting on the four from outside. How many do we have from this mess?"

"The two primaries, Jorgenson and Estrada. There were four meatheads with iron who were cuffed too."

He finally flicked his eyes toward Amber. "Which one is your guy?"

"One of the meatheads. Estrada's right-hand man. He's been working in the family for almost three years now."

Brody wanted to question her about the amount of time the guy'd been undercover, but he wasn't about to initiate a conversation. The less he talked with her, the better. He nodded to the side door and headed out. She'd either follow or she wouldn't. Actually, he'd prefer it if she didn't.

"All in all, the op went well." Amber commented as they drove north heading away from the harbor area.

He grunted in agreement and was met with an exaggerated sigh from her side of the vehicle.

"How are your parents?"

"No." He refused to open that door. His family was *everything* to him, and when she'd dumped him, she'd dumped them too. His mother was heartbroken, not because Amber had left him, but because of what had happened to him afterward.

He watched her with his peripheral vision. She turned her head toward him and gawked. "No? Just no?"

"That's right. Just no." He glanced at the clock. Five more minutes in this truck and he'd be clawing at the windshield to get away from her.

"What the hell happened to you to make you such an ass, Brody? You were never like this before."

He pulled over suddenly, and she grasped onto the 'oh-shit handle' on the side of the truck. The gear shifter slammed into Park, and he spun toward her. "*You* happened. *You* are the reason I'm like this. *My* family, *my* life, *my* friends, everything I care about is *off limits* to you. I have to work with you. I don't have to like it." He threw the truck back into gear and forced his way back into the flow of traffic.

She had the decency to keep her thoughts to herself until they reached the small outbuilding located on the grounds of the Central Precinct. The squat cement block building had a badge-controlled entry and exit. JDET had their own armory holding their tactical equipment and radios, five small holding cells, a bullpen, two conference rooms, and offices for him, the lieutenant, and the captain.

He jammed his truck into a parking slot and slammed his door closed as he stalked to the building. He drew a deep breath. Was it just yesterday he'd bounced into the building wearing a tux? Yeah, yeah it was. He hadn't been home since yesterday morning. Hadn't eaten since the wedding yesterday afternoon, or slept since the night before last. They'd spent the night planning the op, reviewing the plans, and working assignments. He'd managed to avoid talking directly to Amber for damn near twenty-four hours. Now he was back at the precinct, where if he was lucky, he had every intention of avoiding her again.

She yelled at him from beside the truck, "Brody, wait!"

He stopped and glared in her direction. Luck wasn't on his side. Obviously.

"What?"

"I really do need to talk with you."

"Amber, there is nothing you need to tell me you haven't already said. Why did you come back here? Why? There are hundreds of places you could have landed. Did you know I was assigned to this team?"

"No! I had no idea until I walked in that door yesterday."

"Right. How long have you been back in Hope City?"

"I... I never left."

He stared at her for a moment and internalized the razor-sharp syllables which sliced his soul into tiny pieces... again. She'd dumped him to fulfill her grand plan of a life that didn't pass her by, and yet she'd never left Hope City. So, it was him she didn't want. Had she been playing him the entire time they'd been together? What a moron he'd been. He turned and headed into the building.

"Brody, it's not what you think."

He didn't dare stop. He'd been raised to respect women, all women, even the one who had ripped out his heart on her way out the door. Stopping now would be a *very* bad thing. He'd say words he couldn't take back. Words which would be meant to shred her as deeply as she'd lacerated him.

"Brody!"

He swiped his badge and walked into his building, leaving her outside. She had a badge; she could get in.

Derek pounced as soon as he walked in the door. "Sarge, I separated them. The guy in number three is the weakest link. He's sweating bullets and glancing around. His knees are bouncing. The other three are cold as ice." Derek fell into step with him. "When are we talking to them?"

"Captain wants them on ice while we clean up a bit. Have you started your report?"

"Yep. I hate paperwork, so I get it done and out of the way. Man, the leap to the top of the truck was fucking awesome. One day, though, you're going to land on your ass."

"Nah, that's what all those box jumps at CrossFit are for." He motioned Derek toward his desk in the bullpen. "Send me the prints for these guys, and I'll see if I can get some magic help to identify them."

"Dude, who do you know? No one else can get

anything pushed through quickly." Derek plopped his ass behind his desk as Amber entered the bullpen.

He pinned her with a glare. "Do you have a desk yet?"

She shook her head no. Her jaw was clenched shut, and from the flush on her cheeks, she was pissed.

"Derek, put Agent Swanson at Harrison's desk. He's on vacation for the next two weeks. By the time he's back, we'll have a computer for her, and we can pull a desk up from the basement next door. Get her logins and show her how to print."

Derek's face lit up. "Absolutely, I've got her covered."

He didn't doubt it. Derek was a notorious flirt, and if you listened to the man's claims, he never slept alone, although he wasn't strapped down with a relationship. *Whatever.* He spun on his heel and headed to his office. He needed time to breathe without looking at the woman he loved. *Used to love.*

For the next Hope City books, click below!
Brody book 3 by Kris Michaels
Kyle book 4 by Maryann Jordan
Ryker book 5 by Kris Michaels

## ALSO BY MARYANN JORDAN

Don't miss other Maryann Jordan books!

Lots more Baytown stories to enjoy and more to come!

Baytown Boys (small town, military romantic suspense)

Coming Home

Just One More Chance

Clues of the Heart

Finding Peace

Picking Up the Pieces

Sunset Flames

Waiting for Sunrise

Hear My Heart

Guarding Your Heart

Sweet Rose

Our Time

Count On Me

For all of Miss Ethel's boys:

Heroes at Heart (Military Romance)

Zander

Rafe

Cael

Jaxon

Jayden

Asher

Zeke

Cas

Lighthouse Security Investigations

Mace

Rank

Walker

Drew

Blake

Tate (August 2020)

Hope City (romantic suspense series co-developed

with Kris Michaels

Hope City Duet (Brock / Sean)

Carter

Brody by Kris Michaels

Kyle

Ryker by Kris Michaels

Saints Protection & Investigations

(an elite group, assigned to the cases no one else wants…or
can solve)

Serial Love

Healing Love

Revealing Love

Seeing Love

Honor Love

The Fairfield Series (small town detectives)

Emma's Home

Laurie's Time

Carol's Image

Fireworks Over Fairfield

Please take the time to leave a review of this book. Feel free to contact me, especially if you enjoyed my book. I love to hear from readers!

Facebook

Email

Website

# ABOUT THE AUTHOR

I am an avid reader of romance novels, often joking that I cut my teeth on the historical romances. I have been reading and reviewing for years. In 2013, I finally gave into the characters in my head, screaming for their story to be told. From these musings, my first novel, Emma's Home, The Fairfield Series was born.

I was a high school counselor having worked in education for thirty years. I live in Virginia, having also lived in four states and two foreign countries. I have been married to a wonderfully patient man for thirty-five years. When writing, my dog or one of my four cats can generally be found in the same room if not on my lap.

Please take the time to leave a review of this book. Feel free to contact me, especially if you enjoyed my book. I love to hear from readers!

Facebook
Email
Website